Beneath A Midwinter Moon

A WINTER HOLIDAY ANTHOLOGY

ANA BRAZIL   ANNE M. BEGGS   EDIE CAY

MARI ANNE CHRISTIE   REBECCA D'HARLINGUE

C.V. LEE   JONATHAN POSNER   KATHRYN PRITCHETT

MICHAEL L. ROSS   VANITHA SANKARAN

LINDA ULLESEIT

PAPER LANTERN
WRITERS

First paperback edition November 2023

First digital edition November 2023

ISBN 979-8-9871222-3-5 (paperback)

ISBN 979-8-9871222-2-8 (ebook)

Cover design by Jillianne Hamilton

Published by Paper Lantern Writers

PAPER LANTERN
WRITERS

Boiling Point

PONGAL CELEBRATION
BY VANITHA SANKARAN

Pondicherry, India
Mid-January 1941

The first day of *Pongal*, the festival marking the end of the winter solstice and giving gratitude for the new harvest, dawned listless and gray. A waning crescent moon hung like a scythe in the sky; in fact, all of India seemed to live on the edge of a keen blade these days. The country's entry into the world war was imminent, with the British already at the heart of this faraway conflict against Hitler and his Nazi regime. It was disconcerting how easily the Indian masses were swayed into supporting their overlords in a war that ill concerned them, while at home, they were under the bootheels of the selfsame men.

"Fools and dreamers." Mireille Beteille had little patience for either.

She had lived her entire life under British rule and if there was one thing she had learned, it was that anything that took British scrutiny away from their land was something they should celebrate. Yes, war, especially one on a global scale, could scarcely be ignored, but getting entangled in matters that did not concern them was something else altogether.

Matters would soon come to a head. She heard it in the tick-tick-tick whispers of revolution deep in the vegetable market.

"How many of our men will they conscript?"

"If we refuse, will they send us to our deaths anyway?"

"Why not take advantage of their distraction and rise against them?"

She saw it in the countless eyes reading subtle screeds against the British Raj in the local paper for months now.

QUIT INDIA! QUIT THE RAJ!
This government does nothing for our safety.

She felt it in the tension between her own heartbeats as she prepared for the celebration. Even though she had celebrated *Pongal* for as long as her memory went back, this year, she was hosting the festival not just for family and friends but for the entire town. This year, she was in charge of food and festivities for all, and most importantly, the entertainment. This year, her Rosabel would dance in public for the first time.

Every detail, every moment had to be perfect. Achille had arranged a special *fête* this year to show the town, to show the government, that India still had treasures to offer, if only given the chance. In a giveaway sure to delight the local reporters, he was supplying the entire town with the high-quality textiles created in his own factory nearby. Over this four-day extravaganza, he planned to showcase the prosperity of their coastal colonial town and the Franco-Indians who lived here.

Once upon a time, she had found her husband's love of the "Best of India" and the "Best of France" intoxicating instead of suffocating. Once upon a time, she had believed in the propaganda that said their French overlords would help India rise to her pre-British glory. Now, she understood she only needed to count on the jealous enmity between the French and the British to kick the latter out. It would be easy enough afterward to pry off these Franco leeches that had clutched onto their southern coast. No matter her husband was one of them.

Her morning began early, with predawn ablutions and a short prayer to the gods. It was still dark when she crouched outside the front door with her spice box. Stocked with rice flour dyed with roots and petals, fruits and herbs, this palette of seven bright colors was specially chosen for her *kolam* design. It didn't take long to handcraft a street-side mural of a bright green parrot sitting on a vivid pink lotus atop a roiling blue sea. Her rice flour designs were the talk of the town, and she'd practiced this one for months now.

She stopped next at the kitchen, where no fewer than six cooks were directing their younger staff to make today's special treats.

"What is the menu?" she asked Gayatri *Amma*, who oversaw the operation, even though Mireille had set a traditional menu months ago.

The elderly lady had presided over many of the festivities the Beteilles had hosted since settling in Pondicherry a few years ago. Seated on the magenta concrete floor, she never even looked up as she stuffed balls of dough with mashed lentils and sweet jaggery that would then be rolled flat and fried.

"These *poli* are all nearly done, but I don't think we have enough almonds or saffron for the *badam* milk sauce. The *payasam* is ready, though, and the *vadai mavu* is ready."

A relief because the deep-fried *dal* batter fritters studded with a mixture of ginger, black peppercorn, curry leaves, and green chilies were a family legacy, and they were prized in town.

"I can get more almonds, and you can add extra cardamom

instead of the saffron," Mireille decided. "How about the sugar cane sticks and the jujube fruits?" Both were popular with the children.

It took a few minutes to sort the details, but Gayatri *Amma* clearly had everything in hand.

Next, was making sure there was enough fuel for the evening bonfire, plus gearing up for the small and select dance performance that would open the festivities. Which meant she needed to wake her daughter.

Rushing down the long hallway to the sleeping rooms, her ankle bells tinkling all the way, Mireille rapped on the wooden door to the room where both of her children slept. "Wake up. The sun is up, and you are still sleeping!" She rapped her knuckles on the door again, then left to pack the *saris* and paste jewels her dancers would wear tonight. Each costume featured a different style of cloth her husband meant to feature this year, and they had chosen the bright colors and vivid patterns carefully.

Yet, half an hour later, neither of her children had appeared. Could these two not manage to get themselves together one day out of the year?

She stalked back to their room and threw open the French doors. Her son's bed was unoccupied and bare, while her daughter was bundled in a mountain of blankets.

"Maman?" she wailed on the heels of a long cough.

Mireille rushed to her, cursing herself for not checking on her daughter sooner. She peeled off the blankets and pulled the thin, sweat-drenched girl into her arms. Rosa, her beloved Rosabel, was sick. She was listless. She was hot. And yet, she was shivering on her straw bed.

The illness had returned.

Her Rosa suffered from something the doctors could not identify, but despite all their tests, she suffered, nonetheless.

"Oh, my darling." She left for a tense minute and returned

with a cold cloth for her daughter's forehead. Where was her son anyway?

"Krish! Krish! Don't let me catch you hiding from me!"

Unlike her beloved Rosa, small and sickly and so dependent on her for the seven years of her life, Mireille's firstborn had never needed her, had never wanted her. Even in those precious first moments after his birth, when all children reached for their mothers, he'd only turned his face away from her. Her and only her. With everyone else, he was a bubbly, happy child. But with her, he was only ever silent.

Any other woman in this town, in this country, possibly in all the realms of the gods, would prize a son over any daughter. And yet, when presented with the red, squalling reality that was her firstborn, she'd only felt disappointment she'd not been gifted the daughter she'd always wanted. Had her son sensed her dissatisfaction? Is that why he'd turned to Achille, who crowed over how his son was a mirror image of his papa?

"Krish!" she yelled again now. Damn that boy for scampering off when she needed him the most.

Except that the front door opened and slammed, and he called back. "Maman, I am coming!"

He appeared, flushed and out of breath, at the bedroom doorway. If Rosabel was a perfect blend of her parents—thin and tall and slender with silky, brown hair that needed little taming and angular features that seemed cunning and underdeveloped at once —then Krish was fully like his French father, with freckles across his face and a head full of springy coils.

Predictably, that delighted Achille and soured Mireille in equal measure. Once upon a time, when she was younger and in love, she had been charmed by Achille's exotic looks and exotic dreams. This was a far better match than any she could make with a local man, she'd argued to her parents. Her Francophile father agreed. How wrong they had both been.

No, that was too harsh. Achille was not a bad man. Only self-ish. And lacking true tenderness in his heart. His promises to help India thrive once again started with his own fortunes, no matter what he had claimed during their courtship. It had been one thing when he'd reneged on his promise not to take her away from her aging parents. But his coldness when their Rosa failed to thrive—that was something she could not forgive.

She turned to her son. "Where have you been?" She fully intended the snap in her words.

Krish shuffled back. "I called on the doctor. He is ten minutes behind me."

She muttered a few choice words under her breath. The French doctors in this town had no answers for her, no answers for her daughter. They were forever prescribing draughts and potions that left Rosabel too fatigued to leave her room.

"Not Papa's doctors," Krish said, giving her that sideways glance of his. "Yours."

His confession stunned her into silence. Achille mandated the only doctors he would tolerate, especially given how often Rosabel grew sick, were ones trained in the Western ways. She had protested once upon a time.

Achille only scoffed. "Why would we cleave to old, unproven ways when the French doctors have trained on the latest techniques?"

"Dr. Prakash has been seeing my family for generations."

"I have nothing against *Ayurvedic* tendencies. They simply aren't current."

Dr. Prakash had not visited their home again since then. But here was Krish, going against his father to do what his mother believed in.

Had she misjudged him?

The doctor arrived, and Mireille lost sight of her son.

"Your daughter's *Pitta Dosha* is off." Dr. Prakash pressed his hand on Rosa's and examined her fingernails, then checked her eyes, tongue, and internal organs. "See how her skin blisters with rashes, how her sweat smells sour and old? Her body is aflame inside, and it needs cooling."

He dropped his hand and rattled off a list of foods her daughter should and shouldn't consume. Nothing new on the list since the last time he had delivered this lecture, and it was true: when Rosa stuck to her limited diet, her energy peaked. But it wasn't only that. Mireille couldn't help but think Achille's recent arrival from his extended factory tour was to blame. Whenever he was home, her brilliant child wilted under his impatient gaze.

"Sandalwood can also have a cooling effect on body and mind," the doctor continued. "It will help relieve her fever and stop the sweating. You may also administer some rose essence, which will help calm her heart and digestion. I will send an additional mixture of herbs I grow myself that will help bring her into balance."

"Thank you, doctor." Mireille knelt at his feet for his blessing. "I am grateful for your care of my family."

As she escorted the doctor to their front door, she caught sight of her son sitting outside Rosabel's room. When she returned, he was gone.

Bhogi Pongal, or the eve of the true festivities, began that evening. Mireille left their home at the very last moment, kissing her daughter's forehead goodbye. Rosa's fever hadn't broken, but she was breathing evenly now. Her son had been inseparable from his sister, at least until Achille dragged him away to participate in the festivities.

"Come now, son," he yelled from downstairs. "It won't do for us to be late."

"I can't leave her," he mumbled, face buried in Rosa's oily hair. "She can't wake up alone."

"She is getting better." Mireille offered him a smile. "Thanks to you."

Krish rose and wiped his face with one hand. "You'll check on her?"

"As often as I can."

Watching her son retreat with his father, both with the same tight gait and the same squared shoulders, she wondered if there was anything of her at all in the boy. Save his love for Rosabel.

By the time she was able to leave home, a retinue of servants carrying sacks of sweetmeats and snacks struggling to keep up behind her, the sounds of laughter and music filled the air. The small square by the beach Achille had secured for the festivities was centered around a thriving bonfire, with hundreds of people queuing up to throw their old clothes into the blazing flames. In return, Achille and Krish, bedecked in matching green and white *sherwani* trimmed in silver, were busy distributing new cloth from Achille's textile factory, ensuring that everyone received fresh garments to welcome the new year.

It was not an easy proposition, telling their townspeople to burn cloth that could be repurposed as blankets or rags. Even fuel. But that was what Achille wanted.

"Give us your past, and we will give you the future!" he intoned, as he had for weeks about town. His advertisement in the local newspaper had given the details.

Trade your worn saris *and stained* dhotis *for the latest fabrics made outside our own Pondy!*

Burn your rags and take home chintz *and* calico *with all the fashionable patterns!*
Quality fabrics are not just for the British anymore!

Mireille had written the language herself, and although Achille worried they were courting trouble, he was too ambitious not to follow her lead.

Talk in the market only confirmed her approach, with the women deciding they were good enough to wear what the white ladies did, and the men realizing they needed to dress like the British gentlemen they longed to deal with.

Surprising, how many people had shown up to feed the flames with their offerings. But then, wasn't that what *Bhogi Pongal* was about, the renewal and cleansing of the year past?

"Set up beside my son," Mireille directed the servants carrying their sweets and snacks. She hurried toward Achille. He wore an irate expression and, when she neared him, waved a newspaper in her face.

"You're late, Mireille," her husband said between clenched jaws. "Look at this. The government in Madras held a massive *Pongal* celebration of their own last night, and they raised record contributions for the war effort."

WAR FUND FETE IN MADRAS
They surged, school boys and girls, scores of excited men and women, mothers with babies and with chattering kiddies clinging to available fingers, happy young things on the arms of their beaus, while burnished cars and buses squeezed through as well.

9

Mireille read the article claiming thousands of people had attended and scoffed at the photograph of festivalgoers clutching a book of coupons bought to enjoy the food and games. Even though she knew Achille was thinking how small their local effort would fare in the papers against a celebration supporting British war interests, her indignation held little compassion.

"We are doing something true for *Pongal,* caring about our own people instead of worrying about Hitler and his faraway war. And, unlike the British, we aren't using a sacred holiday as an excuse to beg more money from the people least able to afford it."

Achille snatched the paper back. "Does a family on the run care if it's a wolf or a lion chasing behind them? Does a lion or a wolf care if it is a Jew or a gypsy or an Indian it will feed from?" His glare softened as he surveyed the crowded line stretching beyond view. "Are we so miserly, we can only look to our own?"

Her constant irritation with him was papered over with remorse and a nostalgic pride. This was the Achille she had fallen in love with, this man who loved all, who wanted the best for all. Wasn't he giving away cloth to her people, their people, and without asking them to buy books of coupons?

"You are right, of course." Unexpected words between them these days, but then, she had been given an unexpected gift from her own son for her beloved daughter. And surely, those faraway people embroiled in a faraway war had mothers and daughters and sons who did what they could for each other.

Achille moved closer to her and gifted her with that quirky smile he seldom wore now that his days were filled with reports and demands over his textiles. "You are making your family's *vadai.*" He nodded at the heavy carts loaded with frying vats and the terra cotta pots of batter her cooks had delivered.

"They are traditional." She nodded at the growing heap of banana leaf wrappings, still slick with the oil from hot fritters. "We should save those for the cows." The third day of celebrations honored cattle for their role in the harvest.

"And they are your favorite." Achille's voice lowered. "I know you don't agree with me that helping the British in their war efforts may sway their opinion positively about the worth of India. But still, we must stay true to who we are and what we value."

As if they all valued the same thing. Frankly, anything that took the British focus away from India and committed their resources elsewhere, could only be good for India. But that wasn't what she said now.

"Look at Krish. What a little man he has become." It was true. Dressed in the same pressed green and white cotton *sherwani* as his father, he had completely taken over the job of handing out new clothes with a decorum Mireille herself hadn't possessed at his age. Men ruffled his hair, and women pinched his cheeks, but still, he handed them costlier clothes than they had ever seen, with a solemn nod and wishes for a prosperous new year.

"He is. Isn't he? There was no mistaking the pride in his voice. Achille touched her arm, though gently. "And how is Rosa? Is she getting better?"

Mireille startled. It wasn't often he asked about their daughter, much less by name. And for the life of her, she could not remember when he'd ever called their girl "Rosa."

"She is better, thanks to Krish." She didn't explain the details, only said he had been the one to alert her to Rosa's fevered state. "We were lucky."

"Or our boy pays too much mind to his sister. It is good for him to be out among others."

Mireille's sudden affection for the man cooled, and she turned away to keep an eye on the dance performance. She had been working with the young girls for months, teaching them the intricate steps and formations of the traditional dance. The girls, dressed in the beautiful *saris* Mireille had prepared, moved with grace and precision and brilliant smiles.

"Oh, Rosa, you should be at the head of it all tonight." How much her daughter loved to dress in her father's fine cloth and her mother's dazzling jewels. How much care she took in practicing her steps, balancing rhythm and flow with every movement.

As if summoned, Rosa appeared, but not as the vibrant girl exulting at mastering her dance. No, this Rosa was a wraith, sallow and thin, hair hastily braided, dancer's makeup sloppily applied. Krish abandoned his post beside his father and rushed to his sister's side, Mireille two steps behind him.

"Mireille!" Achille snapped. "What is the girl doing here?"

Rosabel stumbled at his words, right into Krish's arms.

"You're not well, *ma frangine.*" Krish cleared up the smudged *kohl* around her eyes with his thumb. "Come, let me take you home."

"Tsst." Achille hissed at one of the servants handing out snacks. "Janak can escort her, and make sure she stays in bed, where she needs to be."

"I need to help her," Krish insisted, meeting his father with defiant eyes.

"And I need you here."

"Maman, please, I need to dance." Rosa's eyes gleamed with determination.

Mireille's heart swelled with love and pride for her daughter's resilience.

"I want to be a part of it, Papa," Rosa whispered, her voice barely audible. "I want to dance."

Mireille placed a gentle hand on Rosa's shoulder, feeling the heat of her fever. "Darling, you're too weak. You need to rest."

But Rosa shook her head, her eyes shining with determination. "I can do it, Maman. I want to dance with the others. Please."

Mireille looked into her daughter's eyes and saw the fierce

spirit that mirrored her own. She understood Rosa's longing and desire to be a part of the celebration, to overcome the limitations of her illness. With a deep breath, she turned to Achille.

"Let her dance, Achille," Mireille said, her voice firm, yet filled with tenderness. "We'll be right beside her, watching over her."

Achille hesitated, his gaze shifting between Mireille and Rosa. Finally, he nodded. "Very well, but take care to keep it simple. I don't want her to make a scene."

Mireille smiled with a surge of gratitude. "Thank you, Achille."

Rosa's face lit up as Mireille and Achille led her to the dance area. The young girls welcomed her with open arms, adjusting their formations to accommodate Rosa's limited movements. The young men who acted as brothers and guardians stepped in, supporting Rosa and guiding her through the dance.

It was a simple movement set to a simple beat. *Thai Tha Tham. Thai Tha Tham.*

The men playing the drumbeat increased their tempo, and the pipers matched the rhythm. Around and around and around, the girls twirled, and Mireille watched with bated breath. It was a delicate and enchanting performance, filled with the beauty of synchronized movements and the bond of family. Every step Rosa took was filled with determination and love, supported by the care and devotion of her dance partners.

And then it happened. Rosa missed a beat. And then another. Before Mireille could intervene, she fell into a heap in the center of the square.

"*Merdre*," Achille swore, but Mireille had no time for him.

Hiking up her *sari*, she stepped off the stage to go to her daughter. Only, once again, Krish was already there.

With a tender smile, he pulled her up and smoothed the tears from her face.

"I ruined it, Krish. I messed up the dance."

"Nonsense. You can only ruin it if you quit. And I won't let you."

He wrapped his silver scarf around her neck and held up her hand in the first step of the dance. The boy hadn't received any formal training, but he *had* watched his sister practice day after day. He apparently knew the steps, the rhythm, and the spirit of the dance.

"Dance with me, Rosa," he said, just loud enough for Mireille to hear.

She was filled with a new love for this son of hers.

Under his loving smile, his sister seemed to gain strength. Her eyes sparkled with newfound energy, and a smile brightened her pale face. Hope surged through Mireille's veins like adrenaline. As the dance reached its climax, her heart swelled with love and pride. The bond between the dancers, the energy of the celebration, and the resilience of her daughter filled her with a renewed sense of purpose.

The dance performance concluded with thunderous applause from the crowd. Mireille embraced Rosa tightly, tears streaming down her face. She opened her arms wider to include Krish.

"You are my treasures, both of you." And both hugged her back.

Achille stood beside them, his expression distant, his body stiff. There would be words to be had later, but right now, Mireille could not bring herself to care as she held her family close. Tomorrow, the festivities would center around boiling milk in earthen pots until it bubbled and overflowed in a symbol of abundance and prosperity. But tonight, they'd had a boiling point of a different kind, filling her heart with love and gratitude for the children she had been gifted. The slivered moon emerged from a mackerel sky, and, in that moment, she knew the coming year would be their best ever.

Change was in the air.

Medhu Vadai, a popular South Indian snack made during _Pongal_

Ingredients:

- 1 cup _urad dal_ (skinned black gram)
  - 2-3 green chilies, finely chopped
  - 1 tablespoon ginger, grated
  - A handful of curry leaves, finely chopped
  - 2 tablespoons chopped coriander leaves
  - 1 teaspoon cumin seeds
  - Salt to taste
  - Oil for deep frying

Instructions:

- Wash the _urad dal_ thoroughly and soak in water for 3-4 hours. This helps in easy grinding and gives a fluffy texture to the _vadai._
  - Drain the soaked _dal_ and transfer it to a blender or a wet grinder. Grind it to a smooth paste, adding very little water if required. The batter should be thick and fluffy.
  - Transfer the batter to a large mixing bowl.
  - Add chopped green chilies, grated ginger, chopped curry leaves, chopped coriander leaves, cumin seeds, and salt to the batter. Mix well to incorporate all the ingredients.
  - Heat oil in a deep pan for frying.

- To shape the *vadai*, wet your hands with water to prevent sticking. Take a small portion of the batter and shape it into a ball. Flatten the ball slightly and make a hole in the center using your thumb.
- Gently slide the shaped *vadai* into the hot oil. Fry 2-3 *vadai* at a time, depending on the size of your pan, to maintain the oil temperature.
- Fry the *vadai* on medium heat until they turn golden brown and crisp on the outside. Flip them occasionally for even cooking.
- Once the *vadai* are golden brown, remove them from the oil and place them on paper towels to absorb excess oil.
- Repeat the process with the remaining batter, shaping and frying the *vadai* in batches.

Serve the hot and crispy *medhu vadai* with coconut *chutney* or *sambar* as a delicious snack and enjoy the *Pongal* celebrations!

·((● ●))·

Vanitha Sankaran writes fiction based on history, legend, and mythology. Her literary historical novel, *Watermark: A Novel of the Middle Ages*, traces the introduction of paper in southern France at a time when heresy was aflame. By day, she works in medical strategy and by night, she capers through collections of folklore. For more about Vanitha, please see her website at www.vanithasankaran.com, follow her on Facebook, Instagram, or BlueSky.

·((● ●))·

The Star Lantern

TWELFTH NIGHT
BY REBECCA D'HARLINGUE

Amsterdam
5 January, 1660

J oanna startled, and it took her a moment to realize she had
fallen asleep in her chair. She looked down and saw she was
dressed. Nicolaes must have helped her, as he always did now,
ever since she had her spell three months ago, right before her
sixtieth birthday. The physician called it apoplexy, as he stood
there in his black robe and coat, his pointed hat, and his collar-
bands. She was lucky she could still speak, he had told her. She was
exceedingly lucky that she could use both hands, which was not
always the case for apoplexy victims.

She could not walk, though. If someone held both of her
arms, she could shuffle along, but that was not walking, so mostly
she sat in her chair.

Ah, she realized now that what had woken her from her nap
was a clattering in the kitchen. It must be the young girl,
Geertruyd, whom Nicolaes had hired to do much of the house
work, work which she used to do. Though he never complained,

Joanna thought surely Nicolaes must begrudge the fact that he had to pay someone to do the work she was meant to do. She found she herself resented the girl, unjust though she knew that to be. Still, she had kindly told Geertruyd she needed to come in for only a couple of hours today and then she could go home to celebrate Twelfth Night with her family.

Joanna had always loved Twelfth Night, the eve of Epiphany, when the visit of the Three Kings to the Christ child was celebrated. As a young girl, she had been envious of her brothers, who might be the "king" for the day, crowned because they had found the bean in their loaf at breakfast. Joanna always wondered whether she would be queen if she found the bean, but that never happened, nor did her two sisters ever find the bean. When she had once quietly asked them if they felt cheated, they looked at her blankly, as though any sense of injustice had never occurred to them, and so she had kept her disappointment to herself. It seemed her three brothers would each find the bean every third year, and it was only when she was older that she realized her mother must have planned it so, taking care to remember which loaf held the bean, and to give it to the appropriate son, but never to a daughter.

As she wondered what Geertruyd was doing in the kitchen creating such a din, Joanna felt anew the old feeling of her mother's betrayal. Joanna had dearly wished she would one day have a girl, but she took some comfort in the fact that, on Twelfth Night, she would never need to let a daughter think it was simply as it should be that a boy always found the bean. Joanna followed her mother's example in giving out the morning loaves on January fifth. Each of her four sons was king in his turn, for how could she bear the disappointment on the face of a beloved son who might never be king if all were left to chance?

"A special day," Nicolaes came in, disrupting Joanna's recollections.

"Yes, special," Joanna replied listlessly, as Nicolaes looked at her expectantly, as though waiting for her to continue. When she didn't, he sighed, and hesitated before turning to leave. As she looked at his back, she thought that in the past, he would have prompted her to say more. Now, he just left her alone.

She remembered her mother was not wholly insensitive to the disappointment she had felt, for she did insist the girls should have a turn carrying the star lantern, when they would go out at night to parade around the neighborhood, stopping at homes to sing songs for the new audience that lingered at the doorstep of each house on their route. Joanna loved her mother for granting her this privilege, for carrying the star lantern seemed to her an even greater honor than being king.

Not every family owned a star lantern, and Joanna thought her family's was one of the finer ones, as it had eight triangles coming from the central circle to form the star. Some people had only six, or even five. The star was attached to a pole, so that it shone above the bearer, and though it could feel burdensome after a while, Joanna never let anyone see her fatigue. She would not have had it taken from her for the world. As their sons grew old enough to carry the lantern, she convinced Nicolaes they should follow her family's example, and the king should not be the one to always be honored with that responsibility.

They did not have the lantern of Nicolaes' youth, as his older brother had claimed it. Joanna was secretly happy about this, though Nicolaes had been a bit sad, because that meant they could use the lantern from Joanna's youth, for she had convinced each of her brothers, when he married, that he should have a new lantern to go with his new family. As her sons and their families always spent the day and night at their parents' home, Joanna exulted in a third generation carrying her lamp.

Looking back, she did not know how the years had escaped her. She worked so hard to care for her sons, though there was never time to reflect on her efforts. One just began the tasks of the day, and the unfinished ones were continued on the morrow. Just like all of the women she knew, this was her life, and she counted herself lucky to have it so.

That is not to say there were never difficulties. Life is never without difficulties. But she and Nicolaes faced and worked through them together. Together. The result was not always the one they had envisioned, but it never destroyed them, and that was lucky, too.

The constant work of raising four sons was never the problem. No, it was the lack of it that had been hard for her, as her sons abandoned their parents' home, one by one, to make their own lives. This was what she had always wanted for them, without having had time to think of what it would mean for her. Slowly, she adjusted, a bit more each time as yet another child left, although the time was already years in the past when she had needed to feed them, help them with their clothes, pray with them at their bedside, sing them to sleep. Still, for years there was food to be prepared, a home to be kept clean, and clothing to launder and keep in good repair.

Even so, those chores became less, until at last, it was just Nicolaes and herself to care for, and he had never been a demanding husband. They were fortunate three of their sons lived in Amsterdam with their wives and children. Their other boy, Dirck, lived in Haarlem, connected to Amsterdam by the *trekschuiten,* the barges pulled along the canals by horses on a towpath. A visit to Haarlem was a pleasant outing when the weather was good.

Before this year, Joanna had not allowed the emptier house to mar her joy at Twelfth Night, and she entered into the preparations with a profound happiness. She spent her days preparing special foods and making sure the house was immaculate. Most of all, Joanna loved retrieving the star lantern from where she had stored it and making sure it was ready for its annual sojourn along the streets of the city. In this time, the busyness of her earlier days seemed to return, like a gift, and she had purpose and felt the joy of it.

In past years, since she had given out the loaves, she had kept track of which of her grandchildren was due to find the bean, and she had distributed the loaves accordingly. She also insisted upon a different child carrying the star lantern, and though each new daughter-in-law at first balked at this departure from the convention, they soon seemed to accept it.

But this year, her idleness cursed her. She had no central role in the preparations or celebration. They would all gather at Thomas's house, and it would be his wife, Susanna, who would give out the loaves. Thomas would be the one to decide who would carry the star lantern. Joanna hadn't even taken it upon herself to ask him to make sure the lantern duty went to a grandchild who had not yet been entrusted with it.

‹‹ ● ● ● ››

"Hester is here," Geertruyd's voice interrupted her.

"Hello, Mama Joanna," the wife of Joanna's youngest son said, nudging past Geertruyd in the doorway. "I've come to help dress you for the special day."

"But I am already dressed, as you can see."

"Oh, I brought you something special, a gift from Frederick and me. He told me how you always dressed up for the holiday, and even saw to it Papa Nicolaes and all the boys had at least one new article of clothing." Joanna knew she should have felt touched, as Hester laid out a beautiful new bodice she had sewn herself. It was made of green fabric and decorated with purple ribbons down the sleeves. Hester had also brought a lovely new collar and cuffs set, with exquisitely-made lace. Joanna understood she should appreciate the thoughtfulness of her young daughter-in-law, but part of her wondered whether her Frederick had willingly spent the money for this extravagance, or if Hester had pestered him to do so.

"You shouldn't have gone to such trouble for an old woman," she said, though when she saw the hurt upon Hester's face, she added, "Still, it is a kindness to have thought of me." Her words belied her feelings, though, as she couldn't help but feel a bit foolish, a doll to be dressed up by this newcomer to her family. After helping her dress, Hester quickly left, saying she would see her later.

How different this morning had been from their custom of years past! Had Nicolaes forgotten that each morning, after the king had been determined, they would all escape to the canal if it were frozen? He must have, for he said nothing about it to her. She had loved those outings, and each year, had fervently wished for the freezing weather that would harden the city's canals. Joanna could only take an hour, for then she must return to the preparations for the evening's celebrations, but she and Nicolaes and the boys would all hold hands, thus daring other skaters to try to separate them. In those moments, she cherished both the strong bond holding her to her family, and a sense of escape from the ordinary constraints of life.

·‹ (● ●) ›·

When Joanna and Nicolaes arrived at Thomas's home, he greeted them warmly, commenting on how pretty Joanna looked. In former times, she would have been as appreciative as any woman at hearing such a compliment, but in her present, reduced state, she didn't see how anyone could find her lovely, and she didn't respond to her son's words.

Thomas settled her a bit away from the activity, and sitting in her chair, Joanna did not revel in the exuberance of her grandchildren as she had in years past. This year it simply felt like chaos. In part, she was glad to be a bit outside its realm, but at the same time she felt sadly disconnected. From time to time, someone would come to speak to her, but then they would get distracted by some new aspect of the day's activities and drift away. When one of Thomas and Susanna's sons found the bean, even though his brother had been king the previous year, Joanna wondered whether this was luck, or some planning on Susanna's part. She didn't feel a strong reaction though, as she would have previously. It was no longer her responsibility to see that the favor was bestowed equally from year to year.

Joanna asked herself what was so engaging to everyone that they seldom came over to have a word with her. Her grandchildren were, understandably, caught up in the excitement of the day, and she would not wish their exhilaration diminished, even if it deprived her of their close company. Her daughters-in-law were preparing the food for the evening feast. There would be capon with Susanna's special sauce, and Joanna found herself wishing it would not taste quite as good as her own used to. Her sons were enjoying the antics of the children, and one another's company, but she forgave them less readily than she did her joyful grandchildren or their busy mothers, for her sons had less excuse for ignoring her and should have felt a stronger bond. At one point, she looked around for Nicolaes and did not see him, but she wondered for only a brief moment where he might be.

She gazed at Dirck's wife as she laughed with her own daughter, as the two of them prepared the batter for the pancakes, and she felt that familiar twinge of envy. They beat the eggs, added water and spices. Even from her spot, she could smell the sharp scent of the cloves and cinnamon, the mace and nutmeg. The pair stirred in the flour, and soon they would put the pancakes on the fire to fry. The evening feast would be on the table before she knew it, and Joanna wondered where the day had gone, and whether she had dozed in the loneliness of her chair.

It was already dark enough that the children had begun to play the game of jumping over three lit candles, symbolizing the three kings who followed the star to find the child Jesus.

"Be careful, children! Watch out for the flames! Do not knock over the candles!" she cried from her chair.

"They are fine, Mama," Thomas said. "We always used to play this game."

It was true, Joanna knew. Why did it only now occur to her this could be a dangerous amusement? She put her worry down to being old, to knowing in her bones that bad things could happen.

"Let us help you to the table, Grootmoeder," said Jan and Tobias, Joanna's two oldest grandsons. As everyone settled into a place at the two large tables Thomas had set up, he stood and said, "Let us give thanks for each other and the bounty of our table. Let each of us, like the Three Kings, always seek the Christ Child in our lives." Knowing of Thomas's propensity to go on at length if given the chance, his brothers all said, "Amen," raising their glasses as though in a toast, and effectively cutting Thomas off.

Joanna enjoyed the happy company of her family more than the food itself, though from everyone else's obvious pleasure, it was delicious. With satisfaction, she judged Susanna's sauce to be inferior to her own, but then realized nothing tasted as good to her as it used to, and perhaps the memory of the flavor of her own sauce was enhanced by the passing of time.

When everyone declared they could eat no more, the youngsters got ready to go out to serenade the neighbors with songs of the season. As they lit the star lantern, Joanna realized that this year, she had not gone up to the loft room to retrieve the lantern and clean it until it shone. She hadn't even thought about it. Nicolaes must have done it. She hadn't known he even knew where she kept it.

She and Nicolaes and some of the other adults would stay at Thomas' house and receive other singers. As her own family's singers marched out of the house, they already heard a group approaching. Nicolaes came to help her to a chair closer to the doorway and tenderly rested his hand on her shoulder as she watched the group's star lantern and listened to them sing:

> *Here we walk, Lord, with our star;*
> *We seek Lord Jesus, we want him dearly.*
> *We already knocked on Herod's door:*
> *Herod, the king, came out himself.*

Joanna looked at the star lantern and was glad she could still appreciate its light and beauty. Listening again, she realized she had missed some of the song, for the next lines, she knew, came further along in the lyrics.

> *We came over the high mountains,*
> *A star remained standing still there.*
> *Oh star, you must not stand so still,*
> *You must go with us to Bethlehem.*
> *To Bethlehem, in that lovely city,*
> *Where Maria sat with her baby.*

She was always taken with the thought of the kings traveling so far to seek out a tiny child. She loved the image of a woman with her newborn babe. As the evening wore on, Joanna experienced anew a sense of joy each time another group with its star lantern approached. This was more than she had felt these past months, and she was grateful. After a while, though, she found herself tiring, and wondered when the children would return.

Just as she was beginning to drowse in her chair, the boisterous group entered, bringing cold and good cheer with them. A couple of the smaller children came up to her and excitedly regaled her with the details of their wanderings, and how many other groups they had seen, and how they had been received at each house. But soon they had conveyed it all, and just as they wandered off to seek out some treats after their hard work of walking and singing, Jan and Tobias came up to her.

"We have a surprise for you, Grootmoeder," Jan said.

"What is that?"

"Oh, but if we tell you, it will not be a surprise," said Tobias, the taller of the two, with a mischievous grin, the same one she had seen many times since he was a little boy. He lifted her from her chair and headed closer to the door, while Jan put her cloak around her.

"Are we going outside? It is too cold, my dears! You forget I am an old woman. And how will I get about?"

"We have blankets to put over your shoulders and your lap, and we will not have far to walk." And with that, the two young men helped her out the door. On the threshold, she lingered a moment to look out and see the star lanterns of several groups. Having felt the sharp cold, she was reluctant to leave the warmth of the house, but the boys insisted and helped her descend the four steps to the path. It was only then she noticed the armchair on runners, like those she had seen older folks ride in on the frozen canal.

Jan picked up the chair while Tobias took a firmer hold of her, and they walked across the road to the Herengracht. There were dozens of skaters on the canal, and from their bulk, it was clear everyone had worn extra clothing underneath to ward off the freezing air. Some young men were racing along, slightly bent forward, with their hands behind their backs. Couples had their arms around one another's waist, and still others formed long snakes of skaters, each holding onto the hips of the person in front of them. This was all a familiar site, and even the horses, whose bells tinkled as they pulled a sleigh of painted wood along the ice, were not unusual. There were one or two other older people, as well as some young children being pushed along in chairs. As Jan put the chair on the ice, then came back to help Tobias assist her to the chair, she felt afraid, and saddened by her fear.

"Do not go fast, my dears," she begged, as the two boys tucked blankets around her.

"Don't worry, Grootmoeder, you are safe with us. All right, here we go!" Although his words suggested speed, Tobias pushed the chair slowly, as Jan skated protectively alongside her. After a few minutes, she began to relax and let herself enjoy the feeling of effortless movement she had been denied since her spell.

"What made you think of this?" she asked the boys.

"Grootvader came up with the idea weeks ago. He searched to find just the right chair, and asked a carpenter how best to apply the runners. He just finished it this morning." Perhaps that was where Nicolaes had gone when she had blamed his leaving on losing interest in her.

"Did you not notice he was gone for a while this afternoon? He went home to get the chair. He said you were downcast all of the time, and he did not know how to make you happier. He hoped this would help, but he thought you would accept it better coming from us."

Joanna was surprised at this. Had she been unjust in thinking her husband was pulling away from her, that it was hard for him to accept a wife who could not take care of them as she used to? He helped her dress every day, and was unendingly patient with her, but she had convinced herself he, good man that he was, would have shown this kindness to anyone in need, and it was not a result of any special feeling he had for her.

She had told herself he didn't care how she felt, but now, gliding along, she remembered the many times after her spell he had asked how she was. At first, she had simply replied that she was fine, and she now saw the look of hurt on her husband's face each time she told this transparent lie. After a while, she would grow annoyed with his question and make no attempt to hide her pique. And so, after a while, Nicolaes had stopped asking. He had never stopped gently taking care of her, but she had not been grateful.

Now, the boys were telling her Nicolaes had done all of this for her, and she had not really thought about his feelings at all. It was her attitude that had kept him from feeling confident enough to offer her this gift, though he would not let his reluctance deprive her of the moments of happiness he hoped this would bring her. Sorrow and guilt threatened to overcome the joy of the moment, but Joanna would forgive herself, as she vowed she would make it up to this husband who loved her, who cherished her, who had also suffered because of her ordeal.

For now, she looked at the star lanterns of the singing groups, some even on the canal, their light doubled in their muted reflection on the ice. Her eyes drank in the sight of so many lanterns shining forth in the night, and she was grateful for the beauty, and for the understanding this Twelfth Night had granted her. Nicolaes had done this to bring her happiness, and she owed it to him to enjoy it to the fullest.

Speaking above the sounds of skates and laughter around her, she said, "Can you go faster, boys? Can you make me fly?"

She heard the immediate effect of her words as the metal blades of her grandsons' long skates, with their curved fronts like the prow of a ship, hit the ice at an increasing pace.

The cold grew greater in the wind of speed, and Joanna leaned back and looked at the pinpricks of stars in the black sky, wondering whether her tears would freeze to her face.

·‹‹●●●›·

Rebecca D'Harlingue writes about seventeenth-century women taking a different path. Her second novel, The Map Colorist, also takes place in Amsterdam in 1660, and features a young woman who dares to create her own map to be published in the largest publication of the century. Secrets, infidelity, and murder threaten her dream. For more about Rebecca, go to her website, rebeccadharlingue.com, or follow her on Facebook, Instagram, Goodreads, Pinterest, or BookBub.

·‹‹●●●›·

Hand-in-Hand Pies

~

FROST FAIR

BY EDIE CAY

London, England
December 1789

Bess shivered in the cold darkness. Around the fire, the watermen swayed, passing a bottle. Bess was so cold that her teeth hurt, so she didn't follow Carver's rule just then about staying away from drunk men. Bess didn't know exactly what drunk meant, other than people not speaking right, words tripping and swirling like when a body turned in circles too many times.

The night was dark, real dark, and the watermen's fire—if watermen was what they were—made her blind, looking only at what the flames let her see: that they stood on the frozen river with a small fire in a pot, wiping their mouths as if they'd eaten not long ago. Bess tried to be quiet in the snow that had just kept falling day after day, but her toes had lost feeling long ago, despite the paper she'd shoved in there that morning for extra warmth.

The whole world had frozen: trees, pipes, and the big river. Her nose and cheeks ached. She couldn't sleep in her regular spot near the church, because Carver told her she hadn't found enough food or coin that day. That was another one of his rules. He weren't but a handful of years older than her, and barely taller, but he sure told everyone what to do.

Bess crept up further to the glow of the fire, hoping to stay out of sight, but those drunk watermen spotted her.

"Oi, Bitsy, this your'n?" A man called out, moving his hand toward her as if he might scoop her up. But nobody ever scooped her up. She was too big for that, even if she didn't feel big on the inside.

"I ain't got none, you know that," the cry came from across the fire.

If they saw her, there was no harm in getting closer to the fire, the cold making her bolder than she would be otherwise. If it were warm, she'd try to slip a hand in someone's pocket, find loose coins, a handkerchief, or maybe even a watch. But Carver said no watches. Too expensive, and enough that might get her into trouble even he couldn't get her out of.

"You hungry, girl?" A lady's voice said that.

She couldn't see that lady, the shadows of the fire playing tricks and making every person seem tall and frightful. Carver said to never let them give you things, because then you owed them something. Safest to not take it. But her stomach growled loudly.

"Poor thing's starvin', Penny. Get her something."

The lady made a coughing noise, and there was a thump, like maybe she gave the man a wallop for telling her to give away their food. Bess kept her mouth shut, not saying yes or no. Her fingers tingled in that way that hurt—like they were first on fire, then so cold she might be able to shake them off like icicles clinging to her palm.

There was a clanking of metal, and the men shifted, laughed, and booed.

"Oi, Penny, didn't say to cook her the King's own feast!"

"Shut your mouth now, Bitsy. I'm to give the girl proper food, and it ought to be warm. Look at her. She's tall, but she ain't but as old as a pup. And it's just a spot of porridge, anyhow. Stick to her ribs."

Bess liked porridge. It didn't taste like much, but she liked how it slid down her throat, warming her up from the inside.

Her feet stung as they warmed, but that faded, and a comfortable, drowsy feeling came over her.

"Tony, poke at her. Poor thing's asleep on her feet."

Large hands gripped around her arm, and Bess' eyes snapped open. She fought like Carver told her, with her teeth and nails. She wailed and kicked.

"Oi, wee girl! Stop! Miss Penny here made you food, and you'll eat it afore you fall asleep on your feet. I ain't tryin' ta take you nowhere." The man's voice was clipped, like the sound of horse hooves on cobblestones.

Bess swung around to face him, ready to bite if need be. His face was covered in a beard, but his lips were pushed together, not in a way that meant he wanted anything from her. She stopped swinging her arms.

The lady with the porridge came over, and Bess could finally make out her face. She was kind, and that made her pretty. Carver said you couldn't tell kindness from the way a person looked, but Bess wasn't sure about that.

Carver's voice telling her not to take food from strangers echoed in her head, but what did Carver know? He wasn't grown, neither. Bess took the bowl, which helped her hands stop aching.

She picked up the spoon and started eating. It burnt the top of her mouth, but she didn't care. She could feel each spoonful slide down to her belly, filling it for the first time that day. Around her, there were more noises, tsks, and shooing noises, and finally, the lady took her by the shoulders, since she refused to stop eating, and pushed her onto a stool near the fire.

"Aw, but I worked all day," one man complained, standing next to the stool where Bess sat.

"Oh, hush now, Bitsy. You've plenty of ale to keep yourself warm, you don't need a stool, too."

"The stool don't keep me warm, Penny; it rests my aching feet," Bitsy whined.

There was a thump, and Bitsy wheezed.

"Shut it," Tony said. "The wee girl needs it more than your fat arse."

Bess ate so fast that when she finished, she had the hiccups. She licked the spoon and waited until it seemed as though the people were looking elsewhere, and she licked the bowl too.

"How old are ye, girl?" That was Tony asking. Bess shrugged, and the people murmured to each other quiet enough she couldn't hear.

A handful of walnuts landed in her lap. Bess was grateful for her skirts, so she didn't lose any bits of the nut meat. The men around the fire cracked the shells, throwing them into the fire, and then handed the meat, one by one, until it reached her. She didn't dare ask questions or say a peep, for fear they might stop.

The big church bells chimed, and then men looked around and began the mutterings that meant they were going to their homes. This was the time Carver said to disappear. Don't let a man promise you a bed. Don't go with them. And she didn't want to. She could sleep right here on the ice, near this fire. She was so very sleepy.

"Penny, you can't keep her," Tony said. His voice was so easy to figure out even with her eyes closed, growly like a stray dog.

But then, Bess was asleep, her belly full and her feet warm.

·‹‹ ◦ ● ◦ ››·

Raised voices took Bess from her dream of running through tall grass to wide awake in an instant. Her heart pounded as she heard the voices get louder and louder. Angry.

"If you're telling me what to do, Tony, then people will start thinkin' you're my husband. And if you're my husband, you better start providing."

"Penny," the low voice growled. "I thought you believed in me."

"Oh, I believe in you all right. But don't be thinking you can tell me how to run my life until you've brought me to church proper."

"That's not what I'm doing," Tony protested.

Bess pulled the woolen blanket up over her head. It smelled like the herb garden down off Hog Lane. Sweet and woody, all at the same time. She could stay safe under that lovely-smelling blanket forever. She didn't know where the blanket came from, or where she was, but right then, she weren't moving.

"No? If I want to bring a girl on to learn my trade, then how is that any different than any of the little ruffians that get plucked out of a crowd to fight? Ain't no difference, and you know it."

"Girls are different, mark my words, Penny, you'll have all sorts sniffing about, wanting to know if—"

"If what, Tony? Any different than those sorts that sniff around your boys?"

"No one is sniffing around my boys," Tony roared.

Bess squeezed her eyes shut. She knew that sound in a man's voice. That meant things were about to hurt.

But there were no words next, just empty air, hanging thick like the fog that sometimes crept through the alleyways and fields.

"Fine," Tony grumbled. "I won't say another word. Take the girl on. At least she'll be fed."

"I'm not about to say thank you for something that's none of your business." Metal clanged on metal.

"I'm not asking you to."

"Good."

"Fine."

"Eat your porridge. I added a bit of that good, dark honey you like." More clanging.

Honey? Bess sat up, letting the blanket fall. Her stomach growled again. It was her first peek at the room around her. It was small, more like a cupboard, filled with sacks of flour, jars of dried beans, and lumpy burlap sacks of root vegetables. Bess was on a pallet on the floor, which had felt like a thousand clouds compared to the hard, cold stone she'd slept on in doorways that Carver said were safe.

"I think I hear our sleeper stirring." Penny pushed aside a blanket hung in the doorway, closing it off from the kitchen. "Good afternoon, wee girl."

Bess stood up, knowing she ought to stand when big people spoke. She still wore her clothes and her coat—thin as it was. She rubbed her eye to remove the crusty feeling.

"You slept a long time. Are you hungry?" Penny moved aside, showing her the door.

Bess understood. This was her time to leave. That fight the big people had was about someone else, not her. She was too young.

The woman pushed her over to the small kitchen table and set a bowl of porridge in front of her. Steam twisted above the bowl, and the woman dropped a dollop of dark honey into it. Bess' mouth watered.

"Here's some of those nuts you couldn't finish last night," she said, sprinkling them in as well.

Bess couldn't help but stare. It looked so delicious. Her stomach growled again.

"Go on, then. Pick up the spoon and stir it in."

Her grubby fingers, still dirty, grabbed the spoon and did as she was told. At least this morning she could wait long enough not to burn her mouth.

"These too." The woman tossed some bits of hard, dried apple and apricot next to her bowl.

Bess popped a bit of apricot in her mouth and stirred in the rest. It tasted so good, and so sweet, even if she had to soften it with her spit before she could chew it.

"You can call me Miss Penny, everybody does." Miss Penny pointed across the table. "And that big lump o' scruff is Mr. Farrow."

Now that it was daytime, and she could see them properly, she knew she wouldn't have gone to their fire. Mr. Farrow was short, not that much taller than the biggest boys in Carver's gang, but he was just as wide. He had muscles on muscles and dark hair sprouting every which way.

"Call me Tony, might as well."

"Oh, you going right soft, then?" Miss Penny teased.

"Hush, now. Girl, you best eat your food afore I do."

Bess set in on the bowl in front of her.

"What do they call you?" Miss Penny asked her. "You have the look of Saint Giles or maybe Paddington about you."

The last place she'd stayed was Saint Giles. But families were moving to help dig the canal somewhere—maybe north?—of town.

"Bess. Bess Abbott." Bess sucked air in around the too-hot spoonful of porridge.

Miss Penny shook her head. "I don't know any Abbotts. Do you, Tony?"

"None I'd let know there was a girl about with the name."

Miss Penny stared at Bess, but Bess didn't care. There was hot porridge filled with fruit and honey and crunchy bits of walnut, and her toes were warm all the way through.

"In exchange for sleeping here and your food, I have a job I'd like your help with. What do you say?"

Miss Penny was pretty—Bess had been right. She had red-gold hair like Mrs. O'Toole and blue-gray eyes. She had some faded freckles. On some people they might seem silly, but they made Miss Penny look kind. Because she was kind. Bess knew that.

"What kind of job?" Bess asked between mouthfuls. Carver always said to ask lots of questions. That way you could know best if it was worth your time.

"I need help carrying my pies to the Frost Fair on the Thames." Miss Penny smiled, her teeth white and almost straight. Oh yes, Miss Penny was the kind of angel that Amy told stories about, even though Carver laughed at them.

"Pies?" Bess was very interested in pies. She kicked her feet that dangled off the chair.

"She'll drop 'em, Penny," growled Tony.

"I'm very good with my hands, even Carver says so." Bess wanted very much to be near pies.

"Very good," Miss Penny said, just as Tony said, "Who's Carver?"

Bess buttoned her lip. She wasn't supposed to talk about Carver. It was the one rule of being in his gang. Miss Penny looked at Tony, and Bess could tell they were having one of those conversations without words that big people sometimes had.

"This is very important to me, Bess. You see, I'm a very good cook. And I want to open my own place."

Bess looked around at the small kitchen they all sat in. It had some light, a table, a fireplace, and an oven. Seemed perfectly fine. Better than fine.

"I'm going to need to sell all of my pies at the Frost Fair. All of them. You saw all the booths set up last night, yeah?"

Bess nodded. The children had all gathered to watch the big people construct booths out on the ice. The watermen all moaned about how they weren't making money, but they spent their time with the keg of ale out on the frozen water, just the same. Some of the boys helped with the construction, earning a shilling for their hard work. None would take Bess. They didn't take girls for that sort of work, no matter that she was just as tall and strong.

"So, we'll carry them all down tomorrow, set up shop, and you'll help me keep an eye out for pickpockets."

Oh, she didn't like that part. "I'll help you carry it all down. And I can keep a watch on your pies, but not for pickpockets."

Miss Penny laughed, and it sounded like bells. Bess liked Miss Penny more than she'd liked anyone in a long time. "Do your best, that's all I ask."

Do her best? Bess could do that. She tried very hard, but it wasn't her fault that she wasn't as smart as some of the other children.

"What kind of pies?" Bess asked.

This time, Tony laughed.

‹‹ ● ◉ ● ››

The next morning, Miss Penny shook Bess awake early, when it was still dark.

"Get up, sweet girl. We have lots to do before the fair today!"

Bess was on her feet in no time. She'd bathed the night before, the water almost warm, and Miss Penny had given her a bit of cloth to wipe herself down with, smelling clean and tidy, just like her. Miss Penny had even found a way to clean up Bess' dress and hung it to dry near the fire while Bess snuggled onto her pallet in the cupboard.

The fire was already blazing in the kitchen, and Bess ran to find her dress stiff but dry. She pulled it on over her head. Felt pretty as a fresh daisy, she did.

"Porridge," Miss Penny called.

Some might tire of it, but Bess didn't. She'd eaten proper food yesterday, with bread and even a bit of meat. She didn't know what kind and didn't care. Miss Penny had made dough and boiled all the vegetables, meat, and herbs in a big pot all day long. Bess had helped with what she could, but mostly watched.

They would make as many pies as possible, and then take them down to the fair, cooking them in an oven they'd set up there on the ice.

Once finished breaking their fast, Miss Penny pinned a cloth over Bess' dress, just like hers. Bess had a pinafore. She smiled. Like a real, proper girl.

Miss Penny rolled out circles of dough one after another, and then handed Bess a scoop, telling her how to fill each one, and to be careful about measuring. The mixture that had cooked and bubbled all day yesterday was now a cold paste. After a few tries, Bess had the understanding, so Miss Penny came behind her and folded over the dough, crimping the edges together. They were thick with cubes of meat and potatoes, and it made Bess' mouth water while they made line after line of them.

After they were finished with a row, Miss Penny tucked the tidy packets into a small handcart, draped with floured cloth. Hours later, after the sun had risen, Tony came to collect them. They hustled about the kitchen while Miss Penny fussed.

"Is the oven lit out there?" Miss Penny asked.

"It's going, middling-like." Tony scratched at his scruffy, black beard.

"We need to take embers then, come on, now." Miss Penny pulled some from the kitchen fire and popped them into the metal pot meant for them. She pulled on her coat, scarf, and hat. Bess looked around for her own thin coat, but couldn't find it.

"Here," Tony said, not meeting her eye as he thrust something at her. It was a thick woolen coat, far too big for her, smelling of horses. "A sight warmer than what you've got."

Bess pulled it on, the sleeves covering her hands. She was used to squeezing into clothing, everything tight and pulling. This was comfortable. She did up the big wooden buttons on the front.

"Gone soft," Miss Penny whispered, kissing him on the cheek.

Tony's face went pink under his black beard, but he didn't seem to mind. "Hush now."

Miss Penny handed Bess the coal embers. "You carry this. Tony will pull the wagon, and I'll make sure nothing falls."

With a nod of her head, they set off for the river.

The cold bit at her face and hands, despite the embers she carried and the woolen coat. All three of them hunched against the wind, relieved when they turned a corner that blocked the wind. They descended the stairs near Blackfriars onto the ice. Already, there was a crowd. Lines of wooden booths with heavy blankets to block the wind lined the ice, and further down, Bess could see skaters twirling in coats of every color. There was a circle dug out on the ice, already set for the bear-baiting. Casks and kegs were being opened and already, tankards were used and forgotten.

Despite the wind and the layers of wool, it felt like a party. They hurried to the booth, Tony leading the way. The brick oven was warm, but not hot, and Miss Penny took the embers and fed the fire. It was an odd thing, built up on bricks Tony had hauled down from the river's edge. But there was excitement everywhere on the ice. People couldn't wait for the fair to start.

"I need to leave at the stroke of half-three," Tony said.

Miss Penny waved him off, still blowing on the fire.

"What should I do?" Bess asked.

Miss Penny thought for a moment and then pulled a ha'penny from her skirt pocket. "Go explore. Find a sweet or doll or whatever you like. Be back at the next clock strike to help me."

Bess nodded, the feeling of a coin in her hand so strange. She went off, hearing Tony in the booth behind her.

"You letting her wander off on her own?"

"She wandered to us on her own. She's fine."

Bess kept on, finding all sorts of strange delights. There was a bookseller, but she couldn't read. There were rag dolls for sale, but where would she keep one? Every booth was filled to bursting with colorful things to look at. Bess hadn't been inside many shops before, as she was usually shooed out because she had no coin. But here she could look her fill while enjoying the feel of snow crunching beneath her feet.

A potter sold cups and plates, and a milliner sold wool hats. Knitted scarves hung on nails, bags of peppermints crowded countertops, and cups of ale dripped on barrels-turned-tables. There was even a silversmith, hammering out designs while customers waited.

A flute player busked on one end of the market, and a singer crooned on the other. Tucked next to the ale booth, an old man squeezed a hurdy-gurdy and another sawed on a fiddle.

But Bess only had her one ha'penny and, much as she liked the music, she couldn't waste it on them. When she got to the roasted chestnuts, she stopped. Those, she wanted. Warm, roasted chestnuts, sweet and that perfect texture between crumbly and soft.

"Oi, Mudface, thought you got lost." Carver was right behind her. His smell, feral and dirty, crowded out the nutty, sweet scent of the chestnut vendor.

Bess turned, feeling less scared than she normally did. Maybe it was all that porridge that made her strong. Maybe, it was because she had her own money in her pocket, and she wouldn't be handing it over, no matter what he said.

"You left me," she scolded, spying Boots and Sam coming up behind him.

Carver shrugged, his dirty, brown hair falling in his face. He shook it out of the way. "You didn't make enough coin. That's the rule. You know that."

"It's cold out." She knew bad weather didn't make rules go away, but it seemed like this kind of cold should be different. If it was cold enough to make a Frost Fair, then maybe it was cold enough for Carver to make the rules easier.

Carver nodded his head at her fist. "You got somefing to gimme?"

She shook her head.

"Then what's in your hand?"

"Nuffin'," she said. It was her coin: she hadn't stolen it or found it, so he couldn't have it.

Carver stepped closer. He towered over most of the children, but she was big. The other two boys with him, Boots and Sam, stepped on either side.

"You can't have it," she warned him.

Carver looked at her in surprise. "Mudface. This is how it works. You get coin, you give it to me, and I show you where it's safe. That's our deal."

Bess shook her head. "But it's so cold, and you didn't show me where it was safe."

Carver sighed like a big person. "It's how this works. You didn't bring home the blunt. What am I supposed to do?"

Bess narrowed her eyes. "If you can't keep me safe, then why should I give you my money?"

"For the next time," Carver said with a big smile, all nice and friendly-like.

Bess shook her head again. This didn't sound right. And she didn't want to go back to sleeping in stone doorways if she could sleep in a warm cupboard under a blanket that smelled like a garden.

"Mudface," Carver said like he was sad. "Give me what's in your hand."

"I don't have to, and I don't want to." Bess backed up, blocked by the barrels of ale and the hurdy-gurdy man.

Carver tsked. "You know what's gonna happen. I'm gonna take that coin from you."

Hot flashed all over her, making her warm down to her toes. "You're not either."

Carver grabbed at her from the front, while Boots and Sam came at her from the sides. Bess did what she could, kicking, biting, and screaming. She knocked Sam down—he was much smaller than her. Boots got her arm and wouldn't let go. Carver tried to pry open her fist.

"Get him lass!" cried one of the ale drinkers from behind her.

She pulled her arm back, trying to get loose from Carver. She bit at Boots' fingers, wrapped around her bicep.

"You got him now, girl, punch his nose!"

So, she did. No thought crossed her mind, no ideas of how a punch ought to be, but her fist was curled around her ha'penny, and she aimed it straight at his nose. Her fist connected. And it was like a bubble burst.

Carver reeled backward, falling on his bottom, his hands covering his face.

Her hand bounced back away and, after a second, it began to hurt, too.

Boots still hung onto her arm, staring at Carver. Boots looked at her, his watery blue eyes wide and confused. Bess was confused, too. She didn't think it would work, that now she could just walk away. Sam took off running.

"You won, girl! I knew you could. Oi, Jacob, you owe me a shilling!" The ale drinkers turned back to their own sport again.

Before she could take herself away, a big arm scooped her up around the waist, separating Boots' fingers from her arm. She glanced over, and Boots was being held up by his jacket in the man's other hand. Boots kicked and kicked, but didn't hit nothing but air.

"Enough!" The man bellowed.

Bess squirmed around until she could see his face. Oh. It was Tony. Oh. She was in trouble. Her fingers hurt, curled so hard around the ha'penny.

"What's happening here? Why you fightin'?" His gravelly voice demanded answers. He swung them over to look at Carver, still sitting on the ground. "Who's this now?"

Carver gave Bess a look that made it clear she shouldn't say. So, she didn't. But Tony kicked out his leg, giving a hard nudge to him.

"This Carver?" Tony asked.

Carver scrambled to his feet and ran off, darting through the people who wandered the booths. Boots started swinging all over again.

Bess knew that both of them were out of Carver's gang for good now, and she'd upset Tony. Tears sprang to her eyes. She really liked Miss Penny. She didn't want to lose the warm, herb-scented blanket in the pantry.

"You can have it back!" she wailed.

Tony's grip on her waist loosened. "What you talking about?"

"The ha'penny!"

"I knew it!" Boots crowed, still dangling from Tony's other fist.

Bess lunged for Boots, but it did no good. Boots swung back at her.

"That's enough!" Tony shook Boots, still hanging from Tony's massive fist. "Who are ye?"

Boots swung out, his legs still scrabbling. "Boots."

"That ain't a name, boy."

"Is what we call him, though," Bess said. "He were the only one of us that had any decent shoes. And they was boots."

"If I put you down, will you run?" Tony asked, looking at her hard, like a raven looks at its food.

Bess shook her head. She had nowhere to run to. Boots kept on waving his arms like he was some sort of crazed chicken.

Tony lowered Bess to the ground, and she slid from him onto the snow-packed ice. She felt terrible. Like she'd done wrong somehow, but it felt more wrong to hand over the coin Miss Penny had given her.

"Peace," Tony bellowed at Boots. It was so loud Boots stopped moving. "Boy, I won't hurt you if you stop flailing about."

"You don't have nowhere to go," Bess reminded Boots. "Not after you got caught, and he knows Carver's name."

Boots glared at her, and she could feel all of his anger. It wasn't her fault he chose the wrong side.

"No place to go, eh?" Tony lowered him to the ground.

Boots shot daggers at both of them. "I do so."

Bess remembered the last time he came back from home. He limped back to the gang, his face all shades of purple, and cuts across his face and arms. He'd been whipped and beaten. Safer on the streets, when that was home. Bess gave him a shrug, but he knew she remembered, she was sure of it.

"Jesus, Mary, and Joseph," Tony muttered.

That surprised her. The only people who said that were Catholics, and well, you weren't supposed to be Catholic. Everyone knew that. No medals of saints, no murmuring of names. That would keep you from getting any hand-outs and definitely would get you sent to a workhouse.

"Well, come on with me—both of you. We'll get you a pasty anyhow."

"Like a Cornish pasty?" Boots asked.

Bess' mouth was watering.

They followed Tony as he trudged through the market, the snow crunching beneath all their feet.

By the time they rounded the bend to see their destination, Miss Penny's booth was swarmed with people wearing their heavy coats, pretty woolen scarves of red and brown and yellow flipping and swaying in the wind. They clamored around, bumping against each other, trying to get a clear view. Tony guided Bess and Boots around to the back, where Miss Penny was frantically checking the brick oven.

"What's the trouble?" Tony asked.

"No trouble," Miss Penny bit out.

"Who's talking to all them people?" Tony asked, peering around the blanket that served as a curtain between the front of the booth and the back.

"What people?" Miss Penny reached in and touched the top of one. Bess was amazed when she didn't seem to burn herself.

Tony waved his arm around. "Them people. Out there. The booth is swamped."

The pink in Miss Penny's cheeks faded. "There's people?"

"A lot of people," Bess said. Wasn't that a good thing? Miss Penny could sell all her pies, and then she would have the money she needed to open her own place.

"Claire!" Miss Penny called.

A woman who looked very much like Miss Penny poked her head around the curtain. She had curly hair where Miss Penny's was frizzy, but it was obvious they were sisters. "I'm busy, Pen. What do you need?"

"How many people are out there?" Miss Penny asked.

"Plenty. Just keep those hand pies coming!" Claire disappeared around the corner again.

"I'm going to need more pies," Miss Penny said, staring into the distance.

"I've got my fight at four bells, but I can help before then," Tony said.

Bess looked at the big man. He had a fight? Who planned a

fight? And did they plan what fight they would be having? Over a piece of bread or a toy or a set of shoes?

"Bess, go with him, duckie, help him gather everything we need to make the pies. The floured board, the bowl full of filling, the measured cup I use, and some eggs. You know, everything we used to make them yesterday."

Bess remembered. She remembered every single step. And, this way, she could prove exactly how useful she was.

"What about me?" Boots whined. He was looking too closely at those hand pies browning in the oven.

"Come with me, do a good job, and you'll get one all to yourself," Tony grumbled. "Probably."

Tony set off with the wagon. Bess ran to keep up, while Boots trailed last. He wasn't as fast. At least if she ran, she didn't have a chance to be cold.

"You gonna live with them now?" Boots asked Bess as they were getting closer to the street where Miss Penny stayed.

"I don't know. I hope so though. Smells better than where Carver has us sleep."

Tony coughed and cleared his throat up ahead of them. "Right then." Tony ushered them up the few steps to the back of the small house, into the warm kitchen. "Let's gather up what we need. Boots, you can..."

Boots looked at him, while Bess shouldered past to get the bowl of filling and the cup Miss Penny had used to scoop it into the waiting dough. There was a bowl full of dough still rising. Bess wasn't sure if they should take that too, but if they didn't, what would Miss Penny scoop filling into?

"Whoa there." Tony stopped her. "Miss Penny didn't say nothing about dough."

"But what else would she put the filling in?" Bess asked.

"I don't know, but she didn't ask for that."

"But she needs it."

Tony narrowed his eyes. "How do you know?"

"Because what else will she put the filling in? Can't have a pie with no crust." Bess put her hands on her hips. She was willing to stand up to Tony if it meant pleasing Miss Penny. Bess liked her better anyway. Boots peered in through the back door.

Tony folded his arms and looked at the bowl full of dough, covered with a towel. Then he looked at Bess. Then turned to look at Boots. Boots gave him a look that he'd given Bess a million times. And it meant, mate, just go along to get along.

Tony grunted. "Bowl of dough goes."

Filling up the wagon took no time at all, and they were back on the way to the Frost Fair before the church bells rang noon.

The crowd was still there, but Miss Penny's sister was not as fresh as she was earlier. Her hair was falling from its pins, and she'd taken off her mittens.

They trooped around to the back of the booth, where Miss Penny was putting in another batch. She wiped the loose hair from her face and smiled. Miss Penny was right pretty when she smiled. And Bess could see Tony straighten himself and puff up like a rooster strutting around the yard, except Tony had a little wagon, not a red coxcomb.

"Saviors!" Miss Penny said, kissing Tony on the cheek. "Every one of you!"

Bess felt her face almost crack open from smiling so hard. She liked this feeling. She wanted this feeling every day. Well, and one of them hand pies, too.

Tony started unloading the wagon, and when he picked up the bowl of rising dough, Miss Penny took it from him and fussed, trying to figure out where to keep it.

"You didn't say to bring the dough precisely," Tony said.

Miss Penny whirled and gave him a look that seemed right crazed, with her eyes all open wide like that. "What would I put the filling in, if I didn't have any dough?"

Bess smirked at Tony, who gave her shoulder a pat. Bess liked that, too. Only Boots looked bored. And he could be on his way, for all she cared.

"If the army is back, I could use recruits!" Miss Penny's sister called through the curtain.

"I'll help take the money," Boots volunteered.

"The hell you will," Tony countered. "I'll help take the money. You two mongrels go make sure people are in line all orderly-like."

Bess wasn't exactly sure how to do that to big people, but there had to be a way. She followed Boots around to the front of the booth where the crowd surged. The mess of people made it hard for Miss Penny's sister to get hand pies to the right customers.

"What should we do?" Boots asked.

"There needs to be a queue for Tony to take their money, and then one to pick up their pasties."

"Are they pasties or hand pies?" Boots asked.

Bess shrugged. "I don't know. They've said both."

Boots nodded like he was thinking it over, and then waded into the crowd of people like he belonged there. "Ladies and gents! If you ain't paid yer money yet, go to this side. That big man there needs to take yer money, so the nice lady on the other side can give you yer food."

Bess was impressed with how easily Boots talked to the big people, herding them like sheep into two tidy queues. She stepped forward and ushered people to where Miss Penny's sister handed out steaming pies wrapped in newspaper.

They stayed like that for some time, sometimes telling a big person where to go if they looked lost. Bess liked watching the faces of customers leaving the line, taking a big bite of the hand pie as they walked away. They had a dreamy look on their faces, like maybe Miss Penny's hand pie was the best thing they'd ever eaten in their lives. It was for Bess. Her mouth watered at the idea that she might get another one at the end of the night. One that was a little burnt, or maybe torn a bit. Not perfect, but still tasted just as fine.

The light faded fast, and before long, twilight was falling on the Frost Fair. The temperature dropped as quickly as the sun. The crowd thinned out, and women and children were the first to leave. Some vendors dropped a heavy canvas over their booth and left with their wares and their money, returning tomorrow when the light came back.

A familiar voice came from behind Bess. "Oi, watched you and Boots working all day. 'Spect you'll have something to share."

Bess whirled around to find Carver. There was a bit of dried blood caught up in one of his nostrils, and a shine of pride warmed her. She'd done that. She'd said no to Carver, and he had to run away. Well, partly because Tony was there, but she'd done that bit to his nose.

"Not givin' you nuffin'," Bess growled. Feeling brave, she gave him a light shove.

A large man ambled past them. "Save it for the ring, young'uns!"

Tony appeared from nowhere and gripped Carver by his collar. "What you doing sniffing 'round here again?"

Carver twisted and swung his fist out, connecting with nothing but air. "Not sniffing 'round nuffin'."

"Oh," Tony's face looked like he'd just heard a good joke. "So, you're here for the fights. I'm on my way there right now. You know, the younger boys start the fights."

"I don't wanna fight no boy," Carver spat, looking daggers at Bess.

"I'll fight you anywhere," Bess said, hands on her hips. She'd already gotten in one good hit, she could manage another one. Did they have to fight with words first? They'd already done that. Could they skip to the hitting?

"Come on, then, all of you." Tony looked around. "Boots! I know you're lurking around here somewhere. You're coming too."

Boots materialized out of the shadows and trailed after them. They were a little parade, streaming towards some other location on the ice. Even if Bess hadn't known where to go, the streams of men and women, whose coats were not fine or rimmed with thick fur, showed the way.

Giant mountains of men greeted Tony as he hauled them all in. He nodded and said his greetings, but Bess could see by the thin line of his mouth that he was angry. Probably angry with her. She hoped he wouldn't tell Miss Penny.

He stopped their parade in front of some older men, whose white hair escaped from their hats. "Got some contenders here," Tony said.

The skinny one pulled a pencil from behind his ear and foolscap from his pocket. His gloves had the fingers chopped off, and Bess could see his nails were ragged and bitten to the quick. Just like hers. "Which ones? All these three?" He pointed at Carver, Sam, and Boots. He didn't include Bess in his gesture.

"Nope. Four. This one, too." He pushed Bess forward.

The men peered at her. The fatter man pushed glasses up his nose as he bent over. "That's a girl, ain't it? Wearing a dress, and all."

"So? She's a kid. They all are. It's the same." Tony shrugged.

Bess tugged on Tony's sleeve. "But—"

"Don't ever agree to a fight unless you mean it. You said you'd fight, so, here you are."

"But—"

"S'pose she could fight the littlest one?" The fat one said as all three old men stared at their crew.

"That don't seem right either," the skinny one said.

The man who hadn't yet spoken finally piped up: "Let's ask them who should fight who. They'd know better."

Even Bess was surprised. She was so used to big people telling her what to do, what to think, what to be, it seemed shocking that her opinion might count. So, fine, if she was to fight, she'd fight the boy she wanted. She pointed to Carver, who was still a head taller than her. "I'm fighting him."

"Puts the two littlest matched up." The skinny one made some scratches on his foolscap. "Names?"

"Bess Abbott," she said immediately.

There was a pause, but the skinny man didn't look up. "And?"

Carver folded his arms in defiance. Tony kicked him. "Ow!" Carver protested, rubbing his leg. "Carver."

"That your Christian name or your family name?" the skinny man asked.

"Ain't none of yer business," Carver sneered.

The skinny man looked up, his eyes so pointed and focused that Bess felt frightened. "Boy, this is a legal fight, so I need your legal name. You ain't yet earned a fighting name that people may know you by, so I need the one the good Lord gave you."

Bess wanted to point out that the good Lord didn't name anybody; it was the parents or the vicar that done so, but she had a feeling this was not the right time to be pointing things out.

"Horace Carver."

"Good lad." The skinny one went back to his paper. "And the other set-to?"

"Samuel Peters," Sam spoke up without being prompted.

But Boots stared at the ground.

The skinny man sighed and looked up at Boots. "Must we do this again?"

Boots huffed. "Everybody knows me as Boots. Everybody."

"I don't know you," the skinny man said. "So, what's the name?"

Boots grimaced, looking at Tony. Tony just gestured to get on with it. "John. John Arthur."

"Good lad. Fine then. I just need to find that lousy nephew of mine to bring these competitors to the ring." The skinny man frowned, looking through the crowd.

"Boy's over there," the fat one with glasses said. "Oi! Basil, get your arse over here. There's work to be done!"

A young man, even skinnier than his uncle, slunk over. "Got some for the first fights?"

"These four," the skinny man said, pointing to them in pairs to indicate each match-up.

Basil peered at the four of them. He pointed a stick-like finger at her. "Even that one?"

"Matched against that one," the skinny older man gestured at Carver. "Now, go, get them settled, and we'll announce and take bets while you explain the rules."

Basil sighed and ushered them over to an area on the ice cleared of people. There was a mound of snow that had been shaped almost like a bench, but Bess didn't think it would be too comfortable to sit on.

Carver kicked at her foot, trying to stomp her toes as they walked.

"One more time, you little shit, and you'll be disqualified," Basil snapped. "Save it for the ring."

The ring? Whose ring? Still, Bess followed Basil as she had been told to do. He gathered them 'round and explained the ring was the markings in the snow, and to stay inside the lines. He would tell them what to do and when to start, and then they would fight, using fists or feet, but no biting. That part was disappointing. Bess was a very good biter.

"Normally, fighters strip to the waist, but it is awfully cold out," Basil said, looking around. He shrugged. "We'll have you take your coats off; it would be hard to fight in something like that anyway."

Basil glanced at the foolscap. "We'll start with John Arthur in that far corner, and Samuel Peters in this one. Whoever gets knocked down and can't get up loses. Understood? After that, Horace Carver in that corner over there, and Bess Abbott in this corner here."

Basil's uncle, the skinny man, entered the area marked for the fights. He talked to everybody and got them to throw in money for betting. He talked about Bess fighting and the other boys and then talked about Tony fighting, too. Soon, Basil was over there shooing Samuel over the line on the ground and past the bench made of snow. Basil brought both boys to the center of the ring and had them put their toes on the line he made there in the middle. He counted down, and the boys just looked at him.

Bess was lost. Where was the ring? Why was there so much money changing hands? Who cared who they were?

Basil threw up his hands. "The fight's started. Get after it!"

Samuel and Boots stared at each other, fists clenched at their sides. Tony appeared in Boots' corner and yelled "Hit him!"

Boots looked over his shoulder at Tony, shouting his directions. The crowd laughed.

"Don't look at me, look at him!" Tony shouted. More laughing.

Boots nodded and turned back around and looked at Samuel. Bess couldn't see Samuel's face, but she doubted he was very happy. Finally, Boots raised his fists, and Samuel did the same. But then, Boots popped Samuel in the nose, and Samuel fell on his arse, holding his hands over his face.

"Round One!" shouted Basil, hustling Samuel over to the corner.

"Come on back, boy," Tony yelled at Boots.

Bess wished she were in that corner, hearing what Tony was saying to him. He probably wouldn't help her as much as he was helping Boots, because she was a girl, and everybody would expect her to lose no matter what. She hated that—knowing she wasn't supposed to win. But there wasn't no reason she couldn't. Carver didn't have much more fighting knowledge than she did; at least, she didn't think so.

Basil sat Samuel down on the snow bench. Samuel was crying, and his nose was bleeding. Bess scooped some snow from the side of the bench and pressed it to Samuel's nose.

"If he doesn't go back in, the set-to is over, yeah?" Bess asked.

Basil narrowed his eyes. "Technically."

Samuel cried still, his nose and his eyes red. "I don't want to go back," he wailed.

Basil pulled his watch from his pocket. "You have twenty more seconds to decide."

Samuel nodded. Bess sat down on the cold snow bench and put her arm around him. They were probably the same age, but Samuel was normal size, and Bess was bigger. Sam blew bloody snot onto his fingers, wiping it on his pant leg.

Across the flat ice, Tony was bent over, talking quickly to John, using his hands to explain something. Basil put his fingers in his mouth and whistled. "Fighters! Toe the line!"

John scrambled to his feet, which made Samuel stand, too. He turned and gave Bess a panicked look. She didn't know why he was going in there if he didn't want to fight.

"Just lay down once it starts," Bess called.

Samuel trudged to the center as if he were being led to the hangman's noose. Basil pulled Samuel to where he needed to stand. Then he whistled again, signaling the start of the next round.

"Please don't hit me, Boots," Samuel begged.

"How else are we ending this?" Boots asked.

Samuel glanced back at Bess and folded himself over until he was lying flat on the ground. The crowd booed. Basil bent over Samuel, bracing his hands on his knees. Then he stood up and declared, "Samuel Peters has declared his forfeit. John Arthur is the winner!"

Basil's uncle was there on the sides of the lines, handing out the winnings for bets. It would be her turn next. Men grumbled and pushed past her, making their way to gather their money. Samuel walked back to the corner with his head hung. Basil dug in his pocket and handed Samuel some type of coin.

"For being in the fights, even if you lost," Basil said.

Samuel took it, glanced at Bess, and then across the ice at Carver. Samuel put his coat on, the coin held fast in his fist.

"What'd you get?" She asked, but Samuel just shook his head and disappeared into the crowd without asking for help buttoning his coat.

"Get your coat off, girl." Basil didn't look at her but at the crowd. There were more now, drawn by the gambling and shouting.

Bess shivered. She didn't want to take her coat off. She suddenly didn't want to step over that line in the ice, putting her toe on the line opposite Carver. But then Tony's giant hand was on her shoulder.

"Good for you, Bess. You can do this. Let's get your coat off first," Tony coached, his voice still low and scratchy, but it felt warmer and nicer somehow. Better than when he was barking at her for doing something wrong.

She slipped her hands out of her coat sleeves, and he took it from her. It still smelled like horses.

"Keep your fists up like this." He held his fists in front of his face. "If that boy tries to punch you, punch his fist with yours, knock him back. If you can, try to get a punch to his belly, that's where the body is softest."

Bess nodded, looking across at Carver. He seemed so far away and so small. Basil was over there by him now, coaxing his coat off.

"If you want to stop the fight at any time, just lie down, like Samuel did."

Bess nodded.

"Did you tell him to do that?" Tony asked.

Bess nodded again.

"Smart girl. Give me a couple of jumps in the air to warm yourself up. It's cold out here."

Bess jumped up and down as he asked.

"Fighters! New set!" Basil's uncle called. They announced the next fight, her and Carver. People called bets out and money was handed over.

Basil got them both into the middle of the scratched-out ring. "Toes on the line!" he called.

Her heart pounded. She hadn't been this scared in weeks. She looked up at Carver, and he looked scared, too. Basil held their hands, counted down, and then whistled the start.

Suddenly, Bess couldn't remember what to do. She looked at Basil, and then Carver hit her in the stomach. His fist hit her elbow first, but it still made her feel bad. She doubled over. It hurt, but not near as bad as she'd had before. Carver didn't have half the strength of the papas in her old neighborhood. She stood up straight.

Carver tried to pop her in the nose, but she remembered Tony's advice and hit his fist with hers. Her knuckles flared with pain, but at least it wasn't her face. Then, she decided she was just going to fight the way she knew how: as hard as she could. She struck out a fist and connected it to his belly. Carver doubled over, and while he was there, she launched herself at him, knocking him down. She sat on his shoulders, as she had other children, many a time when they were being mean. She hit his face with those same hurting knuckles until Basil pulled her off.

She was panting, and her hair was in her face. She brushed it away with the back of her bloody hand, feeling like she might never be able to uncurl her fist again.

"End of round one. Go rest in your corner." Basil pointed to where she'd started, Tony clapping and shouting nice words at her. Boots stood beside him.

Tony piled snow on her knuckles and let her rest. "Nice work, Bess. That was a good job you did, taking him to the ground. Put him at the disadvantage. But it's bad form to hit him when he's already down."

Bess stared at Carver across the way, his face bloodied. She'd done that. It made her feel bad. She'd only wanted to be left alone. It wasn't meant to come to this.

A man came up behind Tony and clapped him on the shoulder.

"Raw talent, this one," he said, motioning to Bess. "Too bad she's a girl. That bottom in this package?" he pointed at Boots. "That's a fighter worth training."

"They're both worth training," Tony growled.

"She won't ever give you returns," the man said.

Tony stood, and his hands were clenched. "Sometimes it ain't about the money."

The stranger put his hands up. "It's your business."

"Damn right, it's my business."

Tony turned back to her, the little bit of skin she could see around his dark beard was flushed.

"What's bottom mean?" she asked.

"Means the fighter can take a hit. They'll keep going, no matter what."

Bess nodded. She was good at that: just keeping on, no matter what happened. "I'm sorry I'm a girl."

He grabbed her hand so fast it made her stomach drop with fear. "Don't apologize for what you are, hear me? Never."

Bess nodded, and while the fear didn't fade, pride added to the mix of her feelings.

Basil called for the second round, and she dutifully went to the scratched line and put her toe on it. He counted down and whistled the start.

This time, Bess wanted nothing more than to make Tony proud, and show that stupid stranger it didn't matter she was a girl. She popped Carver straight in the nose, kicked his knees, so he fell over, and she was on him again, arms flying, even if she wasn't supposed to.

Basil pulled her off once more. This time, Carver didn't get up. He lay there, crying. His face was bleeding. She felt bad, but she also wondered why he was crying. She'd gotten beaten for no reason at all by big people so many times, it seemed pointless to cry. Wasted time and made it harder to breathe through her nose.

Bess returned to her corner as Basil crouched down and talked with Carver. Finally, Basil stood. "Fighter Horace Carver forfeits. Bess Abbott for the win in round two!"

Tony roared his approval, clapping, then picked her up. "That's my girl!"

Bess blushed. That's my girl. She hadn't known some words could make a body feel so wonderful. She wanted to hear those words again and again.

People were shoving past them to get to Basil's uncle and collect their money. Tony took her and Boots over to the man, his big hands splayed on each of their backs.

"My champions," Tony said. Bess thought that was maybe what proud sounded like. It sent another bolt of warmth and comfort through her, better than any coat.

Basil's uncle handed over a small pouch that jangled. "Surprising. Especially that one." He pointed at Bess. "Too bad—"

Tony cut him off. "Too bad there's only one of her. Thanks." Tony turned them around to push them back through the crowd.

"Still fighting your round?" Basil's uncle called after him.

Tony spun. "Of course. Just going to get these little ones fed first, that's all."

"Better hurry or you'll forfeit."

Tony grunted and, turning back, pushed them forward. "Let's get you back to Miz Penny's stall."

Bess stopped him. Her heart thumped hard, not wanting to be disagreeable. "We can get there on our own."

Tony crouched down, so he was the same height as her and Boots. "But this money?" He patted the coat pocket where it sat heavy and jingling. Bess could have picked it off him in seconds. "It's yours. You won it. I want to make sure you get back to Penny safe as houses."

Bess looked at Boots. His face, flush with his win, was pink against his freckles. He nodded at her; he could have nipped that pouch just as quickly.

"We know how to hide it," Bess said, reaching for it.

Tony glanced past her to Boots, and by the time his attention was back on her, she already had the pouch in her hand. He hadn't felt a thing.

"The devil?" he said, seeing the money in her hand, patting his now empty pocket.

"We'll be safe," Boots promised.

Tony wore an expression that Bess had never seen on a big person's face before. She wasn't sure what to name it. He glanced over his shoulder to where the next fights were being called.

"Yer up next, Tony!" Basil called to him.

Tony winced, but then he nodded. "Take care of each other. The best defense is being with someone who wants to defend you. Do that for each other, and you'll be safe. Always."

He squeezed Bess on the upper arm, and Boots on his, too.

Neither Bess nor Boots said anything. She'd never had anyone advise that. Usually, it was, "Don't do this," or "Never touch that."

Tony stood. "You both did good tonight. I'll be back by the booth after I'm finished with my own set-to."

They nodded, and Tony went back to the crowd. Bess tucked the pouch away in the inside pocket of her dress, then looked at Boots, while he looked back at her. "Will you defend me?" Bess asked. She wasn't sure what defend meant, but she had an idea. It meant to fight for, she thought.

"Yes. Will you defend me?" Boots asked in return.

Bess took his hand. "Of course. Let's go."

They ran back to Miss Penny's booth, where there was no longer a line. The heavy blanket had been let down in front, to signal they were closed. Bess let go of Boots' hand and ran around back. She couldn't wait to tell Miss Penny of her win. If Tony had been that proud, how proud would Miss Penny be?

"Miss Penny! Miss Penny!"

Miss Penny and her sister, Miss Claire, were sitting by the stove, drinking from steaming mugs. The oven was empty, but the embers were still glowing and hot. Miss Penny had her feet up on an apple box. They seemed happy, smiling as they were.

"Children!" Miss Penny opened her arms, but Bess was too shy for an embrace. She wasn't ready. "I have two messy leftover hand pies for you. Couldn't sell them to customers, but still very tasty, just for you."

Miss Claire dug around on the floor and found one of the platters they'd hauled over from Miss Penny's house. On it, wrapped in leaking newsprint, were two hand pies, still warm.

Boots and Bess took one each, and while she meant to say thank you, to be polite, the smell of the meat and veg and sauce and crust took over, and she devoured it without looking up.

"Don't forget to chew," Miss Claire said, laughing.

Bess could feel the warmth sliding down to her belly. It felt so good. And she was suddenly so very tired.

"Come here, child," Miss Penny cooed, holding her arms out. Bess couldn't think, she was too sleepy. She crawled onto Miss Penny's lap, pressed her face into Miss Penny's shoulder, and fell asleep. Safe and warm.

Bess awoke being carried. She was snuggled in with her horse-smelling jacket and another blanket over her. It was dark, and she was held tight against an unfamiliar chest. Before she lifted her head, she listened, not wanting to give away that she was awake.

"I can't believe you. Two seconds alone, and you put them in the ring," hissed Miss Penny. There was the clatter of the wagon on the street.

"It just happened. And they both won." The grumble of Tony's voice vibrated in Bess' bones. He was the one who carried her.

"But Miss Penny, I wanted to fight," Boots said.

Bess lifted her head. Where was Boots? He walked between Miss Penny and Tony. Bess blinked a few times. "I wanted to fight, too."

"She awakens," Miss Penny said, and there was a smile in her voice. "You must have been tired."

"Yes. But not because of the fighting." Bess couldn't explain why she'd been so tired. There were so many things. Part of it was being held so tightly in Miss Penny's lap. She'd been so warm.

"Whisht, girl. We can talk about it in the morning." Miss Penny's voice sounded tight.

"I'll do whatever you want me to do. Just let me stay." Bess meant it. If she had to fight every night, she'd do it. If she had to never fight again, she'd do it. Whatever Miss Penny wanted.

Tony made a strange gulping sound.

Miss Penny's laugh sounded sad. "Oh, Bess. We only want to

do what's right for you. If you think you want to cook like me, I'll teach you. If you want to fight like Tony, he'll teach you."

Tony grumbled his agreement. "But only what you want to do. Would you rather cook or fight?"

Bess was suddenly fully alert. She lifted her head all the way, and Tony let her slide down until her feet touched the ground. They stopped as they reached Miss Penny's house.

"You can stay with us tonight, too, Boots." Miss Penny ushered him in through the kitchen gate.

"Thank you," he said, pulling at his cap, as if he were polite.

"Help me unload these, so we can be ready for tomorrow." Tony lifted the wagon up the few steps into the back of the house and Boots and Bess made quick work of unloading the bowls and towels and utensils.

"Cup of milk?" Miss Penny asked, and they all agreed. Miss Penny poured them from the pitcher she had covered. Bess didn't think she was hungry again, but she was thankful to have that cup of milk. It felt nice to have something besides an empty belly. They all sat around the small wooden table near the banked kitchen fire. It was cold, but to make the fire for the night seemed like so much work when they were just going to go to bed.

Bess fished the pouch of money out of the inside of her dress and let it fall hard onto the table.

"Oh, my days!" Miss Penny said. "Where did that come from?"

Tony chuckled. "That's their winnings."

"Not yours?" Miss Penny asked him, her eyes wide.

"I showed you mine already. It was a good purse, but not as good as theirs."

"How much did we make?" Boots asked.

Bess opened the pouch and dumped it all on the table. Coins went every which way. Bess and Boots jumped out of their chairs to chase down the errant shillings. They squealed as they jumped on the rolling coins. When they retrieved them all, they made stacks of all the coins that looked alike.

"That's almost as much as I made today," whispered Miss Penny.

"I'm very good," Bess boasted. "That's what everybody said. Just too bad I'm a girl."

"I told you to never apologize for that," Tony said. "You're a good fighter, same as Boots here. The pair of you, if you train together, you'll be unbeatable."

"I don't want anyone to call me Boots anymore," Boots said.

Bess blinked at him but went back to tapping the tallest stack of coins. She liked the clinking sound it made.

"If I'm going to fight by my real name, then that's what I ought to be called."

"Sounds like an excellent plan, lad. So, what is your name?" Miss Penny asked.

"John Arthur."

"A fine, strong name. John Arthur, it is." Miss Penny watched Bess so hard, Bess could feel the weight of her stare. "Bess, if you would like to train with Tony, that's fine by me. But the second you don't want to do it anymore, I'll teach you to cook, and you'll be my helper. Does that suit you?"

Bess nodded. "I'd like to train with Tony. And John Arthur."

The big people finished their milk—Bess and John had finished theirs ages ago. "Time for bed. John, just for tonight, you can sleep with Bess in the pantry. We can figure out something more permanent soon. The Frost Fair is still going tomorrow, so we have another very busy day. We'll have to be up early."

"Yes, ma'am." Bess stood and took her cup to the washing basin, motioning to John to do the same. She wouldn't let him mess up what she had going here.

"Show John where to sleep. Take care of yourselves. If it gets too cold, there are more blankets on the third shelf. Remember to snuff your candle." Miss Penny smiled at them, and she and Tony disappeared upstairs with their candle.

"We will," Bess promised. She and John tidied the coins away in the pouch. Then she took him to the pantry and they found the other blankets and made another pallet for John next to hers. Bess shucked off her dress and John stepped out of his breeches, letting his long shirt cover him to his knees. They laid down, and Bess blew out the candle.

Staring into the darkness, she was tired, but she was more excited about what Miss Penny would give her: choices. She'd never had a choice like that. But she would fight, and she would make both Miss Penny and Tony ever so proud of her.

"We're going to be the best," Bess whispered into the darkness.

"The best London's ever seen," John promised. He reached out and took her hand. Bess fell asleep, the promise of what was yet to come hovering in the pantry, smelling of herbs and flour and hope.

·‹‹ ● ● ›·

Edie Cay writes award-winning Regency romance about women's boxing in the series When the Blood Is Up. Her next series is about Victorian women mountain climbers, called The Ladies Alpine Society. She is a founding member of Paper Lantern Writers, and speaks on the history of women's boxing, and diverse people in history. You can drop her a line on Facebook, Instagram, or Bookbub; or visit her at her website, www.ediecay.com.

·‹‹ ● ● ›·

Long Winter

CHRISTMAS
BY MARI ANNE CHRISTIE

Philadelphia, Pennsylvania
December 23, 1860

I f Celia Bromley never heard another verse of "Good King Wenceslas," it would be too soon. She would rather never hear another Christmas carol, if only they could be done with them this night. But no, gathered around the pianoforte, with sixteen more hours left to endure of the company at the VanDorns' holiday house party, the collective purveyors of merriment must sing for their supper, whether or not they could carry a tune.

After the caroling, she would learn her fate. When the company dispersed to the holiday dinner or merry dancing, she would learn if her heart truly was in the right place. She would meet Jo in the darkened library; her note had promised news for them both.

"It is endless, is it not?" A voice behind her, not one she recognized, close enough to be heard sotto voce.

She shrugged one shoulder and found her place in the lyrics again, responding by singing a bit louder. She had no interest in meeting another man vying for her dowry, especially tonight, when she hoped to hear from Jo that they could afford premises for the schooling of merchants' daughters.

But she would not be so lucky. After "Silent Night," the conclusion of the guest-powered musical portion of the entertainment, footmen began circulating with cups of hot cocoa and cider, and she found herself accepting one from a young—very young—gentleman with a slight paunch and a serious mien, who introduced himself as Robert Wentworth. "Apologies for interrupting your singing, Miss Bromley. I hadn't thought you were enjoying the program."

"It is nothing, Mr. Wentworth. Thank you for the chocolate." She would have preferred cider, but she would overlook the fact he hadn't even asked. She couldn't just up and run from the ballroom, no matter how much she wished to be in the library. One could never know with whom her father might be doing business, and it would never do to make a scene. The wicked side of her, the one that hoped to needle the man keeping her from her love, found herself saying, "Do you not enjoy Christmas carols, sir? Surely, a rousing rendition of 'Silent Night' stirs the blood?"

He laughed, but the sound was wooden, rehearsed. "No, I cannot say that is what stirs my blood. I would enjoy escorting you to supper tonight, however. And I know your father will not object." When she looked across the room and caught her father's eye, he raised a glass to her. Mr. Wentworth made a slight bow in her father's direction.

Supper? Another hour, at least, before she could slip away to meet Jo, and worse, spent in the company of this little boy in sheep's clothing. She looked around for any obvious reason to decline his invitation, but there was none, barring spending the next two hours in the ladies' retiring room. No one else was offering to take her in to supper, including her father. She couldn't go in alone. She couldn't go in with Jo. She clearly couldn't slip away quietly unnoticed. Ergo, she would have supper in company with Robert Wentworth, then probably dancing. Bother.

·⟨⟨ ● ● ● ⟩⟩·

The clock tolled the quarter-hour after ten; surely Jo had long since abandoned the library. Celia had promised to meet her directly after the caroling at half-past-eight, an event Jo was not even called upon to join. As the widowed companion to an elderly dowager, Jo's absence was not so pronounced in company as Celia, a marriageable daughter of the aristocracy. If Jo's employer went to bed early, and often did, so could she. But Jo would rather spend her time in the library in any house, and could often be found there in the night.

Celia had once spent two weeks here at the VanDorns' for another house party, so she navigated the halls with ease, her path lit by a covered candle. With great good luck, it seemed all the footmen had been pressed into service for the ongoing party and weren't lurking about the halls.

She slipped into the dim—but not dark—library, setting her candle on a side table to illuminate the room even more than the moon had. Before she could go as far as to wrap her shawl a bit tighter against the draft, Jo appeared, exactly as she had the first time Celia had ever seen her, emerging from behind a full shelf of books. Her chestnut hair was gathered in a lace snood at her neck, and she was in a day gown of burgundy silk. As always, she was wearing the brooch Celia had given her when Jo graduated from Mount Holyoke two years ahead of Celia, when they pledged a future with each other.

"Celia. You came. Happy Christmas." Her face was wreathed in a smile.

"Of course, I came. I am shockingly late."

"No matter. I had a book. You are here now, and it is so good to speak to you alone."

Jo grasped her hand and pulled her behind a shelf, close enough to kiss. Then she did, just a little roughly, as ever, as though she couldn't wait to ravish Celia, though they had only reached what Celia would classify as full ravishment twice since they left school, and precious few times while they were there. Their secret love had been, of necessity, a furtive thing, which had the odd effect of strengthening their connection.

Celia moved closer to Jo, pressing against her, yielding herself. Though Jo was as fully engaged, one hand behind Celia's back, the other behind her head, it was but a few moments before she pulled back and stopped. "My love."

"What is it?" Celia asked, searching her face for clues.

"I have news. I do not wish to be distracted just yet." Jo kept her literally at arm's length. What was this news that Jo was so afraid would change the way Celia felt about her, about them?

"There is an action next month against the Fugitive Slave laws. Arrests are expected."

Celia sucked in a breath and held it. It was time to be of use. She broke away, not because she felt any differently toward Jo, but because such decisions were solemn and should be made outside the influence of girlish romance. Jo felt the pressure of it, too, for she couldn't help wringing her hands.

Jo continued, "If we do this, it will be goodbye to a girl's academy. It will likely be goodbye to teaching at all. And anything to do with Society will be at an end." Jo's voice was grave, her face shuttered, though they both knew Celia had more to lose in Society than Jo. "I am inclined to participate. Mrs. Pilchrist is in support."

"In less than a year, I come into my mother's trust," Celia reminded Jo, "and then neither of us need consider a profession if we do not choose it. Twenty thousand dollars covers a multitude of sins."

"Mrs. Pilchrist assures me she has left me a sizable bequest, though what she considers sizable, one wonders. Still, whatever it is, I have more than earned it the past three years, and she cannot hold on much longer."

"Will you not miss her when she is gone?" Celia asked.

"Will you not miss Society?" Jo retorted.

"Not for a moment."

Jo shrugged. "Precisely so. Mrs. Pilchrist is not such a bad sort, but not one to spend the capital of one's life upon. How will your father feel about you abandoning Society?"

"My father would rather I never be useful a day in my life and never express another opinion. His judgments are irrelevant."

"The lawyer says we should expect to stay in jail up to three days. Are you willing, are you able, to risk an arrest record? Are you willing to give up teaching?"

"Like you, there is very little I wouldn't give up on behalf of the downtrodden. And yet," Celia mused, "I am not convinced my arrest is the best way to effect change. Should such a thing not be something we walk into with our eyes wide open, with a plan?"

Jo smiled. "I'd hardly go into such a thing without a plan. I hadn't meant to bring it up tonight, but my darling, the answer is right in front of us: my eldest brother is already there. I propose, after taking such action as our conscience dictates in the march next month, we remove ourselves posthaste to the Western Territories. If we can teach a thousand miles from here without the taint of arrest following us, so much the better, but if not, we will become landowners and shall lobby for legislation to give women the vote."

Celia felt speechless at the thought, but at the same time, she settled into the idea with remarkable speed. "Go West."

"Yes."

"Yes." Celia's stomach flip-flopped as she answered without thinking, purely from her heart. "Let's go West."

"I knew you would say so, dearest." Jo kissed her deeply. "So, you will please remember I love you when I say I am buying a piece of land. I'll buy from my brother, who will hold a note, and I believe him when he says a house with a water wheel is there."

"A house with a water wheel sounds like precisely what we need. I shall pretend you were being romantic and a shrewd businessperson, not high-handed and presumptuous."

Jo had the decency to display a sheepish grin.

"Jo, I—this is all so very much to take in. I will follow you into civil disobedience and jail, and I will follow you West to a water wheel, as I would follow you just about anywhere. I suppose what I mean to say is I love you. "

·‹‹ ● ◆ ››·

Philadelphia, Pennsylvania
March 10, 1861

"You seem to be under the mistaken impression I will marry this man peaceably, Papa." Celia dropped her fork to her plate with a clatter.

"Given your arrest record, you will marry whomever will have you, drugged to docility if need be, like I promised a judge in open court. You are only lucky I was able and willing to secure your release straightaway and they didn't print your name in the newspaper. You are lucky to have any marriage prospects left at all."

"Given I am not six months from my inheritance and independence, sir, I cannot think it fair of you to force the issue."

In fact, she was five months, six days, and seven hours from turning twenty-four and taking control of her mother's trust, such as it was after paying for Mount Holyoke, a Grand Tour of Europe and now, her release from jail. About five months, eight days from leaving for Omaha, Nebraska with Jo. It was long past time for Celia Bromley to be useful, not a pleasant-enough ornament in her father's drawing room.

"Exactly. I have six more months within which you can be prevailed upon to do your duty to this family, Missy. It was always your role to grow up and marry well, to a man of my choosing. All this education and abolition rubbish notwithstanding, and even more so, your dubious plans to cross the country and sleep in a schoolhouse. It was always your role to grow up to marry Robert Wentworth or someone just like him. If your mother were alive, she would tell you the same thing."

"If you push this issue, Papa, you may be sure this will be the last duty I undertake on your behalf."

"That was always the plan, my dear. Your last duty to me is to marry well. After that, you owe your duty to your husband. So do make yourself more amenable to Robert Wentworth."

Celia Bromley had tried to like Mr. Wentworth, but the man simply lacked any redeeming qualities. She had tried to be fair. She had managed to hear him out for the length of supper and dancing followed by an at-home visit. The only thing interesting about the man was his illustrious father, who Celia had been reading in the newspaper since she was fourteen. Robert didn't even want to discuss the man himself unless it was to disagree at volume against P.H. Wentworth's flawless logic, printed every Tuesday, Thursday, and Saturday in the Philadelphia Daily Standard, reprinted by the New York Associated Press.

"You can tell he doesn't want to talk about his father, Celia, so don't. We'll talk about his father once the match is made. His father will have to appear when the families start mingling."

"I do not think young Wentworth will have me, Papa. He won't want a woman who thinks so much."

"Well, then, we shan't let him catch you at it."

"Nor will he want one so old and on-the-shelf. There is a vast gulf between his eighteen and my twenty-three."

"Even more reason to marry him, and quickly. And more reason to increase your dowry."

"I can't believe you would sell me for an introduction to his father. Can you not meet the man some other way? Is that not what chambers of commerce are for?"

Not that she wouldn't love to be introduced to the famous P. H. Wentworth herself, but it wasn't worth her freedom. Not to mention she could think of a hundred easier ways to meet the man, starting with: scheduling an appointment.

"An introduction to his father and an introduction to his trust, my girl. One hundred thousand upon marriage that he very specifically does not want to bank near his father, plus your marriage settlements. The boy wishes to begin his career in banking."

"And yet, he boasted to me not a week ago that he will forgo another quarter million in capital simply to defy his father's advice. I sacrificed a quarter of my dowry and four Seasons of marriage-hunting to gain an education. Can you imagine turning down your choice of universities, a Grand Tour, and a trust? And to brag about it. It is foolish in the extreme."

"He is not smart, it's true, but I expect you to make the best of it. He is rich, well-connected, and easy to manage, and I've got a place for him at the bank. No, Missy, when he asks for your hand, you will accept him, no questions asked."

"If he would stop taking the stupid side of every argument and just follow his father's advice—financial and otherwise—he could turn his trust into millions of dollars, but instead he refuses anything his father recommends. Including a rudimentary university education. No, Papa, Robert Wentworth is the worst sort of human being. He doesn't want to be of use. He is wasteful of everything he has."

"I can't argue the point. Do be nicer next time you see him."

Philadelphia, Pennsylvania
April 10, 1861

"You are restless, my love."

Jo poured a cup of tea at her elbow. She was serving in her own living room for the first time since her brief marriage had ended with her husband's death, necessitating her taking a position as a companion. Mrs. Pilchrist had now also died, leaving Jo enough in her will to fulfill her dreams of emigrating West, and also to rent a small house until she could arrange to leave.

Celia paced once across the room, then back. "What is it you wish not to tell me?" Celia looked away from Jo, ashamed of herself for a long stretch of minutes. Jo pushed the cup of tea toward Celia, so she finally took a seat.

"Is it Robert Wentworth?" Jo surmised. "Has he proposed?"

"Worse." Celia sighed. "He's signed contracts with my father without either of them talking about it to me. My father presented it last evening as a fait accompli. I am to be married as soon as it can be done without being unseemly."

Jo sat with the news for a minute or two before she spoke, sipping her tea and choosing a sandwich. "We knew this was coming when he told a judge in open court he would marry you to a respectable gentleman shortly."

"That makes it no more welcome. I am meant to move West

with you upon receipt of my trust, not tie myself to the nearest jack-about-town. Robert Wentworth, indeed."

"Can you find nothing to love about him?"

"If only it were that easy."

That was how Jo said she had survived marriage to a man, when she was disinclined to ever be touched by one. She had found little things to love about Mr. Abbott, adding up to enough to counterbalance her distasteful wifely duties. Of course, his leaving her with nothing upon his death had negated many of the "good things" about Mr. Abbott.

"Josephine Jane Abbott. He could be the most amiable man alive and not be to my taste. I am not in the market for a husband; rather the opposite."

"Opposite being no husband, or opposite being a wife?" Jo asked with a mischievous grin.

"Both," Celia intoned, knowing she'd get neither. "I am both dismayed and incensed that I will be married to Robert Wentworth in a matter of moments."

"Drink your tea, my love."

Celia did as she was bid. But Jo exhorting her to drink tea was a bad sign for the rest of the conversation.

"I have more bad news, my dear." Celia was not certain her heart could take much more bad news this day.

She put down her cup in its saucer. Jo mirrored her movements, going so far as to slide the teacup onto the table.

"You will leave for Nebraska," Celia guessed. "Your brothers' plans will move forward?"

"How well you know me, my dearest girl."

"We knew this was in the offing, too. We had just hoped for a few months' reprieve."

"Come with us, Celia. Your trust can catch up with you on your birthday. They have banks in Nebraska. Run away with me."

"If I run away with you, you may be sure there will be no trust on my birthday."

"I care naught for your trust."

"That is neither here nor there. I am sure it is now Robert Wentworth's contractually, no matter what I do, and if my father catches wind of your caravan west, I'll be Mrs. Wentworth before you can pack the first suitcase. I do not see a way out of this, barring losing my family, such as it is, and shaming my father publicly—again. We knew this was coming."

For the first time since her father had made her betrothal known to her, Celia felt a tear run down her face. Jo rushed over and brushed the tear out from under Celia's eye. "No, my darling, no tears, for we will have tonight, which is all we may be afforded, and perhaps a few more days besides. We will stay connected, my love, by letter if we must, and I will find a way to bring you to Nebraska if it is the last thing I do. For now, we shall count ourselves lucky to have all we do together."

·‹‹ ● ● ›› ·

Philadelphia, Pennsylvania
August 14, 1861

"I should like to know what kind of marriage you wish, sir."

Celia laid her fork and knife across her plate and took a sip of her wine, settling her hands in her lap as the footman took her place setting. This was their first meal together as a married couple, the first time she had been alone with him, outside the five minutes it had taken him to propose and her to choke out an acceptance. She'd spent more time with the housekeeper and butler than she had with the master of the house.

"Oh, I shall be lenient as long as you refrain from scandal. Your pin money is generous; your father saw to that."

"As long as I refrain from scandal..."

"There will be none of that political nonsense."

"I see."

"You shouldn't have time for such pursuits, in any case. I require an heir. And your father requires a grandchild. With all due speed and urgency. I expect you understand your duties." He coughed and blushed.

His blush was contagious. She felt it heat her cheeks, too. "Yes, sir, I understand."

She understood, she'd daresay, in ways he couldn't. Celia Bromley expected a rude awakening. Her thoughts of lovemaking must turn from two gently fumbling women in love, to whatever Robert Wentworth would require of a wife.

"Perhaps we can forgo dessert this evening?" Robert raised one eyebrow, almost in challenge, standing and holding out his hand for hers. "I'd say you run to plump, do you not, Mrs. Wentworth? Perhaps we should forgo desserts every night."

"Perhaps we should discuss my relative plumpness another time, when I am not so actively trying to find you charming. Shall I not now retire to my room to ready myself?"

How she would do that, she had no idea. It was not a betrayal of Jo, she reminded herself again. They had both known that Celia would be married off against her will and have conjugal duties to undertake. The reason Celia knew as much as she did was that Jo had been married first.

"No doubt you have a night gown planned?"

"No doubt I do." She doubted her lady's maid would let a wedding night go without a special nightgown, no matter how Celia might ask her not to fuss. She was equally doubtful Robert would make anything special of their wedding night at all. Not that she hoped for moonlight and roses, especially from such a green boy, but she'd hoped, at least, for someone who would be kind. Jo's Mr. Abbott had been kind.

As it happened, the night Robert gave her was nothing if not memorable; she would carry the terror and pain and helpless fury the rest of her life.

·‹‹ ● ● ›› ·

Philadelphia, Pennsylvania
December 22, 1861

"We shall spend Christmas with my mother and grandparents." Robert folded the newspaper to more easily read something on an inside page. "While I am certain she is happier without my father there to vex her, she will be lonely without my sisters to keep her company." Thank heavens, Robert's vapid twin sisters had been sent away to school in France.

Celia looked up from the letter she was writing to Jo. "Will my father not be lonely, too? He has no one in the household with him. Can we not split the day between them?"

Robert waved away the problem with a hand, his attention still on his paper. "I make no objection if you wish to have him for Christmas Eve; of course, he should come for the tree lighting."

"But everyone is coming for the tree lighting."

"Exactly. I shall be able to stay well away from your father and his demands, and he cannot make a scene with me in public." Whether demands related to the bank, where Robert was foundering, by all accounts, or Robert's famous father, who Celia's father still insisted could be introduced by letter, or something else entirely, Celia had not the first clue. Robert did not share his life with her any more than her father had.

It was the greatest disappointment, and irony, of her marriage that neither she nor her father had ever met Robert's father, the great P.H. Wentworth. He had left Philadelphia for Charleston well before any Bromley-Wentworth family gatherings were initiated.

"I will be sad to miss my father on Christmas." She would be sad to miss Jo, too, of course, for a day did not pass when she thought of how differently her life might have turned out, had her father not sold her to Robert Wentworth.

"You will learn to live with it. I should like to see the household accounts without delay."

"Oh, Robert, you cannot need to cut costs again." Every time he asked to see the household accounts, she was told she was spending too much on something—servants or wine and spirits or refurbishment of the public rooms—given a new, lower limit, and the difference to be applied to some debt or another, which nature she was not to question. It was not to be overlooked that soon after each of his cuts to her budget, he could be heard whining about fewer servants and less expensive brandy.

"You will bring me the household accounts forthwith, Wife, or you will feel the rough side of my temper. I am in control of you and those accounts, and I will not be gainsaid."

Celia froze. When he started talking about control, he was only inches from its loss. The screaming would start, then the raving, mostly about his father, then finally, he might hit her. So far, only twice, and only one blow each time before he walked away. But she was certain she hadn't seen the last of his fists.

She brought him the household accounts and was told unequivocally she had spent too much on new uniforms for the upstairs servants, and the difference would be taken from her dress allowance. Thank heaven her pin money came from a trust set up by her father upon her marriage, and Robert couldn't get his hands on it. It might end up being the only money they had.

·‹‹ ● ● ● ›·›

Philadelphia, Pennsylvania
April 30, 1862

"Will you put down that traitorous rag and listen to me?"

Robert's most demanding tone of voice cut into Celia's reading of her father-in-law's latest venture, the Wentworth and Hoyt Business Service.

The new weekly investment analysis from around the world was the latest rage among businessmen everywhere—and Celia. She had been afraid, when he resigned from the Philadelphia Daily Standard, that he wouldn't publish at all, but no, he had quickly turned up with this financial advice publication, channeling decades of work and life experience into something that would make millions—billions—of dollars for businessmen the world over. As long as they were smart enough to pay attention.

"Your father is not a traitor; he's a centrist. And a terribly smart one, at that." Celia lowered her copy of his father's advice into her lap.

"Would that I were in control of my own resources," she continued, "I would be up eight percent this quarter." In fact, her invested pin money was up by eight percent. But more every day she resented the money she had been swindled out of through this marriage, and the freedom inherent in spinsterhood. She should be investing the remaining portion of her mother's trust on her own terms.

"Heaven help us if the wives were put in control of their own resources. You'd spend the lot on hats in a matter of days."

How infuriating! Robert was spending her dowry as fast as he could on hats, waistcoats, and walking sticks, to say nothing of clubs and drinking and gambling. The only thing he hadn't yet purchased was a mistress, but that was inevitable. His favorite diatribe lamented her frigidity, relative to the other women with whom he had fornicated. Her dowry would be nothing in no time, and his trust would soon follow. And just what would they do then?

Before she could build up a head of steam to castigate Robert for his spendthrift ways once again, he interrupted her thoughts.

"Might I have your attention for a moment, Wife?"

She laid down the copy of Wentworth and Hoyt in her lap at his suddenly gentle request.

"What is this about, Robert?"

"I've enlisted."

"You've what?"

"Enlisted. In the cavalry."

"Robert, I can't think this a good idea."

"And yet, it is the course I will take. I am hardly the only man to join the Army."

"Your own father discourages all men from joining either army."

"My father is a traitor, no matter which side he falls upon."

Celia resisted the urge to roll her eyes. Just last month, Harper's Weekly had called his father a national treasure. Instead, she extended an olive branch to this little boy she was expected to call a husband.

"Our marriage has not been what either of us expected, Robert, but I do regret you will take this course. Even if you return with your limbs intact, your life will never be the same."

"Indeed, it will not! I intend it should change me to my marrow. I will be a man grown when I return, with adventure to my credit. My father will never be able to look down on me again."

If Celia thought Robert might live up to his father, she would be more hopeful for his chances. She hated herself for the thought, but she would be far better off if he never returned from the war, especially if he left to go soldiering without spending the last of their money.

"Will you go soon?" The sooner the better.

"I'll be away as soon as it is practicable. I should think a week sufficient to tie up my affairs. I need to arrange for your care and oversight while I am away."

"My care and ... what?"

"You can't imagine I will leave you without oversight. Good God, you'd drain the accounts and give everything to orphans. No, I will need to arrange financial oversight, to be sure. I imagine your father would have no objection to acting in my stead."

"Financial oversight? Robert! I need no such supervision. I am not a schoolgirl."

"No, you are not a schoolgirl. You are a woman with a penchant toward politics, who is more than capable of inserting herself into a protest and being carried off by the police. There is simply no chance I will leave a woman so educated and opinionated to shame me publicly in my absence. No, my dear, there will be supervision. Perhaps your father might agree to take you in while I am away. Or my mother."

"I will not be put out of my house and shuffled back and forth between you and my father—certainly not your mother! I do not need minding. Leave the household accounts and my pin money to me and I shall remain here as long as it is safe and join my father only if things become dangerous. If you truly must, leave the funds with trustees at the bank, but I resent the implication that I threaten you with scandal. I have been a model wife to you, Robert, in every way. I deserve the dignity of seeing to my own affairs."

"It is out of the question. Even my father would never have done such a stupid thing as to leave the family finances in the hands of his wife. He tied up every dollar he ever gave to her, with trustees at the bank and stewards at the houses and accounts only at shops he approved. She controlled the household budget, and he reviewed those ledgers himself. My father knew where every dollar went. You can be sure I will have at least as much control over my household."

"I am shocked and dismayed you would think so little of me, Robert."

"I give not two figs for your shock and dismay, Celia. You may remove yourself from my presence, unless you'd prefer to put your mouth to better use than talking."

The very thought made her nauseous. Still, he had given her an out for now, which was better than some nights, to be sure. The bedsport might be contained to the bed, instead of Robert choosing a random time and place and sexual act, even sometimes before the servants, purely to exercise his marital power over her.

"I'll be in to see to you shortly." She could expect to be seen to daily—and shortly—until she should find herself with child or he left for the fighting.

She didn't think she would mind a child. If she loved it at all, it would be more than she loved Robert. If she were honest, she'd much prefer not to have Robert's child. It would complicate things.

·‹‹ ● ● ›·

Philadelphia, Pennsylvania
September 19, 1862

"A Mr. Miles Campton from the Daily Standard, Ma'am." Celia's father's butler inserted himself into her afternoon pianoforte practice.

"Show him into the drawing room, please. I will join him in a few minutes."

Celia took a moment to splash water on her face and hands, drying herself carefully, tidying her hair and dress. When she met Mr. Campton in the drawing room, she felt much better equipped to deal with a newspaperman from her father-in-law's former paper of record.

"Good afternoon, Mr. Campton. I am Mrs. Celia Wentworth. How may I be of help, sir?"

"It is I, Mrs. Wentworth, who is at your service, for I come with the gravest of news. You may not know that we, at the Standard, track casualties for Harry Wentworth—Wentworths, Telfairs, Beaufains, and Woffords—at least as efficiently as the government, and I am sorry to say, Harry's son's name came across the wire today. Mrs. Wentworth, if you haven't been notified already, you will be in the newspaper tomorrow. Your husband lost his life at Antietam."

Celia stood stock still. She was afraid if she moved, the answer to her prayers would disappear. Finally, she said, "Robert? Robert is dead?"

"Yes, Ma'am. And I know Harry would want us to put ourselves at your service at The Standard. If there is anything we can do ..."

"I have no doubt you are in communication with Robert's father, Mr. Campton, but have you told Robert's mother yet?"

"No, ma'am."

"If I might prevail upon you to manage that notification?" Anything that would keep her away from Anne Wentworth another minute. In mourning for her little boy, she would be unbearable. Heaven only knew what sort of obeisance she would require of Celia to pay respect to Robert.

"Of course," Mr. Campton agreed.

"If you'll excuse me, I need to see to my mourning attire."

She would have to see if she could even afford mourning attire. She would have to check with her father, who had been none too pleased at the accounts he'd been handed when Robert left. Not that her father or his mother would allow her to forgo the least bit of what was due her husband's dubious honor.

And she needed to send Jo a telegram at her earliest convenience. Celia lived in fear Jo would find someone else while she was rotting away with Robert, but Jo had never stopped writing to her from her new home in Nebraska. Now, the only question in Celia's mind was how long she would be tied up in Philadelphia paying respect to Robert, and how long after that it would take to get to Jo.

·‹‹ ● ● ● ›› ·

Philadelphia, Pennsylvania
September 31, 1862

"Mrs. Wofford, this is an unexpected visit."

Celia had no idea what her husband's grandmother would want with her, especially not enough to sit and wait while Celia finished her meeting with her solicitor. She was glad, however, her blacks were immaculate today. One less thing to think about after the dire report she'd been handed not moments ago. Robert's will had been filled with accounts accruing to her, but when they got to the holdings, there was often nothing left but debt. If she was lucky, she'd break even before the ramifications were through, but she wasn't counting on being that lucky.

"Shall I call for tea?"

"Tea would be lovely, my dear."

"I'm sorry no one offered while you were waiting." Celia asked the butler to send tea and busied herself arranging seating. When Mrs. Margaret Wofford was seated, her companion off to the side, and Celia had set aside the papers from her solicitor, the tea came, in perfect order to keep them from conversation another few minutes. Celia broke protocol by asking the butler to pour out for all. But finally, eventually, Celia was forced to face her late husband's grandmother over a teacup.

"Now all that is settled," Mrs. Wofford began, "I imagine you wonder what brings me here."

"The thought occurred."

"My dear, I'll come to the point. I am aware Robert left you in rather straitened circumstances, and I do not wish to see you living in poverty. You brought enough to this marriage to expect to be taken care of upon my grandson's death. I am ashamed—well. I won't speak ill of the dead, but my grandson should have done better by you."

What was Celia to say to this? "Yes, Mrs. Wofford, you should be ashamed of so many things where Robert is concerned." "Please, speak ill of him, so I might, too." "Why, thank you so much for not leaving me destitute to live out my days with my father."

"The fact is, Mrs. Wentworth, I knew your mother, and I knew her high hopes for you. She left you that trust with the express purpose you should grow to be an educated, enlightened, thoughtful woman. And so you have done. While we cannot make good the entire trust she left you, we can provide you some dignity in your grief." As she handed over a bank draft, Mrs. Wofford added, "It is only unfortunate Robert's father isn't here, for Harry Wentworth has more money than God and a firm sense of justice."

Celia's eyes widened at the amount. Not half of her mother's trust, but still more than Robert had left her. "Does Mrs. Wentworth know you are here? I am sure Robert's mother doesn't feel as you do about her son."

"My daughter notwithstanding, my husband knows I am here today, and Robert's father would agree, were he here. The money is family money, which we have used to cover Robert's debts as well, and that is all you need to know of that. As a widow, you have no need to look to anyone else for permission to use these funds any way you choose. Certainly not your father or my grandson. I hope you will use it to find a fulfilling, joyful, and useful life for yourself. As to what that means to you, I couldn't venture a guess."

··《 ● 》··

Louden City, Nebraska
December 24, 1862

"You arrived just in time, not only for Christmas, but to shelter from this storm." Jo was warm in the drafty house in wool pants, a button-down shirt, and a sweater, counterpoint to Celia's wool traveling skirt and jacket with multiple petticoats to keep her warm. She had thought to change, but the blacks she was wearing were her warmest, by far. She only wished she'd had the courage to defy her mother-in-law and buy dresses in colors to wear once removed from Philadelphia. She would give up mourning Robert as soon as practicable.

"I should have waited to come, but I couldn't stand another minute of my mother-in-law or my father's new wife. It was worth the risk."

"I am beholden to them both. And only grateful you are not stranded somewhere."

"Clearly I am lucky to be here." Celia shivered. "It is nothing but white out there. I've never seen such a blizzard—and I have seen a blizzard or two in my lifetime. I suppose it will be the two of us alone for Christmas, then."

"The storm has seen to that. But there is an entire town wanting to meet you. Everyone is curious about the two schoolmarms with a water wheel."

"I met a few of them on my way here from the stagecoach." She looked around the room. "We are landowners."

"So we are. We have a house to take care of now. And a class of thirty-seven children, all ages. A much-needed mill, if we wish it, but I haven't wanted to make such a decision without you."

"Surely we must not keep an entire community from access to a mill? I still cannot quite believe the water wheel. How did we end up in possession of this six-room house and grounds?"

"We bought it from my eldest brother, who would like nothing more than to see us open a girl's school, but who had no more sizable property to offer. On that note, my love, as it is coming down hard out there and will soon be deep, I need to make a trip to the barn to see to the livestock. Perhaps you can organize dinner while I do so?"

"Only if you promise you will teach me what's needed with the livestock, as soon as we can dig a path to the barn."

Jo touched her face. "I will, sweeting. You will not be ornamental here, I promise you."

"Be careful out there. If you aren't back in an hour, I will come to find you."

While Jo managed the horses, cows, pig, and chickens, Celia used skills long-relegated to kitchen management in Robert's household. She finished the side dishes and sauces Jo had started earlier, in the hopes that Celia would appear for the holiday. To accompany the roast wild duck Jo had been gifted by a father grateful she was educating his son, Celia mashed potatoes, roasted parsnips, carrots, and onions, heated bread dressing, and made enough gravy to coat the lot of it. She even opened the door to the cold to fill a pail with snow to chill champagne.

This promised to be a most satisfactory Christmas, with a rich meal, good wine, gifts and, heavens willing, no singing at the pianoforte Celia knew Jo had hidden away somewhere. Alone and at the mercy of the elements, but in a sound, weather-proof structure, with plenty of food and fuel, and no shortage of anything else they might need.

Jo had even kept mistletoe in her pocket all day and brought it out whenever she wanted a kiss. Which was often. No less than three times, Jo had referred to marriage, once to the wedding night.

Celia's stomach churned when she thought of it. They were truly alone. For the first time since Jo had left Philadelphia with one brother to meet up with another in Louden City, Nebraska. Celia was embarking on her second marriage, she liked to think, and wiser than the first time around.

Jo opened the door and stomped into the house, dripping snow in every direction. She carried with her a block of ice for the ice box. She slid the ice into its compartment and satisfied herself they had enough wood to make it through the night, then divested herself of her coat, hat, gloves, and boots, hanging things strategically near the fireplace.

When Jo was once again in her stocking feet, she pulled out the mistletoe from her pants pocket once again with a sly grin. "Have a kiss for a hardworking farm girl?"

Celia yielded with great pleasure, though eventually, she put a stop to it, saying, "You've asked me for dinner and it's Christmas. There will be time enough for kisses. Besides, we would do well to grow accustomed to circumspection—and to skirts—for as soon as school starts, there will be no room for error."

"It will be rare, my love—the times when we can be fully

ourselves with each other. We may as well take full advantage while the snow falls," Jo said.

Then she did.

It was everything a wedding night should be, and welcome balm to the travesty that had been her first marriage. They accomplished full ravishment there, before supper, in front of the fire in the wood stove, atop and under several layers of quilts.

Then later, after they had eaten and exchanged gifts—Jo gave Celia a coral cameo and Celia gave Jo a first edition of Epictetus—on the feather tick mattress in Jo's room, just wider than a single bed.

Still again, in Celia's bedroom before the clock struck midnight. They decided as the day turned, they would alternate sleeping in each other's rooms, in each other's arms, any night they were afforded the luxury, starting tonight where they lay.

Mari Anne Christie writes second chances for scarred souls. Her literary historical novel, Blind Tribute, in which Celia Bromley appears as a secondary character, follows the American Civil War through the eyes of Harry Wentworth, an intrepid journalist with controversial views. For more about Mari, check out her website at www.MariAnneChristie.com, or follow her on Facebook, Twitter, Goodreads, or Bookbub.

X Marks the Spot

༄༅

NEW YEAR'S EVE
BY ANA BRAZIL

New York City
New Year's Eve, 1918

"The wheel is made of wood two inches thick and painted blood red with a one-inch white trim on the outside." Emil licked his thin bottom lip with his tongue, like he always did when he wasn't quite sure of something. He never noticed it, but I sure did, especially if he did it while throwing knives at me on stage.

"It'll have four buckled straps to tie down your wrists and ankles," he continued. "Once you're tied up, you'll press your head against the wheel—at my cue, of course—and that hits the button that makes the wheel start moving."

Emil and I were standing in the chilly wings of the Broadway theater on New Year's Eve, waiting for our lead-in act, *Bartholdi's Troupe of Cockatoos,* to finish up. Just moments before, I'd been shivering—it was impossible to stay warm in a huge theater when you were only wearing tights and a corset—but now I felt a trickle of sweat on the back of my neck. Had I heard him correctly? "The wheel moves?"

"It moves in place." He double-checked the location of the long, thin knives secreted inside his sleeveless vest. Realizing I was watching him, he flexed his muscles at me. "It won't be moving all over the stage."

"You're strapping me to a wheel that moves and then throwing knives at me?"

"Yes." He regarded me quizzically. "Otherwise, where's the trick?"

"I'm going to be strapped down on a wheel," I said slowly before pausing. "A wheel turning in circles," I said even slower and paused even longer. "And you're going to throw knives at me as it revolves."

My heart pounded from just imagining the trick. And how much could go wrong from it.

"Can you do that?" I asked. "Throw your knives while I revolve without hitting me?"

"Of course I can," he answered readily.

It sounded crazy at first. Almost suicidal, if you were the one strapped and rotating in front of a dozen brutally sharp, eight-inch knives. Which would be me. Yet, despite the craziness, the idea of succeeding at something so bold, so reckless, so obviously unachievable, made my heart flutter excitedly.

Then, as Emil's smile turned into a smirk, I knew the rest of the story. "You've already got the wheel."

"I've got someone making it," he corrected me. "It ain't cheap, but it's going to make us a fortune. We'll be playing the Palace in no time, and once we play the Palace," he paused his patter, possibly in reverence, because playing the Palace was every vaudevil-lian's dream, "every other vaudeville house will line up to book us. This trick will set us up for life. Even legit theaters will want us."

94

It was easy to catch his enthusiasm, even though I'd never heard of a knife-throwing act making the Palace. Although, the more I thought about it, I *could* imagine myself strapped onto his round, blood-red target. I could imagine the audience gasping at the audacity of the trick, their full attention on me and how I reacted to each flick of Emil's wrist.

Except none of Emil's wild ideas mattered to me anymore, because I'd made a New Year's resolution this morning, just after I'd thrown up for the third time.

"When?" I asked, even though what I really wanted to know was: "How long have you been hiding this from me?"

He put his hand on mine. "There's nothing to be scared of, Lily. I'll mark a large X on the wheel to show where your legs and arms will be. You'll get the hang of it pretty quick."

"An X?" My tights were slipping from my waist. I reached down to my baggy knees and tugged them back into place. "When have I ever needed an X to take my position?"

"Take it easy, Lily. No X if you don't want one. I just thought —" He stared at me like he'd never seen me yank up my tights before going on stage. "What's the matter? You chicken or something?"

I straightened up to my full height, which was at least two inches taller than his. Even in his stage heels. "Do I look chicken? Have I ever flinched while you're throwing?"

He didn't need to respond, because we both knew I hadn't.

"I'm the best target girl in vaudeville," I said, louder than I should have backstage. "But you promised we'd go home after the show closed next week. You promised to get those tickets for the train to Tallahassee."

"Whaddya mean, you want to go home? It's New Year's Eve in New York City and we're performing on Broadway, for Chrissakes. The war is finally over, and the flu is finished. The house is full. There's almost two thousand people out there, all of them waiting to see us perform."

An exaggeration, of course. Today's matinee might be two-thirds full, but even if it was, I was guessing that most of the audience hadn't come for the vaudeville (despite headliners like *The Great Jensen, Master of the Magical Arts*.) No, they were here for the moving picture premiere at the end of the show, Episode 7 of *The Hand of Vengeance, The Secret of the Night*. I was looking forward to seeing *The Secret of the Night* also, even though I'd have to watch it sideways from the wings.

"The Palace is just down the street, Lily," said Emil. "This new trick will get us there. And after that, we'll get booked everywhere. Maybe even the Ziegfeld Follies or the Hippodrome. You'd like to perform in the Follies, wouldn't you? Have your own dressing room? Rub shoulders with Mister Ziegfeld?"

Suddenly, Emil got down on one knee and patted his thigh for me to sit. It was quite the gallant's romantic gesture, except that marrying Emil and traveling the country for six months had already shattered my romantic illusions.

Emil patted his thigh, this time more harshly. "Work with me, honey, won't you? Papa knows what he's doing."

When I refused to sit, he rose and shook out his pant leg, careful that no backstage smudge would be seen onstage.

"I can't believe you still want to go back home," he snarled. "You could be the queen of vaudeville, *headlining at the Palace*, but you want to go back to Tallahassee?"

"I've been telling you that for weeks. I need to see my—"

But he wasn't looking at me anymore. He was watching as Bartholdi and his cockatoos made their final bows and left the stage. The orchestra quickly ended one musical piece and began the introduction to our act. It was showtime for *Conner and Conner, Knife-Throwing Daredevils*.

Even though I needed to focus on our performance, all I could think about was getting home to see Mama. "How much did that new wheel cost, Emil? Is there any money left to go home?"

He still didn't look at me, although, I could make out the edge of his jaw and saw he was grinding his teeth.

Well, it was now or never.

"Either we lay off from performing for the entire month of January and head home to Mama," I said to his back. "Or you can find yourself another target girl."

With that proud ultimatum—because a knife-throwing act was nothing without a target girl—I surged ahead of him, steps away from the stage.

But before I could turn the curtain aside, Emil grabbed a shank of my long hair and yanked me back toward him, his lips pressed upon my ear. "It's bad enough you got yourself pregnant, and we have to lay off for a few weeks this year, but leaving New York will ruin us," he hissed. "I've sacrificed everything to create this act. It's time you gave up something."

One thing about performing in vaudeville: you don't irritate your partner just before you go on stage. Because if you do, things could go wrong. Like, they could talk over your lines, or step in your spotlight, or steal your laughs. Or, if you're a target girl, they could throw a knife so fast and so close that the hair on your forearms stands up and salutes.

Emil and I played our act in front of the curtain, yards away from the audience, so they could see as much as possible. He'd been right about the size of tonight's New Year's Eve audience; almost all of the Broadway theater's two thousand seats were filled with people. I could feel their expectations as I paraded in front of the garnet-colored velvet curtain. Can Emil really throw a knife and not hit her? Can his beautiful wife really stand still and not move? Or will he miss his mark and something terrible happen today?

My scalp still tingled from Emil grabbing my hair, and his threat wove through my thoughts, almost ruining my concentration. Still, I graciously handed him his tasseled knives, hatchets, and machetes, which he threw into balloons, watermelons, and apples without missing. Then we came to the trickiest part of our fifteen-minute show, the damsel-in-distress routine; the five minutes where Emil aimed his sharp weapons directly at me.

This was my moment. I emerged from behind Emil, and while two stagehands replaced Emil's first target boards with mine, I strutted across the stage until I reached my board. It was a large, rectangular piece of wood painted blood red and edged in white, just like Emil's proposed revolving wheel. As the orchestra switched from a waltz to a march, I centered myself on the target, keeping my feet together and hugging my arms across my chest, making myself the smallest target possible, and nothing like the large X Emil proposed for his rotating board.

I sucked in as much air as I could and then released it. I knew I had the audience's complete attention, that I held their expectations of success in every muscle I tensed. I also knew they were on my side. They wanted me to survive the barrage of knives. They wanted me to step from my target board unscathed.

As the spotlight glimmered upon him, Emil licked his bottom lip. The real show was about to begin.

Emil's first knife—aimed at my right ankle, which very few in the audience could see—hit the target board hard; so hard, a splinter of wood spun through my thin tights and into my ankle. It hurt like a mad mosquito's bite, but I bit my tongue and didn't move. His next knife would hit the board in less than five seconds.

In quick order, Emil threw ten more knives at the target

board, each of them about three inches from any part of my body. When he finished throwing all twelve knives, the audience showed their appreciation with applause and cheers and whistles.

I stepped gracefully to center stage and bowed. After giving the audience the opportunity to salute my bravery, I took my place on an oval target board, which the stagehand quickly positioned onstage. This time, I stood with my side to the board, my front to the audience. I arched my back and extended my neck backwards, fully exposing my throat. This was the most dangerous moment in the act, and the audience knew it. Despite the hundreds of people in the audience, the theater was heart-stoppingly quiet.

Emil's first throw landed inches from the top of my head, as expected.

But, in knife-throwing in front of an audience, speed was just as important as accuracy. Faster was better. Even though his throwing was synchronized to the orchestra's precise march music, Emil started throwing faster than the tempo. Almost like he was trying to hit me.

Except both he and I knew he never would. One knife hitting any part of my body—even if it somehow bounced off—would kill the act, and Emil would be blacklisted from working in any vaudeville theater. The audience was eager to see how closely Emil could *almost* hit me, but they would never tolerate one of his knives actually hitting me.

His final knife came closer, less than one inch away. I could feel the knife's tassel whip against my hand. Roars and applause rippled through the theater. I stepped down from the target board and waved my arms at the audience to keep their applause going. After one encore—in which Emil tossed flaming knives at a board of miniature balloons—we stepped off the stage into the wing, not even looking at each other.

While Emil put away his weapons, I went directly to the ladies dressing room, slipped a dress over my costume, bundled myself into my coat, hat, scarf, and boots, and exited the stage door. I hustled toward Times Square and was almost knocked down by a sudden rush of people coming up the subway stairs, one of them carrying a sign on a stick proclaiming: *Helloooo 1919*. New Yorkers might be excited to celebrate New Year's Eve with signs and noise-makers and a big ball drop, but I wanted to avoid it all and turned a block before the commotion at Times Square.

I turned right on 42nd Street, and even before nearing my destination, I heard organ music lofting through the dusky air. I walked up the steps to the front door of Holy Cross Catholic Church and was quickly inside. I wasn't Catholic, of course, being raised in Tallahassee, but days ago, when my need for Mama drove me almost frantic, this church's doors were open to me.

I'd been awed at the huge altar and the painting on the walls and ceilings, and fascinated by the statues of Madonna and child scattered throughout the church. I almost wished I was Catholic, almost wished that this fancy church and its rituals meant something to me.

Now, as I slipped onto a pew near the back, the music ended and silence took over. So, I sat there, far from Emil's grasp and wishing I'd never loved him.

But how could I not? He was handsome. Ambitious. Confident. Precise. Everything I had always wanted to be. No wonder I accepted his offer to train me to be his target girl, and later accepted his proposal of marriage.

But sometime, somewhere, things had gone wrong between us. Emil kept the weekly allowance he'd promised Mama he'd give me. The six-inch knives he threw at me became eight-inch knives, and during one show, a hatchet; the five-inch space between his knife and my skin was reduced to three inches. Then I got pregnant.

I settled my hands around my belly and snuggled into the corner of the pew. Mama could fix it all. With hugs and lemonade and her southern practicality, she could make it all right. She could protect this baby.

The silence, incense, and my worried exhaustion all worked to make me sleepy. Maybe I could sleep for just a moment. Maybe for just a minute. And maybe, when I awoke, I'd know how to get home to Mama. I placed a hand over my stomach and offered the same prayer I'd been moaning to myself this past week, "Don't worry, Junior; Mama'll figure out how to keep you safe."

·‹‹●◉●›·

"Wake up, Lily," a man's soft tones beckoned me from my sleep. "It's time to wake up."

I opened my eyes, focusing first on the altar in the far distance and then on the man sitting inches from me: *The Great Jensen, Master of the Magical Arts.*

I'd never been so close to the magician before; never noticed the jagged scar under his left eye, or that his black hair was bottle-dyed, or that the top hat on his knees reeked of rabbit piss. I'd seen him watching our act from the wings almost every show, standing behind Emil as he threw, staring so intently at Emil's back that I'd wondered if he thought he could magically guide his throw. But *The Great Jensen* was the theater's headliner, the big name act upon which we all depended to draw in the audience, so I'd never challenged his gaze.

Plus, I'd never liked magicians. Never liked how they manipulated the audience into believing something was true when it wasn't. Even though all us vaudevillians were putting on a show, making the audience laugh at our jokes or sing along with our songs or gasp at our knife throws, magicians betrayed the audience's trust, show after show.

I put my hands on the pew in front of me, ready to drag myself up to my feet. "It's late. I need to get go—"

"No, you don't." He pulled a watch from his vest pocket and turned toward me, so I could read it myself. He was right. I didn't need to be in costume and makeup for two hours. "You've got plenty of time before you need to be at the theater."

And then, he let me have it. "Besides, I've got a proposition for you."

My heart sank. Already this run, I'd side-stepped two unsavory propositions from fellow vaudevillians. Still groggy from my nap, I wasn't sure I was up to artfully deflecting our headliner.

"I want you to come work for me," he said.

A job offer? Not at all the proposition I anticipated. "I've already got a job. Besides, why would I come to work for you?"

"Because, my dear," he took a breath, a long, engaging stage breath. "At some performance in the future—soon, possibly even tonight—your Emil is going to miss a throw, and his blade is going to hit you."

I gasped. It was bad luck to even suggest that Emil could hit me on stage, and certainly the magician knew that.

Still, he continued his prophecy. "Something will distract him. Someone in the first row will have a coughing fit. Or something he's tried not to think about will suddenly come to mind. Or that new red wheel will suddenly spin too fast."

The magician must have been backstage before our last performance. Must have heard Emil boast about his new target wheel. I wondered what else he knew about. I resisted putting my hand on my belly, and all I could say was, "Emil's never hit me on stage."

"But he has hit you."

That much was true, and I looked down at my gloved right hand, which was marred by two scars from Emil's practice.

"What about those girls you saw in half?" I'd been watching

the magician's act for the last week and knew it well. "You're telling me you've never cut into them?"

He smiled. "My dear, everything I do on stage is an illusion. There's nothing real about it. The box isn't real, the saw isn't real—"

"Your assistants are real," I replied. "And they sure react like everything's real."

"Pure illusion; the saw never touches them and never will." He stared at me, as if staring long enough would reveal all of my secrets. Maybe it did. "Let me tell you something about yourself."

The organ began to play just then, and a soft series of scales accompanied the magician's story. He turned to face me completely in the pew. "I performed at the front for the soldiers. I took my entire troupe. My props, my costumes, my animals. We performed our entire act to any Allied soldier we could, in any place we could. We were there in the spring, when the great offenses were launched. And when the influenza came through the camp."

His mention of the war and influenza brought up all my bad memories, and I interrupted him with, "I thought this was about me."

"Soldiers were dying around me every day, from battle and snipers and the flu. Being this close," he held up his thumb and index finger, less than half an inch apart, "to the possibility of death was the most thrilling time of my life. I loved every moment performing onstage, even knowing we could be hit by enemy fire at any time."

Almost against my will, I wanted to hear more of his story.

"You love it, too, Lily. Knowing Emil could hit you with his knife at any time."

I clutched my coat tighter around me.

"You love it," the magician went on, "but someday it could kill you. Or someone you love."

How could the magician know so much about me? How could he know that I craved my time on the target board? That having Emil's knives hit so close to my skin made me tingle with a triumphant thrill? That from the first moment on stage, I knew I was home?

"Train tracks," I whispered.

"What?"

"Train tracks," I raised my voice slightly. "Like in the moving pictures?"

He shook his head.

"Didn't you see *Teddy at the Throttle* last year? Where the wealthy heroine is chained to the train tracks by her evil, money-snatching uncle? And she can't get out of the chains. And then the train starts down the tracks, smoke streaming from the chimney, whistles blowing from the orchestra, the cowcatcher grinding toward her. She can't escape from the heavy chains tying her to the tracks, and the train's going to run her down."

Whether or not he'd seen the picture, I had his attention now.

"Who do you think the audience cares about? It's the damsel-in-distress. The audience cares about her, they're rooting for her. They love her." *How do I give that up*, I wanted to ask.

"If it's love you need," he smiled gently, "I can make the audience love you. There are tricks I'm working on, ones that rely less on illusion and more on a woman's nerves. And I've never seen anyone with nerves like yours. Never."

I relished his compliment for seconds before replying, "Like I said, I already have a job." I forced myself to not put my hand on my belly. "I don't need—"

"You say that now, but when Emil's blade ends up in your fingers—or worse—

you'll need someone. You and your baby both."

So, he had overheard us backstage. Or he was a very keen

observer. This time I did put my hand on my baby, not caring who knew about it.

The magician swooped past me to the center aisle and placed his top hat firmly on his head. "Think about my offer, Lily. And don't say I didn't warn you about Emil. Accidents can happen at any time."

A few minutes later, I stood alone in the church's doorway. Daylight had evaporated and an almost-full moon had risen above the tall buildings. I searched the sky for a star, and wished upon it, because all of the magician's talk about accidents had spurred an idea in my head.

By the time I reached the Broadway theater, I'd decided to create an accident of my own.

·‹‹ ● ◉ ›·

Still in costume, Emil bounced from foot to foot on the landing outside the stage door, jabbing his bare arms out in front of him like he was a prize fighter, his nervous energy almost toppling him.

"Lily!" He pulled his fists back toward his heaving chest, as if tensing to deliver the knockout punch. "Where'd you go? I've been looking all over for you."

"I went—"

"Never mind." He left off punching, put his arm around my shoulders and led me through the stage door. It was hours before the 8:15 show, and not even the stage crew was backstage. Emil stopped suddenly, clutched me hard and put his mouth to my ear. I shivered, wondering if he was going to threaten me again, but held my ground.

This time, he spoke sweetly. "It's here, Lily. It's here."

Now, gripping my shoulders, he walked me away from the

stage and down the wing, until we almost reached the backstage wall. He led me to a large object sheathed in thick canvas and positioned me in front of it. He pulled the cloth away, rolled it into a ball, and threw it behind him. "My wheel, Lily. It's finally ready."

The wheel was thick, round, and blood red, just as Emil said it'd be. It was much larger than I'd imagined and, for something built for the rough-and-tumble vaudeville stage, it was almost beautiful.

"Let me strap you in," he whispered almost reverently. And then, "So you can see how it feels."

The four straps for my ankles and wrist were in thin red leather; I didn't need to be strapped in to know they weren't strong enough to keep me from sliding across the target. Also, I'd need a thick belt around my waist to keep me in place, and there was none. Since my arms and legs were long, I could also use a strap around my knees and elbows.

But how, I wondered, would the audience react to all those straps? Would they think I was playing it too safe? That I wasn't really in distress? Or would the red leather bonds excite them even more?

As all these thoughts flew through me, I felt a sudden disturbance in my belly. And although it was something entirely new, I realized right away that it wasn't fright or anxiety pulsing through me. For the first time, Junior let me know he was there. I put my hand on my belly, but the sensation had left me. Still, I knew what Junior was trying to tell me.

"I won't," I told Emil. "I won't let you throw knives at me up there."

"What do you mean *won't*? It's your job."

"I'm four months pregnant. I need to stop working now."

"You can't stop working. It'll kill the act. Besides, I said I'd give you two weeks off once the baby came."

"I need to go home to Mama." And then, wanting to give

Emil one more chance to avoid the accident that was taking shape in my thoughts, I added, "Just give me money for a train ticket and let me go."

He put his hands on my shoulders and shook me hard, like he could rattle me enough to see things his way. I thought he might slap me, but we were too close to curtain time for him to leave a visible mark on my face. "I'm so tired of you talking about your Mama. I've sunk everything into this act. That new target board cost three months' salary, and it's going to make me famous."

His fingers dug into my shoulders, creating so much pain I knew he'd leave a bruise. "You're the most selfish bitch in the world, and you're going up on that board if I have to nail you on it."

·《●●》·

I hid in the ladies' dressing room until just before showtime, refreshing my makeup, pulling up my tights, and fretting about whether I had enough nerve to follow through with my accident. I did, didn't I? Hadn't the magician just told me, "I've never seen anyone with nerves like yours?"

And it wasn't such a large accident. All I needed to do was spread out my left arm directly in the path of one of Emil's knives. Once the audience realized he hit me—and saw my reaction—the stage manager would pull us from the stage.

I joined Emil in the wings as Bartholdi's Cockatiels began their big finale. He was bouncing on his feet, and I stood clear of him, experiencing an unexpected twinge of guilt that in a few minutes, I would wreck his career in vaudeville. Because once his knife struck me, I had no doubt he'd be blacklisted; no theater would ever book him again.

Maybe because it was New Year's Eve and the Times Square

ball drop was only blocks away, the theater was packed and the audience noisy and restless. The squawking cockatoos were also restless, and they muffed their big finale and left the stage without performing an encore. It was showtime for *Conner and Conner, Knife-Throwing Daredevils;* but this time, it was the final showtime.

We took our places in front of the curtain in our usual positions, Emil stage right and me stage left. But, instead of launching immediately into his opening balloon throw routine, Emil faced the audience directly, waited until he had their almost-complete attention, and addressed them.

"Ladies and gentlemen," Emil's voice glided over the audience, even reaching the cheap seats in the loge. "Tonight, for the very first time on a New York stage, you'll witness a knife-throwing demonstration that will boggle your mind and excite your senses. On this very special night, in this very theater, I will premier an astounding exhibition of knife-throwing excellence. You will marvel at this demonstration of my skills."

My stomach roiled, but this time, Junior wasn't responsible. Emil's impromptu introduction could mean only one thing.

"Tonight," he announced, "I will introduce you to The Wheel of Doom!"

As the orchestra launched into a foxtrot, the curtains opened just enough to expose Emil's large, red wheel. He extended his left arm toward the wheel, encouraging the audience to applaud. They did.

I couldn't believe Emil thought he could try the rotating wheel tonight, without practicing; I'd already told him I wouldn't mount it, and there was no way he could force me to do it with an audience of two thousand looking on. At least, I didn't think he could.

"But first, dear audience, let's warm up our knives."

The orchestra launched into the music used for the first part of my damsel-in-distress performance. Enough of the audience had seen our show before that they gazed toward me and started to applaud. Stunned as I was by Emil's announcement, I moved toward the target. This might be my best, my only, chance tonight to cause an accident.

I mounted my rectangular target board without giving any appearance that anything was amiss. I clutched my feet together and wrapped my arms around my chest; I was the same firm target I'd always been.

Normally, Emil threw twelve knives at me in rapid-fire succession, plucking the knives from a table placed waist-high before him. But tonight, he lingered before each throw.

His stage patter—and the promise of a new trick featuring the impressive Wheel of Doom—had riled up the audience. Their earlier restlessness had turned into rapt attention. People scrambled down the two main aisles and jostled each other to stand just outside the orchestra pit, ten feet from the stage.

Their focus was entirely on Emil and me, and I'd never felt so connected to the audience before. Tonight, I was the girl chained to the train tracks in *Teddie at the Throttle,* and the hearts of everyone in the theater ached for me, the damsel-in-distress on the target board. My heart thumped so fast, I was sure the people in the cheap seats could feel it. This was what succeeding in vaudeville was like, and I was greedy to keep the feeling as long as possible.

Over a few minutes, Emil threw nine out of his twelve knives, each landing safely away from my ankles, hips, knees, chest, and right ear. After each successful hit, the audience applauded—not politely, but with real gusto—something that had never happened to us before.

Emil selected the third-to-last knife on his table and pointed it at the audience, rotating it toward them, as though he was going in for a kill. Despite the warmth of the stage lights, I shivered.

I was going in for the kill also. I was going to kill any chance of Emil staying in vaudeville. But suddenly, I realized, I might be blacklisted from appearing in vaudeville also. I'd no longer command the target board, no longer hear the audience gasp or bask in their applause, no longer feel that surge of power from having never flinch—

I'd turned my eyes from Emil for just seconds, and he launched the knife at me. It landed inches from my left ear. The audience went wild, and I had a vision of Emil and me taking this bodacious new show on the road, eventually ending up as Emil intended, at the Palace Theater. How could I give up this audience adoration?

Emil took the second-to-last knife from the table, bending down to display it to the audience leaning over the orchestra pit.

I looked past Emil and his knife to see *The Great Jensen* staring at me from the wings, so close, he was almost on stage. *I've never seen anyone with nerves like yours*, he'd told me. And then, *Accidents happen.*

Suddenly, my thrill at the audience's applause for me dimmed. I knew what I needed to do, I really did. I knew that Emil's anger would boil over at me one day, or worse, at Junior. I had to protect Junior from Emil, just like Mama had protected me from Daddy.

But I also craved these moments on stage. I loved being the only person in the theater, perhaps in the entire city of New York, who had the nerve to stand tall and still while knives were thrown at her.

The second-to-last knife whizzed from Emil's hand to inches from my right shoulder. He must have thrown with additional strength, because the thud of the knife hitting the target board was the loudest I'd ever heard. The audience roared. Tonight, Emil and I were the greatest knife-throwing daredevils ever to perform.

Finally, Emil had only one knife on the table in front of him. This knife would go a few inches from my left shoulder, in full view of everyone in the audience. And if he missed the board and hit my arm, it'd be a perfect accident. Emil seized the knife and waved it high above his head in a grand gesture, encouraging the audience to cheer his final throw.

As my mind raced from Emil's prowess to the audience's cheers to The Great Jensen's premonition to Mama's hugs, unsure if I could walk away from the applause, Junior made himself known once more, kicking my belly so hard, I strained to keep my arms crossed against my chest.

And just as Emil hurled his last knife, I spread my feet out slightly for balance and thrust my arms in a V above my head. I'd created a large X on the target board that Emil's knife had to strike, keeping Junior safe not only from Emil, but also from me.

Many years ago **Ana Brazil** inherited the theatrical memorabilia of vaudeville songstress Elsie Clark. This treasure trove inspired Ana to create Viola Vermillion, the smart, sassy, and bodacious vaudeville heroine of THE RED-HOT BLUES CHANTEUSE and also to write the short story *X Marks The Spot*. Ana's currently writing the second of her Viola Vermillion Vaudeville Mysteries, THE MAGNOLIA VOODOO BRAWLER. Join Ana on Facebook, Instagram, or at www.AnaBrazil.com.

A Wicked Turn at Christmas

CHRISTMAS
BY JONATHAN POSNER

Grangedean Manor, England
December 19, 1569

Lady Mary de Beauvais stood back with her hands planted firmly on her hips.

"I told you, William, we are having a full tree this Christmas." She waved a hand at the tall fir reaching nearly to the ornate plaster ceiling of the Great Hall. It had just been brought in by their servants, and was commanding attention as it glowed a vibrant green in the morning light from the high windows. "There it is," she continued. "Tell me it is not magnificent."

Sir William de Beauvais put his hands on his own hips, assuming a stance that mirrored Mary's own. She shook her head slightly. There was no need to psychoanalyze his body posture; the deep frown and red mottling coming up from under his ruff told their own tale. And anyway, such analysis had its place in the twenty-first century, not the sixteenth.

"Why must we have the whole tree, Mary?" he asked. "When we have long been content with but a few branches, some holly and mistletoe, like norm..." He stopped himself with a brief clearing of his throat.

"'Like normal people,' you were going to say?" she asked, putting a little sweetness into her voice to take the sting out of the accusation.

But William's wavering was true; they were not 'normal.' Oh, for sure, on the surface there was nothing to distinguish the de Beauvais family from other minor nobles in Elizabethan England. Grangedean Manor was a fine house. Sir William spent most of his time hunting in its extensive woods and parklands, and oversaw the farms, rents and lives of its tenants. Mary herself was the model lady, managing the supply of meats, vegetables, beer, wine, and sugar that came to their table, as well as looking after the household accounts and the welfare of the staff. Their son, Ambrose, was a lively, boisterous two year old, if slightly too keen to cling on to his mother, and ten-month-old Kathryn was just starting to crawl around on her chubby little hands and knees.

But Mary knew the real truth. They were not normal—far from it.

For a start, Mary herself had not been born in the late 1530s as she told everyone. No, she had been born later. Much later.

In 1988.

It had been in 2015, when she was Justine Parker, working as an event organizer in Grangedean Manor, a historic building, that an electrical storm had sent the whole house spinning back 450 years to its Tudor past—and landed her, confused and frightened, in 1565.

She had made her first mistake almost immediately. Sent to work in the kitchens as a 'spit-boy', she had made a casual expletive in front of Margaret, a superstitious servant. This resulted in an unwarranted accusation of witchcraft—and with that came pursuit by the local Witchfinder and a hurried change of name to 'Mary.'

But she had also met and quickly fallen in love with Sir William. So, the accusation of witchcraft had been extended to him by association, meaning they both had to fight to clear their names.

And while all this had been finally resolved more than four years earlier, Mary thought there was every chance that some of the villagers still harbored their suspicions. No smoke without fire?

Mary shivered slightly. Best not to think of fire, when death by burning had been the threat she had faced if found guilty.

"Normal people—yes, I was going to say that, as it happens," William replied. "A full tree—'tis most unusual. Grangedean managed with just evergreen boughs last year, and the year before. And every Christmastide for decades 'ere to that. So why do we need to bring this..." he waved at the fir, "...this monstrous piece of the forest into our dwelling now?"

"Because last year, I was confined before Kathryn was born, and the year before, I was recovering after the birth of Ambrose. So, your lovely and much-missed mother was in charge of the decorations, just as she had been the first two Christmases after we were married. But this year, I am in charge, and I say we have a proper tree." She raised an eyebrow, as if to challenge him. "Which I plan to decorate."

"You plan to...?" William's eyes widened. "With what, by all the Heavens?"

Mary shrugged. "Red ribbons, silver trinkets, and the like. And I have a star for the top, to symbolize the star at Christmas that brought the wise men to the manger." She made a small pout. "We can decorate it together as a family. It will be fun. And I have had Cook bake some small cakes we can hang from the branches, then pick off and eat on Christmas Day." She paused. "With honey glaze and a hazelnut inside... Your favorite..."

He did not reply immediately. She held his eyes and smiled,

noting after a while that his neck was finally starting to assume its more expected color. So, she pressed on. "We have had many challenges in our time together, William, and I want this Christmas to be a lovely one for us all. I want it to be full of peace, love, and above all, family harmony. We can have all the usual celebrations. The Yule Log will be lit on Christmas Day and burn 'til Twelfth Night. We can give small gifts to show our love. I will put mine in folded packets and place them beneath the tree, so we can look forward to opening them together on Christmas morning." She paused to see how this was being received and was pleased to note the frown was now gone. "I have asked the servant, Simon, to act as the Lord of Misrule, and to organize games, dances, and entertainments, just as he did so well before Ambrose was born. And if he wants us to don disguises and take part in masquerades again, then that we will do. They were fun, too!"

Mary stepped closer to her husband and looked up at him with her widest, most guileless eyes. "So, if I want us to have a tree in the house, and decorate it with colorful ribbons, shiny trinkets, and baked fancies, then how can you deny me?"

William stood tall, as if to assert himself, but even he must have known his wife was going to get her own way. As she usually did. "But, as your husband, Mary," he tried, then hesitated a moment. "It is my word that..."

"Shhhh," she whispered, putting her finger on his lips. "As my ever-loving and kind William, I am certain it is not for you to say me nay, but indeed, it is your pleasure to indulge me in this." She slid her hand 'round his neck and pulled his lips down onto hers. After they had kissed, she pulled back and said, "Is it not, my love?"

All he could do was shrug helplessly.

‹‹●●●››

Dusk was creeping across the parklands, and heavy snow was now starting to fall, as Mary took a last look at the fully decorated tree before heading down to the kitchens. The red ribbons and silver trinkets set the green branches off beautifully. She wished she could add fairy lights and coloured baubles to the mix, but accepted that the tree would have to make do without such twenty-first century fripperies.

She gave a small chuckle. William had finally stopped being such a grump and really got into the decoration, hanging the silver trinkets on the branches while she put up the ribbons. The trinkets were things like cups, spoons, and bits of old jewelry Mary had found around the house and added loops of twine. She had smiled as she watched William hooking them on the tree, his tongue part way out of his mouth in concentration, before he stood back and checked each one with a critical eye. He had even encouraged Ambrose to decorate some of the higher boughs, holding the boy up by the waist as Ambrose fumbled the branches with his little fingers.

She had then brought up the tray of baked fancies from the kitchens, and the three of them tied small lengths of twine to each, then hung them on the tree amongst the other decorations. She cautioned William not to eat any, on pain of her eternal disapproval. He assured her he would not, but she made sure to count them all once he and Ambrose had gone. Sadly, no matter how many times she counted, she always came up two short. One she knew about; she had sneaked it into her own mouth when William and Ambrose were looking the other way, but the other must have been down to her husband. She hoped he had shared it with his son, and decided he probably would have done—the child would not have let his father get away with eating it all himself without shouting in protest.

The star had proved a problem. Not in its construction—she had asked one of the servants to make a simple star-shaped wooden frame, onto which she had sewed a yellow linen cover— but in its placement. The tree must have stood at least twelve feet, which was far too high to reach without a sturdy ladder. It was William who suggested getting a team of men to move the whole tree slowly and carefully over to a new position by the gallery, so he could lean over and put the star in place. Mary chuckled to herself again, this time at the memory of her husband clutching the star like a prize teddy bear as he scampered up the stairs to the gallery to implement his master plan.

Mary arrived in the kitchen and saw Ruth, the housekeeper, talking with the cook at a table in the center of the room. She waited while Ruth gave a small curtsey and the cook, who was a sturdy fellow with unruly gray hair under his cap, gave her a nod of the head.

"My lady," he said, "what is your pleasure?"

"I would we go through the list of provisions for each meal one more time," Mary replied. "I want to be certain we have not forgotten anything. Especially as the snow is now falling hard. It will start to settle, and we may not be able to get to the market."

"That is so," the cook replied, then walked with Mary and Ruth towards a small table in the corner, on which were several pieces of paper, held down by a large inkwell and quill. As he went, he barked orders over his shoulder at the various kitchen servants who were grinding powders in pestles, rolling out dough, and cutting joints of meat.

"Now then, my lady," he said when they were seated on stools round the table, "today we have but a simple family repast." He shuffled the papers and pointed to one. "With a goose that is even now cooking on the dry spit. To that, we will add a selection of the season's vegetables from the gardens here at Grangedean, followed by a pudding of stewed apple pie using fruit harvested from our own orchard. And tomorrow, we will have a side of mutton."

Mary nodded. "That is good. And you have all the oils, herbs, and salt you need for the cooking?"

"We do, my lady," Ruth answered for the cook. "I secured these and all we need for the festive season in the market."

"Wine and beer?" Mary asked.

"Indeed, my lady," answered the cook, shuffling his papers. "I have checked the barrels in the cool store, and they are all good." He looked up. "We will also have plenty of wine to mull for the wassail."

Mary nodded again. "And the twenty-first? Midwinter solstice?"

"The repast that night will be the five-bird roast. It starts with a pigeon, which has been filleted of its bones and put inside a partridge. Likewise, this is placed in a chicken, which is itself within a goose, and finally, all these are put inside a peacock and roasted. The vegetables alongside will be parsnips, carrots, sprouts, and cabbage.

They discussed the menus for the twenty-second and twenty-third, then turned to the Christmas Eve dinner. "We have invited around forty guests for the feast," Mary said. "Assuming the snow does not become too thick, and they can make their way here. Are you still certain we can cater for all of them effectively?"

"We plan to have a roast venison," the cook said. "Can I assume the master will be successful in the hunt for a stag or a hind?"

Mary smiled. "I have no doubt if William and his friend Thomas Melrose set out for a deer, they will get one, even with these snows coming down."

"I am sure also," the cook replied.

"And Christmas Day?" Mary enquired. "We will have only the close family."

"There is a brace of turkey from the farm, my lady," answered the cook. "We also have a plum pudding and will soon be starting to make mince pies, each containing thirteen separate ingredients to honor the Lord Jesus and his disciples. The fruits are well dried, and we have the particular spices through a merchant who brings them from the Orient. There is only the pastry to roll and the mutton to chop for these." He paused and nodded to Mary. "I warrant that will be plenty for the family to enjoy. I can promise you fine Christmas celebrations."

"Excellent, Master Cook. I thank you."

Mary waited while the cook went back to his table and put her hand over Ruth's. "And you, my friend, how do you fare?" she asked. "I know Christmastide has bad memories for you."

Ruth nodded slowly. "It has been nigh on six years to the day since God took my Daniel to his side," she replied. "And each Christmas, I must remember and mourn what a good man he was. But, I have our daughter Sarah, and I have you and the master and little Ambrose and baby Kathryn, and the villagers still call on me for my herbs and remedies, so I am content with my lot."

"And we are fortunate to have you, Ruth," Mary replied. "I know I would not be here if it had not been for you."

Ruth gave a small laugh. "Indeed, my lady. Not a word has ever crossed my lips, nor Sarah's, about how you appeared here one day from the distant future. We are both silent on the tales you told of polished flat stones that show pictures and give forth voices and carriages that move, even without a horse to pull them."

"And I am forever grateful," Mary said. "And grateful also that you were able to become our valued housekeeper when we had to turn that treacherous girl, Martha, out."

"Aye, 'twas good fortune indeed."

There was a companionable silence, while the noise, bustle, and heat of the kitchens swirled around them. "I wonder what became of her," Mary said eventually.

"Martha? I know not," Ruth replied. "Nor do I know of Margaret," she added, "that other girl who would have seen you burned for being falsely accused a witch."

"Nor her."

Ruth moved her hand and they both stood. "Then let us hope we never find out," she observed.

‹‹ ● ◆ ● ››

Mary was to remember the housekeeper's words only a few hours later.

The family had finished their supper and she had taken Ambrose to bed, his little legs clamped around her waist as she carried him up the stairs.

"Night-night, sweet Bambi," she said, as she tucked him in and kissed his forehead. "Sleep well, my precious." She checked Kathryn was asleep in her crib, then crept out.

It was as she was coming down the stairs that she heard voices, including a female one that was strangely familiar.

"What in the name of all that is holy are you doing here?" This was William, sounding as if his usual bluster had been knocked out of him.

"I had to see you."

"Nonsense," replied William.

"It is important."

Mary paused on the stairs, frowning to herself. There was definitely a familiarity to the voice, and it was not a pleasant one, but for the life of her, she could not place it.

"To you, perhaps, but not to me," she heard William snap. "Now, get out!"

"I will say my piece first."

"Say what you like, it is as naught to me." William's voice was rising, and Mary could sense he was about to explode in anger. "It is Christmastide, and I am with my family!"

"Is that the family you have by the witch?"

"GET OUT!"

"And not let you come to know your son? Your oldest son, your true son, named for you?"

Mary gasped, and her hand flew to her mouth. Now she knew who it was—by the way the voice said, 'the witch.'

She lifted her skirts and almost fell down the stairs, then ran into the Great Hall.

William was standing up from his chair, leaning forward with his clenched fists supporting him on the table, a dark-haired woman in a peasant dress standing before him, her hand holding a small boy of around three years of age. As Mary entered, William looked over at her, and the woman turned slowly.

Mary found herself staring into a pair of cold eyes—the eyes of the very person she had told Ruth earlier she would never want to see again.

It was Martha.

"I have returned, witch," Martha hissed, "to claim what is rightfully mine."

·‹‹ ● ● ● ›·

December 20, 1569

Lady Mary sat up in bed, pulled back the curtain, and peered out. The dull morning light coming through the diamond-paned window was depressingly gray, and the snow was falling heavily and settling in great drifts across the gardens.

She flopped back on her bolster and stared up at the carved wooden roof-panel suspended from the bedposts.

Why had Martha returned, and why now?

The answer to the first question was easy enough. The woman was claiming her son, Will, was the product of a sexual encounter with Sir William, one that had happened a few weeks before Mary had evicted Martha from Grangedean Manor. Was that possible? Martha had been the housekeeper at the time—which was no more than a servant position. Would William have even noticed her, let alone bedded her? True, she had been around twenty-one or twenty-two and passably pretty, but even so...?

Mary turned on her side to face her husband. He was fast asleep on his back, breathing gently. A stray lock of blond hair had fallen across his eye. She reached across and pulled it back.

"You did not deny it last night," she whispered, so quietly it was no more than a breath, "when that woman claimed her son was yours. Why did you not deny it?" William gave a small grunt, and Mary withdrew her hand. "Was the woman speaking the truth?" she continued, "for all we threw her out as a treacherous liar four years ago? After she sided with that dreadful witchfinder against us?"

William's breathing deepened a little. "You sleep well, my husband, but I have scarcely slept a wink this night," Mary whispered, "after Martha once again accused me of being a witch, and not only that, claimed to be your rightful wife! The real Lady de Beauvais! Just because she says you bedded her and gave her a son!"

Mary rolled onto her back again. The accusation was one thing. For all it was deranged nonsense, it would still need to be fought, refuted. But there was the other question. Why was Martha here now? Why had she come at Christmas with her dreadful accusations? Mary frowned. That was a difficult one to answer. It would need more information from Martha herself, and Mary resolved to find out.

Indeed, Martha and the boy were still in the Manor. Tempting though it had been to throw them out, the snow was falling so fast and lying so deep that Mary had decided to allow them to sleep in the kitchens on a spare truckle bed alongside the other servants. In all conscience, she could not throw a small child into the cold and risk him freezing to death.

·‹‹ ● ● › ›·

Mary found Martha in the kitchens, sitting on a stool with her son on her lap, watching the hustle and bustle of activity swirling around them.

"I see you have engaged a new cook," Martha observed drily when Mary came up. "Was the previous one thrown out as well, for thinking you a witch?"

Mary could not suppress a small sneer as she replied. "Nay, the last cook stayed with us despite your treachery. Sadly, she passed away a year later."

"Passed away?" Martha asked with a cold smile, as she bounced the boy on her lap. "Was that by God's will, or perhaps you called a devil's curse down on her?"

Mary took a deep breath and forced a smile of her own. "I shall ignore that. And as you are currently a guest in my house, I will thank you not to make such ungodly accusations."

"Ungodly?" Martha stopped bouncing the boy. "I find that hard to take from one accused of witchcraft."

Mary felt her upper body tensing and for a moment allowed

herself to imagine pulling back her hand and throwing a knockout punch at Martha's jaw. Then she took another breath and consciously relaxed her shoulders. "I have allowed you to stay in my house, Martha. Would you rather I had you and your son thrown into the snow to die of cold?"

"It would be easily understood as the actions of a witch."

"Well, I have not done so, and will not while the snows still fall, for as you know in your heart, I am not a witch." She paused a moment for emphasis. "But be assured, when it is safe to do so, I shall have you and this boy sent hence from here."

"You say I know in my heart you are not a witch." Martha lifted the boy off her knee and put him down on the flagstones. She stood and turned to face Mary, her head barely reaching the height of Mary's chin. "But the truth is the opposite. I know you are such a person and nothing said—by God or any mortal—would give me cause to change my mind."

She gave an offcut of pastry from the table to her son. He sat down heavily and began stuffing it into his mouth. Mary studied the boy a moment. Could he be William's? His hair was blond, that was true, but many children had blond hair in their early years, before it went darker. Ambrose had just such hair and was not yet three.

"What is his date of birth?" Mary asked suddenly.

Martha gave a knowing smirk, then answered, "The twenty-third day of April, these three years past."

Mary did a quick calculation in her head, then sucked through her teeth in annoyance. It fitted with William having bedded Martha just before she, Mary, had arrived in 1565 as a frightened and confused time-traveler from 2015.

Martha gave her a look of triumph. "Aye, Justine, which I believe is your real name, it gives no room for doubt. My Will is the oldest son of Sir William de Beauvais, and I have the stronger claim to the title of Lady de Beauvais."

"Why should you think to claim anything of the sort?" Mary snapped. "You were a mere housekeeper. Get real, woman."

"Oh, and you were so much better, I suppose? I was a house-keeper, but you were nothing more than a soot-covered spit-boy in these very kitchens." Martha put her hands on her hips and looked up at Mary with a defiant set of her jaw. "How does that make your claim any more valid than mine?" Martha took a step closer and looked up so their chins were almost touching. "Unless you used witchcraft to ensnare him," she said softly. "For that is the only way he would think to take one such as you to wife."

Mary could hold her anger back no longer. "It was for love, you filthy little piece of shit!" she shouted. "Something unknown in your cold heart!"

The kitchen went silent, as everyone stopped what they were doing and started watching the two women squaring up to each other.

"The noble Sir William de Beauvais falling in love with a common girl?" Martha snapped back. "One no more than a dirty spit-boy?"

"That is better than a traitor!" Mary yelled. "Who would have seen him condemned!"

"But who was carrying his child at that very time!" Martha shot back. "Which he did not deny when he met the boy last night!"

"He will deny it. I will make sure of that!"

"What, with an enchantment?"

That was enough!

Mary swung the flat of her palm hard. It made contact with Martha's cheek with the sound of a thunderclap, causing the woman's head to snap away.

Martha stepped back, her eyes burning into Mary's, and put her hand up to her face. "You will regret that, witch," she whispered. "And it will not be you throwing me out. I will do the same to you, so you can stand trial on the charge of witchcraft you should have always faced. Then you will be rightly condemned, and you will be burned. As the mother of William's child, I will become the rightful Lady de Beauvais." She rubbed at her jaw, where a red weal was coming up. "And do you know? When you burn, I will be there." She took a step forward. "I will be there to rejoice as you scream for mercy." She gave a slow, cold smile. "As the flames take hold of your flesh and turn it into charred waste."

‹‹ ● ● ● ● ››

December 21, 1569

Sir William shifted from one foot to the other and avoided Mary's eye, for all the world like a guilty schoolboy caught with his hand in the cookie jar.

"Why have you been avoiding me all this time?" she demanded. "You were out hunting with Thomas all day yesterday until dark, then drinking with him until the early hours of this morning." She frowned at him. "I need to talk with you about this wretched woman and her son."

"But we killed not just a stag, but a hind as well," he muttered. "We have all that Cook needs for Christmas Eve, and more besides."

"I know; he told me so," she answered, "and it is good news, believe me." Mary actually found herself stamping her foot. "But what of Martha and this boy she claims as yours? It is nonsense, William, is it not? You would not have bedded a housekeeper, would you?"

William did not answer but seemed to be studying the toes of his shoes with excessive interest.

"Would you?" she repeated, starting to find his lack of response concerning.

Then it seemed her fears were justified. "Might have done," he muttered to the floor.

"I beg your pardon. What did you say?"

He looked up. "I... um... might have had a quick tryst with her," he said a little more clearly. "I... er... do not recall exactly."

"You might...?" She raised an enquiring eyebrow.

"Yes, but it meant nothing. It was of no consequence."

"I beg to differ!" she snapped. "If it led to a son, as she claims."

"I mean it was of no consequence to how I feel for you, Mary. That is what I meant."

"I know that," she answered. "It was before we met." She put a hand to his cheek and gave it a stroke. "She is trying to get you to set me aside, William. She wants to become your wife in my place."

William's face assumed a stern look, and he put his hand over hers. "Well, that is indeed nonsense, Mary," he said. "How can she say such a thing?"

"Exactly," Mary replied. Suddenly, she found herself unable to speak, as a lump filled her throat. William was never going to cast her aside in favor of Martha—he was her true husband, and he loved her, of that she could be certain. Not only was the woman delusional, but her threats truly were empty and hollow.

"But what if the boy really is yours?" she asked.

He thought a moment, looking over her shoulder. "Then, I will give her a few shillings for his care, and send her about her business." There was a pause, and she could see the moment when pride in his ability to father sons crossed his face. "But truly, Mary, the boy is mine?"

"So she claims," Mary sighed.

"Well, if so, I would not have him want for aught." He

scratched his beard a moment. "Maybe... maybe I will make regular payments as the boy grows."

Mary shuddered as her feeling of relief disappeared like chaff in the wind. The thought of William supporting the boy was horrendous. It would mean, at the very least, that Martha would become a permanent feature in their lives—and an ongoing thorn in her own side. No, this could not be allowed. The happiness of her family relied on keeping Martha as far away from it as possible.

"I think not, William," she said. "It would not be fair on Ambrose, Kathryn, and me, if you accepted this child as well."

"Nay, Mary," William replied. "If the boy is mine, my own flesh and blood, then he is also part of our family. I must provide for him. It would be the Christian thing to do." He fixed her with a stern eye. "I have conceded to you on many things, Mary, but not on this. I will not be swayed."

·‹‹ ● ◉ ● ›› ·

The midwinter moon shone down on the snowy parklands as the family filed into the Great Hall that evening for the solstice meal. Mary could not hide her disgust as Martha appeared as well, clutching tightly at her child's hand.

William seemed oblivious to Mary's feelings as he settled Martha and the boy at their places, fussing over Martha's comfort and making sure the boy's chair had a wooden plank across the arms so he could reach the table with ease. Mary caught Martha's eye as William pushed the woman's chair in. Martha gave a small triumphant smile that fair turned Mary's stomach.

"Thank you, my lord," Martha simpered, before washing her hands in the silver saucer of water proffered by a servant, then throwing her napkin over her shoulder. For a peasant housekeeper, Martha seemed to be settling into the role of a lady with worrying ease. Someone had even clothed her in a fine-looking gown and dressed her hair. Mary leaned across to Sarah, her lady-in-waiting and Ruth's daughter, who was seated beside her. "Is that gown one of mine?" she whispered.

"Aye, madam," Sarah replied, "but it is one that you last wore before you fell pregnant with Master Ambrose."

Mary frowned. "Where did she get it?"

"It must have been in the back chamber," said Sarah. "We still keep the storage chests there. She would have known where to look."

Mary studied the gown a moment. "We should have let it out so I can wear it again."

Sarah nodded. "I will see to it."

"I must say," Martha observed sweetly as she smoothed the skirts with a small smile, "'tis indeed a most singular thing—a full tree inside the house. Decorated with spoons and cakes and such-like, too. Most odd." She gave a silky smile to Mary. "I am sure such a thing would not be allowed were I the mistress of the house."

"On second thought," Mary hissed to Sarah, "have the gown burned. I cannot bear to wear it again after that woman has been inside it."

A servant entered carrying a platter showcasing a magnificent peacock, its head held proudly aloft and its tail feathers spread out behind. The servant carried it over to Sir William, who nodded his approval. The servant set it down and stepped back as William stood up and raised his goblet.

"Good family!" He gave a smile to little Will. "Old and new. Welcome to our midwinter celebration. Let us give thanks to Almighty God for this magnificent feast and look forward to the retreat of the snows and the start of spring."

"It cannot come soon enough," Mary muttered under her breath. Aloud she said, "Amen!" and gave an acid smile at Martha.

William put his knife under the peacock's skin and lifted it. It came away in one piece, revealing the cooked meat below. "A fine five-bird roast," he observed, as he carved slices onto a platter. "A magnificent dish. My compliments to the cook."

·‹‹ ● ● ● › ›·

Mary made her way up to Ambrose's nursery with her son clinging to her waist like a small limpet.

"Shall I tell you a story, Bambi, before you go to sleep?" She squeezed his hand. "What would you like?"

"Cind'rella!" he squeaked. "I want Cind'rella."

"Not the tragic Princess Diana?"

"No, Cind'rella!"

"Very well." She pushed open the door and stopped dead at what she saw inside. Martha's son was sitting on the floor, playing with Ambrose's favorite toy, a carved wooden horse.

Ambrose gave a small squeak and wriggled out of her arms, then ran over to the boy and snatched at his possession.

"Tha's mine!" he yelped. "Give it over!"

"I got it!" the boy replied, jumping to his feet and holding the horse up high. "S'mine now!"

Ambrose tried to stretch for it, but the other boy was taller. Ambrose turned a desperate face to Mary. "Ma, make him give it to me!"

Mary walked towards the boy and said in a stern tone, "Will? Will? That is not yours." He seemed to ignore her completely, continuing to keep the toy just out of Ambrose's reach. Mary whipped it out of his hand. "It was a present for Ambrose at his last birthday."

"My boy will have it soon enough," came a hard voice from behind her. Mary spun 'round, to see Martha emerging from behind the door. "When I have you cast out, as you did me, I will be the mistress of this house, and I will be the one to decide which playthings are appropriate for each of Sir William's sons."

Mary did not answer. Instead, she deliberately turned her back on Martha, then handed the horse over to Ambrose. "Here you are, Bambi," she said with a motherly smile. Her son snatched it to his chest and ran to the far corner. He sat clutching it with a defiant expression on his face, as if daring Martha's son to try and take it back.

Mary turned slowly 'round again, and fixed Martha with her hardest stare, breathing deeply to stop herself from striking the woman again. "I beg your pardon. By what reason do you think I will be turned out by you?"

This time, it was Martha who ignored Mary. She gave a haughty flip of her head, then walked over and sank down in front of Ambrose. "Now then, Ambrose," she said in a sickeningly honeyed voice that nearly made Mary throw up, "I think you should share this horse with To... with young Will here. I am sure you have been taught to be a good Christian boy, and what is it that good Christian boys do with their toys?" Ambrose must have shaken his head. "No, you have most likely not been taught, have you? But I can tell you; they share them. So, I would ask you, as one who loves you like a mother, to do as I ask. You must think of Will as your own brother. And good Christian boys share toys with their brothers."

But Ambrose jumped up and dodged around Martha with the horse still in his hand. He flew across the room to Mary, threw his arms 'round her legs, and buried his face in her skirts. There was a loud sob from within the material, then another. She put her hand on his head and stroked it gently.

Then she looked up. "Get out," she snarled at Martha. "Get

out of my son's chamber and take your vile little thief of a boy with you. There's a bed for him in the kitchens, and I suggest you put him in it before I decide to have you both thrown out into the snow after all."

Martha put her hands on her hips. "I shall go now," she replied, "but be assured, I shall not forget this. When I am mistress..."

"Oh, grow up!" Mary snapped. "You are living in some dreamland, you stupid woman! I am mistress here. I am married to William under God's holy law. And do you know what?" Martha stared at her, not moving a muscle. "William loves me truly, and I him. He will never accept you in my place. It is madness to even think such a thing. So, be assured, I will do everything in my power to make sure you never come between us!"

Martha's face suddenly drained of all color, until she was ashen white. "Do you curse me, witch?" she asked in a strangled whisper. "Does 'everything in your power' mean you will call down Satan's magic on me and my son? Is that how you protect your so-called marriage, with witchcraft and curses?" Martha grabbed her son by the hand and scooped him onto her own hip.

"Come," she said to the boy, "we cannot tarry a moment more in the presence of such evil." She looked back at Mary. "Oh, yes, we will be away as soon as the snows recede. Have no fear of that. But it will not be to leave my precious Sir William in your evil clutches. It will be to bring the authorities here to Grangedean Manor, and to have you arraigned and burned for witchcraft. Then, this so-called marriage will be over. And, as the mother of William's oldest son, it will be my claim above all others that he will recognize."

She marched to the door, then stopped and turned back. "You think on that, witch," she snarled, "and remember it as the flames start to lick at your toes!"

‹‹‹●●●›››

December 22, 1569

Mary poked a log on the fire and watched as it blazed briefly. "The woman is impossible," she observed to Ruth and Sarah, who were sitting with her in the little back parlor. "She seems to believe she can have William set me aside, so she can assume my place."

"Madness," agreed Ruth. "She has taken leave of her senses."

"If she ever had them," muttered Sarah. "She always had ideas well above her station."

"As may be," Mary replied. "But now she threatens to have me accused of witchcraft once again."

"That bird will not fly," said Ruth, with a knowing smile.

"I know," agreed Mary, "but it just might, and I cannot take that risk."

"Surely the Master would not countenance such a thing?" asked Sarah.

"He might, if I am condemned and burned, so he needs a new wife," Mary said, rubbing her neck as she stared bleakly into the flames. "Martha believes that as the mother of his oldest child, she has the best chance to assume my place."

Then, something Martha had said the night before flashed into Mary's mind. "Except..." She stopped, unsure if she recalled it correctly.

The other two women looked at her curiously.

"Except..." she repeated slowly, giving the memory time to take hold. "She said when she first came back that her son was named Will, for his father, yes?" They nodded. "Yet... I swear she nearly called him by a different name last night. I was too angry to pick up on it at the time, but now I think back, she almost called the boy..." Mary drummed her fingers on the arm of her chair. "I think she was going to say 'Tom,' but she changed it to 'Will'."

Then another image came to mind—the boy ignoring her when she had called him Will. Of course! Why would a three-year-old readily respond to a name that was not his own? If he was even the age Martha had said. Maybe she had lied about his date of birth as well? After all, it had been conveniently appropriate to support her claim.

Mary frowned at Ruth and Sarah. "I am beginning to think she has told us all a falsehood about the boy. Belike the child is not actually named Will. And if so, then why should we believe that he is even sired by William at all?"

The other two nodded, looking almost relieved. "I could countenance it of the woman," Ruth said. "She is truly capable of such deceit."

Then Sarah asked, "But how can you prove it? It is her word against ours. The boy could have been sired a few weeks later, after she was turned out. But it is not as if he would look any younger."

"He has William's hair, to be sure," said Mary, as a piece of the log fell away and flared briefly. She looked up, "But, if it is so, then we must get Martha to admit it, or we will never be rid of her."

Sir William looked moodily out of the bedroom window.

"I would be out in the park hunting again," he muttered. "Two days ago, I could ride through the snow, but now it is too thick." He peered through the glass. "For all I warrant that it might be starting to recede again."

"Belike you should not look to spend time apart from your family?" Mary asked softly. "But be content to spend the Christmas celebrations with us?"

He turned back to her and gathered her into his arms. "Of course," he said, giving her a brief kiss on the tip of her nose. "That is indeed my wish."

"And, by your family," she continued, pulling her head back so she could see him properly, "I mean myself, Ambrose, and little baby Kathryn." She searched his eyes. "And no others."

He broke away and stood back with a small frown. "Oh, come now, Mary, I cannot ignore my son. He is named Will for me. He is my flesh and blood. We must welcome him to our hearts. We must provide for him."

"And what does that mean, exactly?"

William shrugged. "I will see to his welfare."

"And Martha?" Mary raised an eyebrow. "She was a traitor to your cause four years ago. Will you see to her welfare now?"

William gave a deep sigh and looked out the window again. He tapped his fingers on the sill. "It was a long time ago," he said eventually, then looked at Mary with a frown. "And she has borne me a child. It would not be Christian to abandon them now. I will find them a place to live near the Manor."

Mary could not help thinking that the Christian thing would be for Martha to abandon such spurious claims on her husband, but she did her best to keep calm. "And if he is not your flesh and blood?" she asked. "But is, in fact, sired by another?"

"He is, though. Martha has been most clear that the date of his birth means he is mine."

"And you believe her?"

He looked down. "I do not deny that I bedded her. So, her claim is most likely true."

Mary resisted the temptation to do a face-palm, but instead, she smiled sweetly. "Martha has much to gain by such a claim. As I told you before, she believes herself the rightful Lady de Beauvais, and means to take my place."

"And I have told you before, my sweeting, that I will not countenance such a thing to happen."

"Yet, you would give her a place close by?"

He paused a moment, frowning as he considered this. Then his face cleared. "It would be made clear to her that she can have no thoughts of advancement." He took her in his arms again, then whispered in her ear, "and certainly not of ever becoming my wife. Not while I have you."

Mary smiled, but her own thoughts were racing. *But what if you do not have me? What if I am once more accused and burned as a witch?*

"And again," she asked aloud. "What if the child is not yours?"

"If that were the case," he replied with an easy smile, "then I would have nothing more to do with her." He nodded. "Or with the boy."

Mary thought, 'Then let us make sure that is so, for the sake of our marriage.' She took a sharp breath. 'And my life.'

Mary, Ruth and Sarah met once again in the back parlor.

"I would we could get the boy on his own, so we can find out his true name," Mary muttered. "But the woman does not leave his side."

"He is but three years of age," Sarah observed. "She must know he would answer to his real name, whatever she has taught him to say."

"I warrant she has coached him most thoroughly," Ruth observed. "In case he gave it out by chance." She looked at Sarah. "When you were but three, you would chatter away for hours. I recall your blessed father and I, God rest his soul, took you to the market one day when you were that age, and you would tell any man that asked your name, your age, the names of your parents, and the name of the wooden doll you carried every place. It was all we could do to stop you talking."

Sarah gave a small gasp, "Oh, my doll! That was Katherine! I forgot her. She was named for the Queen!"

Mary once again tapped her fingers on the side of her chair to help her think. The wooden doll! Why did the doll matter? Then she gave a small gasp. "I think I might have an idea," she said slowly. "How we can get the child alone, get Martha to admit her lie, and be rid of her and her threats forever."

·‹‹●●›·

December 24, 1569

William squeezed Mary's hand as they stood in the hallway outside the doors of the Great Hall.

"You are truly a vision of beauty, my dear," he said, his voice raised slightly against the loud noise of their guests laughing and shouting on the other side of the doors. "And will be a fine hostess this Christmas Eve."

Mary twisted slightly to ease the pressure of the tight-waisted gown on her stomach and patted her swept-back hair. Why did fashion need to be so constricting? She looked enviously at William in his comfortably fitted doublet, roomy breeches, and silken hose. "Indeed, my husband," she answered, "And it is good the snows have now receded enough that our guests could make a path here for the banquet."

They heard a wooden staff being knocked on the floor, and the noise of the guests faded down to a low hum. "Pray silence!"

came the voice of Simon—normally a lowly servant but elevated as the Lord of Misrule for the duration of the Christmas celebrations. The hum reduced to total silence, broken only by the occasional cough. "It is my solemn duty to make sure that we all have the most miserable time this Christmas Eve!" There were a few nervous laughs. "Nay, honored guests, I jest!" he shouted. "I jest, indeed! For that is not my duty at all… Nay—it is to make sure you have the best time possible! The most fun that is in my gift!" There were cheers and some clapping at this. "But first, it is my onerous duty… nay, not that at all… but, in truth, my greatest pleasure, to ask you to give your loudest, most enthusiastic welcome to your host and hostess for this truly wondrous occasion! I give you the noble, the magnificent, the most honorable, Sir William de Beauvais, and his bounteous, beautiful wife, Lady Mary de Beauvais!"

The doors opened, and a great cheer went up as Mary and William swept into the Great Hall. She wanted to shade her eyes against the light of what seemed like a thousand candles, but instead, she smiled and nodded at the various guests standing behind the tables that ran around the room. There were many faces she recognized, including Thomas Melrose, William's one-time adversary, but now firm friend. Thomas was with his wife, Elizabeth, widow of Oliver Dowland. He had been another of William's friends—and had fought bravely when the accusation of witchcraft was made by the awful witchfinder, Hopkirk.

She glanced at the table on the left, where she had asked for Martha to be seated. The woman was there, again wearing Mary's gown. Her son was clamped to her waist, and she had a twisted grin on her face, as if she had already seen Mary off and taken her place.

Mary carefully arranged her features into a flat mask. 'You wait, my girl,' she thought. 'We will soon see who has won this battle.' Then, she gave a warm smile to the guest next to Martha, just to make it perfectly clear how unwelcome the woman was in her house.

Once Mary and William had taken their places at the High Table, Simon once again banged his staff on the floor and led everyone in a loyal toast to the Queen, followed by the traditional prayers of the season. Then, the banquet began in earnest. Servants brought out two great roast beasts lying on enormous platters. One was a large stag with his head reattached and antlers standing proud, while the other was a smaller hind. To wild cheering and clapping, these were brought to the High Table. William acknowledged the kills with a smile and a nod to Thomas, then carved a slice off each. Both platters were then removed to a side table, where a servant proceeded to carve the meat onto separate plates. These were then brought 'round the tables and served.

"Fine beasts, William," Mary murmured, putting her hand on her husband's arm. He smiled and nodded, putting his own hand over hers. "Indeed, they are," he said. "And they led me and Thomas on a merry dance when we gave chase in the snows."

"I am proud of you," she said, giving him a little peck on the cheek.

"And I you," he answered, returning the kiss.

Mary could not help but let her eyes slide over to Martha, who had clearly seen the exchange, and had a face like thunder. Mary treated her to a beaming grin, then turned back to William, nodding and smiling at everything he had to say.

Eventually, the meal was finished, and Mary glanced around the room. It seemed that everyone had had their fill of the venison, seasonal vegetables, and finally, the stewed plum, pear, and apple puddings. The men were sitting back in their chairs and clutching their bellies with satisfied smiles, while the women were looking as if they had taken as much food as they could possibly fit inside their constricted stomachs. Servants were still refilling goblets with claret, and there was definitely a raucous edge to the conversations and laughter that suggested there had already been plenty of wine drunk. Mary gave a small nod at Simon. He clambered to his feet and again banged his staff for silence.

"Most noble ladies and gentlemen!" he began. "As your Lord of Misrule, it is my pleasure to lead you in our topsy-turvy revels." He glared around the room with an exaggerated frown. "But first, it is my sad duty to tell you there have been some people who will be called out for their misdemeanors!" This brought a mix of loud groans and expectant laughs from the guests.

William stood. "But you are not yet crowned, my lord!" he shouted above the noise.

Simon stepped out from behind the table and walked towards the main doors, where a large, wooden chair had been placed facing the room. He turned to the guests and bowed, then settled himself in the chair, just like a king on his throne—except he was bareheaded. He nodded to William, who came over holding a wooden crown decorated with lush holly and deep red berries.

"I crown thee the Lord of these revelries," William intoned with mock solemnity, placing the crown on Simon's head. "The Lord of Misrule!"

As the crowd cheered and William returned to his place, Simon looked down his nose at the revelers a moment, then banged his staff again. "Let the first miscreant be brought forth!" he called out.

There was a flurry of activity behind him, and the cook was brought into the room between a couple of servants.

"You are the cook, are you not?" asked Simon.

"Aye," the cook acknowledged, hanging his head in mock shame.

"Then you are charged with the most heinous of crimes!" admonished Simon.

The cook looked up. "What is it?

"That you willfully, and with malicious intent, prepared the bodies of both a stag and a hind. Then, with knowledge afore-thought, you did use your best skill to roast their carcasses. And you did coat them in sundry herbs, that they may taste most deli-cious, and you surrounded them with diverse vegetables, that these good folk here may be sated at this most sacred Christmas-tide!" Simon glowered at the cook. "How do you plead?"

"Guilty, my Lord." This brought a wave of cheering and thumping of hands on tables. Simon held up his hand for silence.

"Then I pass sentence," he announced. "You shall be taken from this place and made to suffer your punishment."

The cook asked, "Which is?"

"You are to be taken all the way... over there," Simon pointed at the nearest table, "and made to sit with these good fellows and ladies and forced to drink as much of Sir William's finest claret as you can hold."

This brought more cheering from the room, as the cook was led to an empty seat, smiling and waving at the guests. Then, he accepted a large glass of wine, threw it back in one draught, and held it out for more.

"I trust that will teach you not to serve up anything less than your customary perfect fare!" shouted Simon over the noise. Then, he became solemn again. "And now, we have another miscreant or two to admonish before we have a masquerade! Bring forward Ruth Tanner, the housekeeper!"

Ruth was brought before Simon. Mary glanced at Martha, who had a small frown of curiosity.

"Are you Ruth Tanner, the housekeeper?" Ruth nodded.

"I heard you not!" Simon barked.

"Aye," Ruth replied. "I have been housekeeper here these past four years."

"Four years, eh? And on what grounds did you attain this honored and responsible position?"

"I was appointed when my predecessor was cast out for disloyalty."

"Disloyalty? In truth? And what became of your predecessor?"

"I know not where she went at the time, except she is back here now, with her son."

Mary glanced at Martha again and was pleased to see the woman was now looking nervous, clearly unsure where this was going. Mary smiled to herself. So far, the plan she had agreed with Ruth and Sarah was working. Especially as Simon was playing his part in it to perfection.

"And I understand you have been accused of behaving in a most Christian and charitable fashion towards her son?" Simon continued.

"If you say I have." Ruth hung her head, as a few of the guests laughed, although many were now looking serious, as if they appreciated that something had changed. That this was no longer light-hearted frivolity.

Martha must have realized the same. Her face was again like thunder.

Simon pointed at Martha and the boy. "You took the same son, who we can see is but three years of age, and last night you picked him from his bed while his mother slept, and you let him play with a wooden horse toy he so desired, then you treated him to some sweet marchpane. Do I have this correctly?"

"Aye," Ruth said. "You have."

"And while you were entertaining this boy so kindly, what did you learn of him?"

"That he likes to talk, and when his mother is not by him, he chatters away most freely." Ruth paused and looked directly at Martha. "I learned he is called Tom and is named for his father, one Thomas Webb, a weaver in the town of Wokingham."

Martha tried to stand up, but the guests on either side who, like Simon, had been well briefed by Mary, held her sleeves and made her sit again.

"I learned his mother told him to answer to the name of 'Will' while he is here at Grangedean Manor," Ruth continued. "And was most insistent that he must not answer to any other name." She paused, then added, "He likes it not that his mother says he must pretend such things." She shook her head. "But he said his mother threatened to hit him if he got it wrong." There were gasps from a few of the women. "Indeed, he said," Ruth paused and took a deep breath, "that she has oft beat him with a leather belt—so, he knows well her threat is real."

At this, the entire room turned and stared at Martha, all laughter and merriment gone. One or two of the more drunken guests gave nervous titters, but even they now realized this had become serious.

Mary stood up. "My Lord of Misrule," she asked quietly. "If all this is so, what is your verdict?"

"In the case of Ruth Tanner, I say, she is guilty... of nothing more than the kindness and Christian love we have long known is in her heart."

Ruth nodded and scurried back to her seat, accompanied by a couple of muted drunken cheers.

Simon continued. "As for Martha," he turned and looked directly at the woman, "then I say this. You came to Grangedean Manor with the express aim of displacing the good Lady Mary of her rightful position, through dishonesty and lies. You cynically chose Christmastide as a season of goodwill, where you might find a better reception for your untruths. You used the falling of snow and the goodness of Lady Mary not to turn you out, as a reason to stay in the house. You allowed this would give you enough time to complete your mission. The plan you constructed was false, deceitful, and ungodly. But, by good fortune and through God's good grace, your lies have been exposed."

There was total silence in the room, apart from the quiet crackling of the fire.

Martha seemed to be about to say something, then stopped with a look on her face like she had bitten a sour fruit.

Mary looked down at William. "What say you, my lord?"

William stood, a look of disgust on his face. "I agree; this woman has set out to deceive. She has preyed upon my good nature and made a mockery of me, when all I would do is my Christian duty to one who I thought was my own flesh and blood, but I now see is nothing of the kind. She and her son have no place here and must leave us now. The snows have retreated enough, so she has a clear walk back to Wokingham, or wherever it is she is now living."

"Take my gown if you wish," added Mary. "I have no wish to wear it again, now your scrawny little body has been inside it."

Martha stood, and this time, the guests on either side did not stop her. Two well-built servants came up and took an arm each, then marched her and her son away from the table.

At the doors, she turned back and struggled briefly to resist them.

Mary said, "Let her speak."

Martha scowled at her. "Very well, my Tom is not Sir William's son. So be it. But, for this, I will see you in hell."

Mary smiled sweetly. "I rather think you might be there without me, Martha."

"You twist my words," Martha retorted. "Once a witch, always a witch!"

"Or never, as the case may be," answered Mary, broadening her smile.

This seemed to break the tension, and there was even a little laughter around the room. Mary gestured at the guests. "As you see, your threats are easily dismissed," she observed. "These are my friends, and they have borne witness to your lies. Your word will never again carry any weight, and such accusations as you make will be seen as they are—hollow and baseless. So, go now and leave us to celebrate Christmastide in peace from your madness." She nodded at the servants, and they marched Martha and little Tom out of the Great Hall.

There was a moment's silence after the doors closed. Mary glanced around at the faces of her guests and was pleased to see smiles and nods of approval as the room returned to chatter and laughter. She banged her goblet on the table for silence. "My Lord of Misrule," she said once there was quiet. "You said you had another miscreant to admonish before we have a masquerade." She put her head on one side. "And who might that be?"

Simon got to his feet. "It is you that I call to account, my Lady Mary!"

"Me?" Mary put her hand to her chest in mock surprise. "Why? Whatever have I done?"

"A crime of the most heinous proportions!" Simon gestured at the Christmas tree that dominated the corner under the gallery. "The crime of having a perfectly good tree felled and brought into the house, and for," he paused for effect, "decorating with such trinkets as silver spoons, ribbons, and baked fancies!"

"Guilty as charged," Mary replied with a smile. "As it happens, I think it most festive, but 'tis no matter. What is my punishment?"

"You, my lady, are to be forced to enjoy the friendship of these good people and the love of your family this Christmas Eve! And to have your close family and friends sing your praises on the first day of Christmas tomorrow, and on each of the twelve days thereafter!"

"I accept this punishment." She looked up at the star atop the tree. "I am sure one day, all houses will have a tree such as this for Christmas—but for now, I am content that it is only for my beloved Grangedean Manor, my great friends here tonight, and my lovely family."

To cheers and applause, Mary nodded her thanks to Simon, Ruth, and Sarah, then leaned over and embraced William. "You can be difficult," she whispered in his ear. "And you can be thoughtless, stubborn, and sometimes downright annoying. And what is more, you can be easily led by your sense of Christian duty. But, do you know what, William de Beauvais?"

"What is that, my lady?" he whispered back, his breath tickling her cheek.

"For all that, I love you. I love you so much."

"And I love you, too," he replied. "Very much, if not more. Happy Christmas!"

Then, to the accompaniment of shouts of approval from their friends, he kissed her on the lips.

·‹‹ (● ● ● ●) ›·

Christmas Day morning, 1569

William watched as the small flame caught on the side of the large Yule log.

"There," he said. "That will burn for at least the twelve days of Christmas and bring us good fortune." He turned back to Mary, Ambrose, Sarah, and Ruth sitting by the tree. Kathryn was ensconced on the floor, stuffing one of the baked decorations into her mouth. "The least we deserve after the strange events of the past few days."

"I agree," Mary said. She reached down to the parcels wrapped in paper below the tree and picked out a large one, which she handed to William. "There, my love," she said. "For you."

William gave her a sideways glance as he ripped off the paper. Inside was a wooden box, which he prised open. He smiled as he reached in and withdrew a silver hunting horn. "A fine piece, Mary," he said, then gave it a blow. The pure-sounding note rang out around the room. "Thank you. I shall always think of your love when I take it out to the hunt."

Mary selected a packet and handed it to Ambrose. He ripped it open to reveal a carved wooden dog. "For you to enjoy without anyone else trying to take it," she observed with a smile.

"Thank you, Ma," Ambrose squeaked. He sat admiring the dog, turning it each way to see how well it had been made.

Mary picked out a small package for Sarah. "Here, this will suit you well, I warrant." Sarah opened it carefully to reveal a small box, which contained a silver brooch. She studied it a moment and looked curiously at Mary. "It is a partridge in a pear tree," Mary explained. "The partridge is Lord Jesus, and the sweet pear tree is his virgin mother."

"It is, for sure, a thing of beauty," agreed Sarah with a quizzical smile, as if to ask if this was another item from the future of Christmas, like the tree in the corner. Mary gave the tiniest nod, then reached for another package, which she handed to Ruth.

"This is yours," she said. Ruth opened it and took out a different silver brooch—this one a small silver arrow.

"A token to remember your fine husband, Daniel," Mary explained. "I believe he was a fletcher by trade?"

Ruth looked up and gave Mary a slightly watery smile. "He was, indeed."

"Then wear it in his honor."

"I thank you, Lady Mary," Ruth replied softly, putting the brooch carefully back in its box. "I will." She gestured at the empty base of the tree. "You have no need to give us such gifts. There are none for you in return."

"I have all the gifts I need from each of you," Mary replied. "I have you all in my life and that means everything to me."

She smiled at them in turn.

"Let us now enjoy the rest of this Christmas together."

‹‹ ● ● ● ›› ·

Jonathan Posner writes action adventures set in Tudor England. The Witchfinder's Well tells how modern-day Justine Parker falls through a worm-hole in time and lands in 1565. There, she is accused of being a witch. In her fight to survive, she tries to counter Tudor superstitions, including those of Martha the housekeeper. For more about Jonathan, visit his website, or follow him on Facebook, Instagram or Goodreads.

‹‹ ● ● ● ›› ·

Frontier Christmas

CHRISTMAS

BY LINDA ULLESEIT

Prairie du Chien, Michigan Territory
Christmas Eve, 1832

Sarah Knox Taylor loved Christmas, and this Christmas she was in love. Standing on a chair so she could reach the mantel above the fireplace, Sarah arranged cedar branches and artfully nestled paper cones filled with nuts in the hollows. She hummed "Adeste Fideles" as she worked.

The front door opened and Sarah turned to see who had arrived, just as she heard her sister call, "Knoxie!"

"Ann!" Sarah climbed down from the chair and greeted her sister with a warm hug and kisses for the baby in Ann's arms and the toddler clinging to her legs. "Merry Christmas!"

Ann looked around the room and smiled. "The decorations are coming along nicely. I suppose you've banished Betty and Dick to a corner somewhere?"

"Upstairs trying to string popcorn and cranberries."

The sisters laughed. Their sister, Betty, was ten years younger than Sarah, their brother, Dick, two years younger than that. It wasn't always easy to keep them busy and out of the way. This year was especially hard, since Sarah had turned eighteen, finished her schooling in the east, and returned to live with the family. She wanted privacy, mostly to dream of her handsome lieutenant, but Betty and Dick were on a mission to prevent that.

"Remember when we were the ones who had to make the garlands?" Ann asked. She was the oldest of Zach and Peggy Taylor's children, married to a surgeon at Fort Snelling. It had been a mild December, so Ann and her family had been able to make the trip downriver to Fort Crawford to spend the holiday with her family. Sarah could hardly wait to tell her sister all about Lieutenant Jefferson Davis.

"They were never long enough to reach across the mantel. We ate too much popcorn." Sarah's eyes twinkled.

"Easier to eat it than string it," Ann said, laughing.

Heavy footsteps on the stairs up from the basement kitchen drew both women's eyes to the door. Sally had been with the family since Ann was small. Her dark face lit up when she saw Ann's young sons. "You give those babies to me, now," she said, folding the boys into her ample arms.

Peggy Taylor came into the room just after Sally, wiping floury hands on her apron. She kissed her grandsons before Sally headed upstairs with them, then embraced her eldest daughter. "Glad to see you," she told Ann, "but you're too early to smell the mincemeat and cranberry pies baking."

Ann laughed. "As long as I'm here when they're served!"

Peggy led her daughters to the chairs in front of the fireplace. "Sit, girls. We deserve a break."

Ann and Sarah joined her, and they chatted about the unseasonably warm weather and past Christmases in army outposts similar to Fort Crawford. Peggy urged Ann to tell them all of the gossip from Fort Snelling, and Ann shared tidbits of her boys' antics. Sarah smiled and nodded, absently twirling the ringlets in her long brown hair. She caught Ann giving her a quizzical look and tried to enter the conversation, but it was no use. Her mind, and heart, were on Jeff Davis.

It wasn't long before their mother had to scurry back to her pies, leaving the sisters alone. Sarah felt her entire face light up. "I'm in love, Ann. He's wonderful." As much as she tried, she couldn't help gushing like the schoolgirl she had been until recently.

"Tell me everything," Ann said.

"He's here at the fort. Last summer, after the war, he was chosen to escort Chief Black Hawk to prison in St. Louis."

Ann waved her hand. "Less about the lieutenant and more about the man."

"He's God-fearing," Sarah began. "Everyone speaks of his integrity and decision-making."

Ann pretended to yawn.

Sarah leaned forward, her hazel eyes sparkling. "He's handsome, and I can't breathe when he's in the same room."

Ann laughed. "And that sounds like love! How does he feel about you?"

Sarah's smile dimmed. "I don't know. We've spoken when Mama and I encounter him on the street, but it's not like he has calling cards in the wilds of Michigan Territory." Sarah thought about Louisville, where she'd gone to school. There, a man didn't even have to speak to a woman he wanted to court. He'd send a card to indicate his interest, and maybe write letters. She had no idea how a soldier on the frontier would proceed.

"Knoxie? Are you sure about this man? Papa won't like it."

"Papa says he doesn't want me or Betty marrying army men, but Mama did and so did you!"

"Life is hard for army wives," Ann said. "He wants a better life for you."

"Army life is all I've known," Sarah said. "Love is more important than comfort. Oh, Ann, what do I do?"

Her sister patted Sarah's arm. "He's an officer, so he'll be here for tomorrow's dinner. You make him a special treat and serve it to him. Stay near him and talk to him, so when the dancing starts you are the closest available partner."

Sarah nodded, imagining the scene in her head. "I have another problem. Mary Street claims Lieutenant Davis likes her, and they are about to begin courting."

"General Street's daughter? Isn't she at school?"

Sarah said, "She's sixteen and home to help with her younger siblings. She has five older and four younger ones! And we think two younger ones is hard." She laughed.

"I'll distract Miss Mary Street at the party tomorrow," Ann promised. "And Papa, too."

Sarah hugged her sister. "Thank you, Ann." She picked up a stack of paper and some scissors from the table. "Help me cut?"

Ann agreed, and they spent the next hour cutting and folding snowflakes, paper doves, flowers, and fans to hang around the room. Peggy Taylor always made sure her household was decorated with elegance and taste, as if Prairie du Chien was New York City.

·‹‹ ● ● ››·

Christmas Day dawned as clear as if the angels themselves had swept the sky with their wings. Lieutenant Jefferson Davis stopped outside the makeshift church to take a deep breath and square his shoulders. He bit his lip. Did God know his interest this morning centered less on the Christmas service and more on a girl with bright brown eyes and ringlets?

Reverend Lowry welcomed all Christians to his Christmas

Day service, held in a house that was designated as a church whenever a man of God was in town. The other officers arrived, and Jeff entered the house with them. For Christmas service, the house had been decorated with cedar branches and candles.

Jeff sat down before he swept the room with his eyes. Sarah wasn't there yet, but Mary Street actually waved to him. Waved. In church. Or what passed for church in Prairie du Chien. He nodded at her but looked away. Jeff didn't like her forward ways. She made him uncomfortable. Not like Sarah, who always filled him with optimism.

He'd first seen Colonel Taylor's daughter when he returned from St. Louis several months ago. He'd been swaggering a bit as he walked up to the fort from the dock, feeling a bit cocky after completing his mission to deliver the captured Chief Black Hawk to prison. He'd passed the house where the Taylor family was staying and seen Sarah and her mother come out with baskets over their arms. Later, he'd learned they were bringing cheese made by Mrs. Taylor to the soldiers at the fort. At the time, though, he could only see Sarah. How could brown eyes shine with so much light and joy? He'd mumbled something to Mrs. Taylor.

"Welcome home, Lieutenant," Mrs. Taylor had said. "Have you met my daughter, Sarah? She's just returned after finishing school in Louisville."

"Miss Taylor," he'd said, acknowledging the introduction. Her smile enveloped him in warmth and welcome. He followed them like a smitten puppy up the street.

Later, he couldn't remember exactly what they'd discussed. The words weren't important, though. Sarah responded to him as if he were her oldest friend, as if they'd known each other forever.

On that Christmas Day, when the Taylor family arrived for church, it was as if the sun entered on Sarah's shoulders. How was it possible that one woman could shine so brightly? Jeff watched her look around the room, much as he had. His heart leapt as

Sarah's eyes settled on him and she gifted him with a brilliant smile. Behind her, though, was her father. Colonel Taylor's glower gave him pause, but not for long.

Throughout the service, Jeff's eyes strayed to Sarah. Or, rather, they strayed away from Sarah so as not to appear to be staring. His attention never wavered.

Ever since he'd met her, he wondered how he had managed to make it through days that now seemed gray if he couldn't see her or talk to her in passing on the street. He'd executed complicated maneuvers to accidentally encounter her, but now he wanted more. He had to know how she felt about him, and determined that this Christmas was the day he would find out.

After the service and the singing, Sarah and her extended family filed out. Her father lingered, his eyes fixed on Jeff. "Lieutenant Davis? A word?"

Jeff took a deep breath to steady himself. "Yes, sir?"

"I am aware of your interest in my daughter. She's a fine young woman, but I've forbidden her to marry an army man. Best to look elsewhere." Zach Taylor's glare burned into the lieutenant. "Understood?"

"With all due respect, sir, isn't that somewhat up to her?" Jeff met his commanding officer's eyes.

"We'll see." The colonel gave him a cold stare and turned to join his family.

"I'll see you later at your house, sir. Merry Christmas."

Colonel Taylor didn't turn back. He tossed a hasty Christmas greeting over his shoulder and marched outside.

Jeff didn't know why Zach Taylor didn't want his daughter to marry a soldier, but he didn't believe it was personal. He and the colonel respected each other too much for that. A vague warning wouldn't deter him, though. He felt alive when Sarah Taylor was near him, as if the rest of his day and night, he was merely existing. He must speak to her today at the party.

He left the church and almost walked right into Mary Street. Her family must have gone on without her. She'd waited for him. He swallowed a groan and forced a smile onto his face as he tried to navigate the awkwardness of speaking to her alone. Mary couldn't help it that she wasn't Sarah Taylor. He must find a way to discourage her politely. "Miss Street. Merry Christmas."

"Oh, Lieutenant Davis, Merry Christmas to you, too!"

She actually slipped her hand under his arm and walked beside him like she belonged there. Jeff prayed Sarah had arrived home before she could see this. Mary's hand was cold, her grip clawlike. He shuddered despite himself.

"Are you cold, Lieutenant? Maybe later we can share a hot drink near the fire?"

Mary looked at him with a glint in her eye. Not a sparkle like Sarah's eyes, which he chose to interpret as love. No, Mary's glance was more like that of a hungry bear. He gently removed her hand from his arm. "I really must be going, Miss Street."

"I'll see you later at the colonel's, Lieutenant." She flounced off toward her father's house.

‹‹ ● ● ››

Meanwhile, at the Taylor house, Sarah and Ann hurried upstairs to change from their good day dresses into their party finery, while their mother went downstairs to the kitchen to make sure Sally's preparations were coming along.

Sarah had brought her dress from Kentucky when she moved back after finishing school, hoping for an occasion to wear it, or someone to wear it for. The yellow silk gown had a full, pleated skirt decorated with couched cording from waistline to hem on each side. Tulle roses down the front of the dress matched the edging on the puffed sleeves. It was the prettiest dress Sarah had ever owned, and it made her feel like a fashionable debutante even as she twirled in a circle like a child to admire it.

"You look beautiful," Ann said. She helped Sarah arrange her brown ringlets on top of her head.

"I'm nervous," Sarah said.

"One step at a time," her sister advised. "First, you need to discover if he has feelings for you. Second, you encourage him to court you." She held up an index finger to halt Sarah's protests. "Third, you convince Papa he is the right man for you. Finally, you accept the lieutenant's proposal and let me help you plan a wedding."

Sarah smiled. "You make it sound so easy. Step three is daunting, however."

"Papa loves you. He'll come around." Ann patted her sister's hand and led her downstairs.

The family gathered in the parlor before guests arrived. Small gifts had been tucked amongst the greenery Sarah had arranged on the mantel. Her father handed striped candy sticks and apples to Dick and Betty. The younger children knew the treats had come with their Auntie Ann from Fort Snelling, and they ran to hug her. Dick also got a penknife from his father, and Betty a doll's dress her mother had made.

Sarah fidgeted impatiently. When would the guests arrive? She fell into daydreams of dancing with...

"Sarah? This is for you," her mother said, handing her daughter a hand-embroidered pincushion.

Sarah thanked her mother and forced herself to remain focused on the celebration. Her family appreciated the handkerchiefs she'd embroidered for them, and they exclaimed over gifts of ribbons, mittens, and scarves.

Finally, officers from the fort began to arrive. Zach Taylor greeted the guests to his home. General Street arrived as usual, amidst a raucous crowd of family. His wife hurried to take the youngest three upstairs to Sally as he sought out Sarah's father. Mary Street sashayed over to Sarah with a smug look on her face.

"Merry Christmas, Miss Street," Sarah said. She tried to imbue genuine good wishes into her words.

"And to you. Have you seen Lieutenant Davis yet? He said he'd like to dance with me tonight. I want to make sure he doesn't stuff himself at the feast beforehand." Her trill of laughter sounded as false as Sarah's greeting. Mary didn't wait for Sarah's response. She moved across the room, finding a place to watch the arriving guests.

The door opened and the room brightened. As if a heavenly choir announced him, Lieutenant Davis joined the party. No one noticed except Sarah and Mary. Sarah headed toward him, but Mary was quicker.

"There you are, Lieutenant!" Mary said. Turning to Sarah, just a few steps away, Mary said, "Oh, Miss Taylor? My brother, Thornton, says to tell you he can hardly wait to come home from school in the spring to begin courting you." She flashed a tight smile that became sweet when she turned back to Lieutenant Davis.

Stung by Mary's statement about her awful brother, Sarah didn't know what to say.

Jeff Davis said, "A very merry Christmas to you, Miss Taylor."

Sarah's heart fluttered. He was so handsome, and he was talking to her, not Mary. "Thank you, Lieutenant. Merry Christmas. Have you sampled the eggnog? My mother makes it with my father's brandy. Or the wine? I believe Mama is serving one of her better vintages today." She stopped talking, mortified at her chattiness.

Jeff laughed. "Can I bring you ladies a glass of eggnog?" He crossed the room to the punch bowl.

Mary hissed, "Don't embarrass yourself by intruding where you don't belong."

"Why, Miss Street," Sarah said, "I do believe you are jealous." She turned to smile at Jeff, who approached and handed a glass to each girl. Sarah talked to Jeff, sipped her eggnog, and pretended not to notice Mary hovering.

·‹‹ ● ● ● ›·

Jeff sipped his eggnog, which was truly excellent, and talked to Sarah of the weather, the construction at the fort, and her family. Every word was heavy with subtext he couldn't quite read. Certainly she felt something for him? When Mary Street gave up and left them in a huff, Jeff wanted to take Sarah's hand and pull her close. He wanted to know how she felt in his arms, how soft her hair was, how her skin smelled, what it would be like to be alone with her, but he couldn't keep himself from checking to see where her father was. Colonel Taylor's powers of observation, and his dogged attention to details, made him a good commanding officer. Jeff would be a fool to discount his warning.

When dinner was ready, it seemed every one of the fifteen dinner guests started talking at once as they looked for their assigned seats at the table. Frowning, Jeff took his place at the opposite end of the table from Sarah, across from Mary. It would take a lot of effort to be polite while she prattled at him.

·‹‹ ● ● ● ›·

Sarah spotted Ann across the table and a few places down, and Jeff almost at the far end. She leaned forward to see who sat across from Jeff. Mary Street! It took every bit of grace Sarah possessed not to express her dissatisfaction. Mary must have moved the

160

name cards. There was no way her mother would seat her next to a much older officer who smelled of tobacco.

Lieutenant Davis looked up and smiled at her, and suddenly they were the only two in the room. Conversation dimmed, colors blurred, and Sarah's chest tightened as she smiled back. Then Mary leaned forward and said something that drew Jeff's attention, and the spell was broken.

Sarah turned her attention to the table, focusing on the details rather than the people seated around it. A large roasted turkey on a bed of evergreens occupied the center. At Sarah's end of the table sat a boiled ham, and at Jeff's end was a roast pig. In between were platters and bowls of mashed prairie turnips, boiled onions, and bread with last summer's strawberry jam. Mama's famous cheeses, served on a plate with pecans, dotted the repast. At each corner of the table, pitchers of sweet cider and iced water waited to be poured.

The officer next to her had started a story about the informality of pioneer marriages. He said, "Women married in this way believe they are married lawfully. They get these ideas from the Indians. Even at a fancy ball at Fort Snelling a woman left with a trader who proposed to her. She stepped out of the ballroom into his canoe, believing herself married. They lived together several years and even had a couple of children."

Head shaking and snorts of disbelief greeted his story. Sarah thought that if such a thing had happened, Ann would have told her.

Eating only a few bites, Sarah couldn't help but look down the table at Jeff. He laughed at something Mary said, and a knife slashed Sarah's heart. Then he looked her way and smiled, which delighted and embarrassed her at the same time. She hated to be caught staring. Sometimes, though, she'd look up and he'd be looking at her. Then she smiled with warmth and as much love as she could put into a smile from the other end of the table.

When the guests had finished eating, the men pushed the table against the wall. Sally was upstairs with all the children, so Peggy Taylor brought in the pies and cakes to fill the table again.

The sounds of a fiddle signaled the guests to create squares for a quadrille. Ann started a conversation with Mary, subtly turning so Mary's back was to the dance floor. Following her sister's advice, Sarah had managed to work her way closer to Jeff so she was close by when the fiddle started.

Jeff bowed and held out his hand. "May I have this dance, Miss Taylor?"

Sarah nodded and placed her hand in his, thinking he could have every dance he wanted.

He was a smooth dancer, leading her confidently through the steps. She didn't need to worry about her footwork since she was floating on air. The quadrille required too much thinking and physical activity to converse, but Sarah wasn't sure she could speak anyway, with her head in the clouds as it was.

On one spin, to her delight, Sarah noticed Mary standing alone near the dessert table, glowering. Sarah gave her what she hoped was a condescending nod and ignored her on every subsequent pass.

Sarah noticed her father, standing to one side. His face thundered disapproval, but it couldn't dim her smile. Next to Papa, Ann did her best, proffering a dessert as she tried to engage him in conversation.

When the dance ended, Jeff bowed over her hand again. He said, "I hope we have the opportunity to dance again."

Was it Sarah's imagination or did he hold her hand a bit longer than necessary? Would he offer to bring her a drink as other men were doing for their partners? He started to speak, but then Mary appeared at his side with a glass of water.

"I thought you might be thirsty," she said to Jeff. "Unless you want something stronger?" She tilted her head and batted her eyelashes in a pose that made Sarah's stomach sicken. Jeff Davis inclined his head to Mary in a gesture that was more bow than nod and accepted the water.

Sarah wondered if he was just being polite or if he was taken in by Mary's flirting. Sarah touched Jeff's arm lightly. "I enjoyed our dance very much," she said. "Have you had dessert? I made a cider cake. I'd love for you to try it."

"That sounds delicious," Jeff said. Still sipping the water Mary had brought him, he followed Sarah to the table laden with cakes.

Sarah cut a slice of cake and handed it to him, but before he could take it, the music started up again. Mary appeared at his elbow, and Jeff asked her to dance, leaving Sarah holding the plate of cake and fuming. She refused to watch them dance as if she were pining away. Setting the cake back on the table, Sarah went to find her sister.

Ann stood near the door to the kitchen, chatting with Mrs. Street, Mary's mother. When she saw Sarah coming toward them, Ann excused herself and walked toward the fireplace. Sarah joined her.

"I saw you dancing with the lieutenant," Ann said.

"Yes, but look who he's dancing with now," Sarah said. It was a relief not to have to pretend. With her sister, she could be irritated or overjoyed. She didn't have to maintain the serene exterior her mother said ladies must have.

"He looked happier to be dancing with you," Ann said. Her eyes twinkled.

"Don't tease me," Sarah said.

"I'm not. Remember, he's an eligible bachelor required to dance with every single girl in the room or else be embroiled in gossip." Ann leaned toward Sarah as if telling a secret. "But he doesn't have to like it. See his smile? It looks forced. It didn't look like that when he danced with you."

Sarah looked back at the couple on the dance floor. She

couldn't see what Ann did. To Sarah, Jeff smiled at Mary the way she wanted him to smile at her and only her.

Ann waved to someone across the room and left Sarah by the desserts. Sarah picked up the plate of cider cake and began to eat it. She scanned the room for her parents, and found them talking in a corner near the door to the kitchen, heads together as if conspiring. Sarah kept her gaze anywhere except the dance floor. She even contemplated going upstairs to visit the children.

Peggy Taylor joined her daughter. She pretended to be straightening the desserts as she said, "Lieutenant Davis, is it?"

"Oh, Mama, I love him," Sarah said.

"Sarah..." her mother began.

"I know Papa disapproves. But Lieutenant Davis is a good man, you know that! Please help me convince Papa not to scare him off before I have a chance to know how he feels about me." Her mother looked up from the dessert table. Sarah touched her arm. "Please, Mama?"

"He is a good man," her mother conceded. "I will see what I can do." She brushed off Sarah's exclamations of gratitude and headed for the kitchen to replenish the pies on the table.

‹‹ ● ● ● › ›

On the dance floor, moving mechanically through the steps, Jeff struggled to keep his mind on his movements. He saw Sarah standing with her sister and smiled. Mary's face lit up, clearly responding to a smile not intended for her.

During a pause in the dance, Mary said, "What a good dancer you are, Lieutenant." She flashed the sort of eyelash-intensive smile that always made Jeff nervous.

"As are you, Miss Street," he said.

When the music stopped, he bowed to Mary hastily, almost

being rude. Mary reached out to catch hold of his arm, but he pulled it away before she touched him. She overbalanced and tumbled forward, falling to her knees. Jeff heard gasps from several directions, but when he looked up all the women were turning away, unsuccessfully hiding smiles behind their hands. The men laughed. Mary's face flamed. Jeff started to help her up, then saw Sarah turn quickly and walk away toward the kitchen. He couldn't let her go. He raced from the dance floor. General Street waddled past Jeff, glaring at him, on his way to assist his daughter.

Jeff caught up with Sarah by the dessert table. "Is there any more of your cider cake left, Miss Taylor?" he asked. "Or did you eat it all?" He focused his attention on Sarah, refusing to look back to see how Mary fared.

Sarah's eyes flicked past him toward the dance floor, then back to Jeff. "I'll get you a piece," she said. She cut him a good-sized piece and handed him the plate and fork. His fingers grazed hers as he took the plate, sending tingles up his arm.

He took a bite and savored it. "This is very good. Tastes like the cakes my grandmother used to make." He ate another bite.

"You're very busy with the new fort, Lieutenant," Sarah said.

Jeff nodded. "I spent some time on the Yellow River, managing the felling of timber for the fort. But then I caught pneumonia and came back here."

"Oh! I wasn't aware you were ill."

Jeff noticed Mary approaching. He squared his shoulders and tightened his lips, but Ann caught Mary's arm and drew her away. Jeff relaxed. "I recovered in good time. But that was last year. Earlier this year, I led a detachment to Galena to remove miners from land claimed by the Native Americans. Your host, James Lockwood, was there with his brother Ezekiel, the postmaster in Galena."

"I wondered where he was staying while my family occupies

his house. It sounds like you were lucky to be able to return in time for our holiday festivities."

Sarah was more than smiling now. She glowed. Surely that meant something? Jeff set down his empty cake plate and fixed an intense gaze on Sarah. "It was important to me to be here tonight."

··‹‹●●●›››··

Sarah looked up at him, her mind muddled with emotional signals from her heart. The fiddler started up again, this time playing "Adeste Fideles." Everyone sang the carol. Sarah remembered yesterday's joy while decorating the parlor and humming the song. The music filled her heart, chasing out all nervousness that had plagued her this night. Sarah smiled at Jeff, not wanting to shout at him over the music and song.

She remembered a few weeks ago when Jeff came into Mr. Lockwood's store. Her mother had been at the counter, talking to the clerk about something she'd ordered. Jeff smiled when he saw her perusing a new shipment of ribbons and asked what color dress she was trying to match. "I've seen my sisters rustle through a box of ribbons like that," he'd explained.

"I'm hardly rustling," Sarah said, smiling. "It's important to select the right shade of green for my new hat."

"Oh, a hat ribbon. I see." He'd affected a knowledgeable air that made her laugh.

"So, what do you recommend, good sir, for an emerald green hat? Would a forest green or sage green ribbon complement it better?"

"I leave the decision to the lady." They had laughed together as if they were old friends.

Sarah's mother had come over then and spoken a few words to

Lieutenant Davis. He went to examine the store's selection of tools, and Sarah finished her ribbon purchase. Mama had looked at her curiously, but said nothing, leaving Sarah free to relive every laugh and dream.

‹‹ ● ◉ ● › ›

The music soared, perfect for dancing but too loud for talking. Jeff tilted his head, nodding toward the door, and started in that direction. He looked back to make sure Sarah was following. "Shall we step outside?" he asked as soon as he could be heard. It was a daring request, since her parents were still inside. "We'll stay on the porch," he promised her. "And come back inside before we are missed."

She nodded, and they stepped outside. Jeff let out a breath he'd been holding when he saw they weren't alone. Others had come outside to cool off from dancing, or have a private word. There would be no scandalous chatter about him disappearing with the colonel's daughter if they stayed on the porch.

Candles danced in the windows of houses along the street, and the clear, cold night spread above them. With the music in the background, Jeff looked out across the Mississippi River, dotted with reflections of the stars. "The North Star," he said, pointing. "A symbol of hope for eternity."

Sarah shivered. He wished he could take her in his arms to warm her, but touching her was not allowed. Sarah looked up into his face. His eyes were brighter than the North Star, more hopeful.

"I hope I'm not out of line," he began.

She took a deep breath and held it.

"I know I haven't been acquainted with you for long," he said, starting again, "but I have come to care for you, Sarah. May I call you Sarah?"

167

"Yes," she said, exhaling.

"I will do so only if you call me Jeff and tell me how you feel."

"Jeff," she said. "I care about you, too."

"Do I need your father's permission to court you?"

"When you ask him, make sure Mama is there."

Jeff looked down at the beautiful face that filled his dreams day and night. With this woman, he could build a home, a stable foundation that appealed to him more than the nomadic life of a soldier. He had to make his intentions known, to prevent other girls from wasting his time. He had to show her father he was the best choice for Sarah. His brother had a plantation in Louisiana and had been trying to convince Jeff to leave the army and occupy the neighboring plantation. Jeff hadn't given it serious thought until now. With Sarah, he could envision a life after the army.

·‹‹ ● ●› ›·

Standing next to him, close enough to feel the warmth of his body beside her, Sarah looked up at Jeff and joy filled her heart. Since she'd been old enough to know such things, she'd wanted a loving marriage like her parents and her sister had. In all her dreams of the future, she worked together with a man she loved to have a happy home and a family. With Jeff, she might find such love and respect.

Ann's advice echoed in her head. *First, you need to discover if he has feelings for you.* She smiled. Step one complete. She hadn't needed to do anything to complete the next step. *Second, you encourage him to court you.* Her next task dimmed her smile. *Third, you convince Papa he is the right man for you.* Papa respected Jeff as an officer and a man. That would surely help her cause. Her mother and sister would help Sarah change his mind. Snippets of possible conversations darted through her head. She could do this. She had to, in order to complete Ann's final step. *Accept the lieutenant's proposal and let me help you plan a wedding.*

Sarah laughed with delight as her mental images focused on the wedding she and her sister would plan, on the life she and Jeff would create together. The promise of the future dazzled her as much as the stars in the sky.

·‹‹●●›·

Learn more about Sarah and Jefferson's story in Linda Ulleseit's novel The River Remembers.

·‹‹●●›·

Linda Ulleseit is the award-winning author of heritage fiction about her female ancestors. Under the Almond Trees follows the lives of a suffragette, an architect, and a photographer in pioneer California. The Aloha Spirit is set in territorial Hawaii. The River Remembers, her most recent, is set in 1835 Minnesota and explores the intertwining Native American, Black, and white cultures. Find out more about Linda on her website, BookBub, Facebook, or Instagram.

·‹‹●●›·

Dear Santa

❧

CHRISTMAS
BY ANNE M. BEGGS

San Jose, California
December 1969

K atie Rose pulled into the familiar driveway, a typical tract home in the expanding community of San Jose, California, with the Christmas tree up in the window, the lights along the eaves, and a welcoming wreath on the door. She was home. Home from college for the brief holidays, with so much on her mind— graduate schools and bald tires to replace. Yes, she had to work, and was so grateful she had been hired at the Sears Santa Photo Studio at the new mall.

Her mother came out the door to meet her, still wiping her hands on a dish towel.

"Katie," she called, extending her arms.

"Mom," Katie said as they embraced.

"I can't believe you have to work. At least today, when you just got home. 'Til nine o'clock, you say?"

"Mom, look at my tires, I need the money."

"That graduate school nonsense. Business school!" Her

mother was not a fan. "If you managed your money better, you would have new tires and could spend the Christmas break with your parents."

"Mom," Katie said, deciding graduate school was not worth arguing about at this moment.

"If you must return to school, why won't you listen to me and go to nursing school. How else will you find a doctor to marry?"

Another argument. Katie had no intention of marrying. A doctor or anyone. Her mother was relentless, prattling on about meeting a future husband, as if college was nothing more than an extended dating ritual.

"My Katie Rose, home for Christmas."

Katie Rose. Always such a disappointment. That was the reason she chose Kate Thorn as her pen name. She was a thorn in the side. She had actually brought home copies of the college newspaper and journal with her writings, along with her three letters. What would her parents' think? She still wasn't sure how or when to share them. What a complicated time. Her life and 1969.

After quickly unpacking her suitcase and boxes, Katie was back in the car, the radio playing "I Heard it Through the Grapevine" while driving to the new mall. What an amazing thing, these malls. All the stores inside one large building, with benches and a food court, turning shopping into a social occasion, with so many shopping options and no traffic to dodge once inside. She parked near the Sears department store: this was her first day.

"Miss Bennett, I am so glad you are here," said the floor manager, Mrs. Parker, who was easily as tall as Katie, perhaps five foot, eight inches, with her dark brown hair, obviously too dyed, in a short and curled cut, so like her mother's. She wore a navy-blue dress suit. She extended her hand in a warm and friendly shake.

Katie had chosen to wear a lime green dress suit, with a black belt at the waist, and now wondered if she had made a bad decision, with something so markedly youthful.

"Come into my office. We have some changes to discuss."

Wardrobe mistake, she thought, as she followed Mrs. Parker. Gosh, she needed this job, and already a reprimand, maybe a dismissal.

"Have a seat, we have a new opportunity. Katie, I see you took the initiative to put on your application you have applied to business school. You are motivated," Mrs. Parker said.

"Yes, thank you, I know this is a temporary job, but I—" Katie didn't finish.

"You are motivated, and you are enthusiastic," Mrs. Parker continued. "I find myself without a studio manager at this most critical time of year. I think you might fit nicely into the job. Are you interested?"

"What does the job entail?" Katie asked, already wondering how difficult it might be.

"It pays one dollar an hour more and is full time through Christmas Eve. You will assist the Santas, Bob Morris and Tony DeMatteo, with costumes and make-up, directing the Elves, overseeing the photo and camera supplies, photo orders, timecards and more."

Katie could barely calculate the salary and added hours, but it was an opportunity to try her hand at business.

"Yes, please," Katie heard herself saying, thinking how unprofessional it sounded, not knowing what else to say.

Mrs. Parker walked her through the entire day, smiling, encouraging, and trusting that Katie could do it.

"See you tomorrow, Katie," Mrs. Parker said as Katie left at nine, spent but excited.

Driving home, the radio blasted "Crimson and Clover" then "Come Together." How would she have survived without *Abbey Road*, easing her through the tough autumn semester—the MBA application process, and the one token social services application, which was mostly a nod to her mother, but there was a spark in her own soul, she had to admit; even if she didn't understand the full implication.

And her writing. Where did Kate Thorn fit in all this? Writing was not a viable career. Even *she* understood that.

As she drove, she enjoyed seeing so many Christmas lights already decorating the houses. It was all so festive, so promising, ever changing, yet still the familiar streets of her home. One of the homes had the most amazing black light display, with the white trees and bulbs glowing with psychedelic yet calming splendor.

She pulled into her driveway, singing a blast from the past, "I Can't get No Satisfaction," leaving the engine running until the end. No one turned off the Stones.

"Katie," her father greeted her as she came in. Setting down his *Field and Stream* magazine, he stood, and they hugged.

"Dad."

"How was your first day as Santa's Helper?"

"More like Mrs. Claus. I was promoted. I'm the studio manager."

Sitting on the couch with both parents, she explained.

"I am thrilled. So much work. So much responsibility. It will be like an internship. Perfect for a business degree."

"You still have your heart set on an MBA?" her father asked. "I know you're driven. Are you letting all this women's lib go to your head? Business is tough. Men are—" he paused. "I don't think you understand. I am glad you know how to type. Shorthand would have been helpful," her father said, not for the first time.

"MBA!" her mother said with a scoff. "We are proud of you, Katie, but this is so impractical. What do you expect to do? Run the mall? Lockheed? You need to find a good husband, a lawyer, or the next boss of Intel. And give me grandchildren. My arms are empty. Please, Katie."

"Please, Mom," she said, mimicking her mother, and shrugging.

"And are you working all day Sunday?" her dad cut in. "The 49ers are playing in Minnesota, so we can watch that game. But it's radio for the Raiders/Chiefs. What a game that will be."

"I'll be working, Dad. The Santas were talking about the game. Tony is working that day. Bob said he would phone in the scores."

"Your tires," her dad said, changing the subject. "Sears does tires. Do you get an employee discount?"

"I'll ask."

"Good. You got a good promotion. Get your tires replaced while you are working. We'll pay up front and you pay us back. That is good business. Bald tires are not."

"Thanks, Dad. Great plan. I'm excited about the job."

Her father studied her.

"Maybe I should take your car in. I don't want those mechanics cheating you because you are a woman. Selling you more than you need."

"Thanks, Dad. But when would you have time? I can do it tomorrow. I'll go in early."

Katie got her car to Sears, and was pleased to find she was entitled to a meager employee discount, and was assured her car would be done in three hours.

Walking to the studio, she enjoyed the quiet in the store before it opened to customers. The decorations were bright and so modern in bold hot pink, orange and lime green. 1969. The end of a decade. A new beginning—the 70s. It seemed the store reflected the hope and prosperity of the coming years. Neil Armstrong had landed on the moon; Kennedy's promise was fulfilled. Such tumultuous times as well: War, protests, civil unrest, two Kennedy brothers had been assassinated, as was Martin Luther King, Jr.

Santa Bob and the elves would be arriving. Soon the kids and moms. *Leave the outside cares behind*, she reminded herself. The harrowing news and depressing adult things had no place in the children's Christmas. Her job was keeping the magic alive and selling photos to be a lasting memory. Like the ones she and her parents had made.

Katie liked being the first one to arrive, finding everything where she left it last night. Mrs. Parker met her, bringing a paper cup of coffee.

"Black, right?"

"Yes," Katie said, taking the cup.

"Any questions? Something you thought about last night?" Mrs. Parker asked.

"No, I think the first day went very well."

"It did. Though it will get busier the closer we get to Christmas. Last minute rushes. Keeping the studio bright and fresh. You have a good staff this season. It will be fine."

"Thank you, I feel lucky," Katie said.

"Thanks, and don't forget to call if you need me, at least in these first days."

"I will. And thanks again for the coffee."

Katie heard some crackling and scratching as the mall's audio system kicked in and started playing Christmas music. Bob walked in. Time to apply his makeup.

"Day five for you, my second," she said as she gently wiped his face with cotton balls.

"How many years have you been working as Santa?"

"This is my first time. I was laid off on Halloween."

Katie didn't know what to say. So much prosperity, but some companies didn't make it.

"I am sorry to hear that."

"Me, too. That was one hell of a trick, instead of a treat. I didn't see it coming. Unemployment wouldn't get us through

Christmas. So here I am. Maybe something else will open here at Sears."

Katie nodded before starting the light makeup. So odd to apply foundation to a man, no matter how light. She had no experience with beard stubble, and it made her giggle.

"I'm still not used to this either," he said, as she added the exaggerated blush to his cheeks and nose. "Go light on that, I don't want to look like a drunk," he mumbled as she touched up his nose.

"We don't want that," she said, chuckling at the thought. "No repeats of Miracle on 34th Street." In the movie, the original man hired to play Santa was drunk, and the real Kris Kringle showed up to save the day.

"I always enjoyed that movie. And Natalie Wood. She grew into a beauty, hubba hubba."

"She is an amazing actress." *Actress*, Katie thought, *or should I say actor? Must we differentiate by sex?* She wasn't sure. So much to consider these days. These were the questions Kate Thorn wrote about.

Bob was still talking, but she hadn't been listening as her mind wandered.

"I said, I'll go change into my costume now."

"Yes, of course. I'll help fit it when you come out," Katie said as he stood.

Cindy and Cathy were both waiting in their elf costumes. Once again, Cindy's hair hung long and straight.

"Mrs. Parker wants your hair up in the hat," Katie reminded her.

"Mrs. Parker is old-fashioned. I think elves should reflect the times. It's not like I'm wearing bell-bottoms," Cindy said, hands on hips.

"Cindy, I rather agree with you. In fact, I think bell-bottoms might be a cute update. But it isn't my call. Mrs. Parker and Sears chose our costumes and the look."

"Oh, wouldn't red and white, candy cane bell-bottoms be far-out? Or maybe a twirling, red and green pattern, and big sunglasses!" Cathy said in a gushing tone.

"Psychedelic Santa and the Outta Sight Elves," Bob said, returning in his traditional red and white suit, still buckling his black belt.

"Let's get that beard on you," Katie said.

"Hair up, Cindy," Katie said again. "Sears isn't paying you to protest. But I will bring it up with Mrs. Parker. It might be more fitting with the modern theme the mall is presenting."

"I really think we need a Woodstock elf. If only I had been there. That's where I belong," Cindy lamented.

"Finish high school," Santa Bob said, as Katie helped him with the beard. "Then travel. And no hitchhiking!"

"You're Santa, not my father," Cindy said, but with a pleasant smile.

"Hair up, do your job, and let Katie do hers," Santa Bob said. "Is it showtime yet?"

"Almost," Katie said, checking her watch to be sure they weren't late.

Santa and the elves started their shift walking around the mall as it opened, greeting the shoppers and reminding them Santa's photo shop was located in Sears. All children were welcome to come sit on Santa's lap and tell him what they wanted. Paid photos were not required. But who didn't want to capture the magic moment forever in a photo? The screaming, fearful little children, along with the brave and smiling ones. How would the kids look back on this?

·‹‹●●●›·

The first few days were challenging, and Katie wondered if she would be able to keep up. The moms and children came in large rushes, with long lines, and anxious families. Occasionally, in a lull, Katie could catch up on the orders, and make sure the paperwork and payments were correct.

"Katie, you are so quiet tonight," her mother said, as they all sat to eat dinner, the TV blaring the nightly news her mother found necessary. Images of the war in Vietnam, helicopters and men being carried on stretchers, were all so brutal. Then came the images of student protests and more violence. How was she supposed to eat dinner with all this? Yet they did, every night: weather, politics, the economy.

"I—" Katie paused. She had so much on her mind. Those graduate school letters were still waiting for her reply: business school, social work, or that writing internship. "Just so much to contemplate, I guess."

After doing the dishes she went to her room.

She had only received one acceptance letter to an MBA program. Not only was it at the bottom of her list, but it also came with no scholarship or financial aid. Not her ideal, but an acceptance. Coming so late in the year, it also felt like she was at the bottom of their list. A cold, disappointing form letter of acceptance. *Rally, Katie, you knew it wouldn't be easy. MBAs still aren't for women. You show them.* This had been her pep talk during the whole process.

The other acceptance letter was for the grad program in social work, also without scholarships or financial aid, at an expensive, private women's college. She loved the campus and felt welcome, but it was too expensive. Why had she applied? No husbands there, her mother would protest. *Mom.* Yet, it was with thoughts of her mother that she applied.

The writing opportunity was with a burgeoning feminist periodical that had published a few of her articles. They wanted her to join the team, as an intern, not only writing for the New Woman, but learning publishing. Such an opportunity. Such an adventure. Such a privilege. No pay. The long hours of work and learning were all contributed for free. Cheaper than staying in school, they argued. Growth and opportunity. Isn't that what entrepreneurs did? Was that the career she wanted? Did Kate Thorn have the fire in her soul?

·◦‹‹ ● ›› ◦·

"Katie," her mother said, as they sat down to coffee and breakfast. "Your father and I, and you, need to get passport photos. Sears still does that, don't they?"

"Sure, Mom," Katie said, wondering why she needed a passport.

"Do we need an appointment, or can you do it?"

"You need an appointment, and no, I can't do it. That is a real photographer. Passports! That is big. Where are you going?" This was a new development. Passports.

"Your mother has always wanted to travel. Especially to Ireland. Her maiden name, those Dahlquin roots," her dad said from behind his morning paper. "Connacht, didn't you say? Nowhere near an airport. And one of the most dangerous places on the planet right now."

"Genealogy is fascinating. Wouldn't you like to know about your Bennetts?" her mother asked. "Yes, Connacht. There is an old castle ruin, Dahlquin. Isn't that amazing? Maybe we are royalty."

"If the castle is in ruins, unsuccessful nobility. Serfs, most likely. Didn't your ancestors come steerage? Or did they swim?" her father asked from behind his paper.

"I certainly want to know more about Cormac and Echna Dahlquin, and their children, Lando, Sean, and baby Aine. Such unusual names. And tragic times, that potato famine."

"Mom, that is exciting. But Dad is right, the IRA terrorism is frightening. Not a safe place at all."

"Well," her mother said with a sigh, before continuing undeterred, "Since I went back to work as a teacher's aide, I have been saving. It is not much, but enough for a trip in September," her mother said, her smile as wide as a jet plane. "That is when your father can take off."

"We wanted to wait until Christmas to tell you, but it is too much, especially with relatives here," her father said, leaving his thought unfinished.

"Katie, I know we always said we could not afford to send you on a European holiday for your graduation, but we believe we can all go to Ireland. You, too, if you don't mind coming with your stodgy parents. I will have saved enough money by autumn."

"Too dangerous," her father said from behind his paper.

"That sounds great! Unbelievable! But September?" Katie said, "I will be starting grad school then."

"Grad school," her mother sighed. "Have you actually committed yet? Why not take a year off? Travel with us to Ireland. I need you. Work for a year and see if you even need grad school."

"You mean, if I have found a husband by then," Katie said sarcastically.

"You never know, but grad school can surely wait. You will have a year's more experience. Decide then," her mother said.

"Mrs. Bennett," Katie said, in her silliest English accent, "You are proving yet again that nothing has changed in two hundred years since Jane Austen wrote *Pride and Prejudice*. You obsess over finding me a husband, when I am not in need of one," Katie said, seeing her father bend his paper down to stare at her, then her mother.

"Oh, hang Jane Austen. What did she know of motherhood or grandchildren? Or the Irish plight? These are modern times, yes, and getting married and raising a family is timeless and natural. I am a Mrs. Bennett who works outside the home, earning money to take the trip of a lifetime," her mother said, obviously trying to reel in her feelings of disappointment.

"Much as I love the entertainment," her father said, also trying for an English accent, "I will be late to work. Goodbye, my love," he said to his frowning wife. "Goodbye, Katie Rose, ever the thorn in your mother's side."

"Don't forget your lunch," her mother said, getting up to fetch it for him.

"Thank you," he said, heading out the door.

"You will be late, too, Katie," her mother said, putting on a smile. "Will you at least think about Ireland? Just think. Here's your lunch."

"Thanks, Mom. I love you."

"I love you too, dearest."

Kate Thorn carried her brown paper bag to her car. Damn! Ireland. September. She was not a child. She wanted to build a life, a career. Then she would have money to spend, to travel. With a business degree she could manage a travel agency! Hadn't her parents taught her to work hard and plan for what she wanted? Wasn't that what she was doing? She only applied for the Social Work program to appease her mother, didn't she? There was little income in social work if she wanted to travel. Her writing, no matter how good, was gratis—it cost her to be published. Suddenly it seemed planes and suitcases with travel stickers pasted all over them filled her mind—her own passport. She would be writing behind the scenes from Ireland.

She pulled into the parking lot. Whatever was playing on the radio went unnoticed. As Santa Tony said, *Time to make some magic.*

· ‹ ‹ ● ◉ › ›

Tuesday, December 23, 1969

Two days left before Christmas.

Katie was tired from arguing with her parents again. Holiday tensions were high with disappointment and unfulfilled expectations. And it wasn't even Christmas.

She wasn't done with school. There was so much more to learn and achieve. Maybe she should pursue journalism or creative writing. Wasn't this the time to explore? Her parents disagreed heartily. Even the women's movement—Women's Lib—was not unified in this. Go to work, have a career. Don't support the old school. Create yourself. Ireland.

Arriving early, the phone was ringing and there were already notes on her desk.

"Good morning, Santa's Photo Shop, this is Katie," she said, answering the phone.

"Katie, so glad I got you. Did you get Tony's message?" Bob asked.

"I see messages here on my desk, but I answered the phone first," she said, picking up the messages.

"Tony is sick. Very sick. He can't work today. Fever, chills, cough. He called me this morning. He sounds terrible. He asked me if I could fill in. Gosh, Katie, I would love to, but I'm in training for my new job. They are already working around my

Santa gig. I can't miss the training. I'm sorry Katie. I need this job," Bob said.

He needed that job, she knew. Her mind was spinning.

"Call one of the boys," Bob was saying. "Craig would be good, but any of them can fill in."

One of the boys. She wracked her brain to remember who was working today.

"Yes, thank you, Bob. I will look at the schedule and start calling. Good luck with your training. See you tomorrow." She hung up and grabbed the schedule.

Cindy, Cathy, and Barbara. She grabbed the elf list and looked for the phone numbers.

There was no answer at Craig's house. *Where was everyone?*

She called Dan, but he was babysitting for the whole neighborhood. He started to explain his plans to take the kids to the park, the creek and then make popcorn.

"Thanks, Dan. Have fun. I gotta go, more calls," Katie said, hanging up before he could answer.

Ron wasn't home. He and his girlfriend had gone to Santa Cruz early to get in some surfing.

Katie hung up the phone. Staring at the useless device. Then it rang, and she jumped as if a ringing phone were a miracle.

"Good Morning, Santa's Photo Shop, this is-"

"Katie, this is Cindy."

Katie hardly recognized her voice.

"I'm so sorry. I have a cold. Will you call one of the boys to fill in for me today?" Cindy said.

"Cindy. No. Oh no," Katie said, her mind further whirling, another elf down.

"I'll call if you are busy, just give me the numbers," Cindy said.

"No need. They aren't available. Cindy," she paused, trying to sound businesslike. "We have no Santa. Tony is sick with the flu.

Bob is working his new job and all the boys are busy. I really need you. What am I going to do with no Santa and two elves?"

"Give me Craig's number, I'll keep calling," Cindy said.

"Cindy, please come in. Call him from here while I think. Please. I need help."

"Shoot, okay," Cindy said, sighing.

Cathy and Barbara were both late, rushing into the shop.

"Katie, what's wrong?" Barbara asked.

"Are you coming down with something?" Cathy asked.

"No," Katie said, explaining the crisis.

Both girls stared at her for a moment.

"Should we put on our costumes, or cancel the day?" Cathy asked.

"You have to be Santa," Barbara said, already putting her purse down and going to the dressing room.

Katie glared at her. Of all the ridiculous things, yet—

"I am considering it," Katie said, rather surprising herself with the revelation.

"You know how to do everything. We'll help you get the costume on," Barbara said.

"Forget Craig, you need to get dressed now," Cathy said.

"I do," Katie said. "Let me call Mrs. Parker first."

Mrs. Parker appeared just as Cathy and Barbara were putting the Santa hat on.

"Ho, ho, ho, Mrs. Parker, Merry Christmas to you," Katie said, practicing her Santa voice. Knowing it would never fly. What was she thinking?

"Well, I'll be damned," Mrs. Parker said, breaking her own rule about swearing on the job.

Cathy and Barbara both giggled at the slip.

Cindy came in, red nosed and sniffling.

"Ho, ho, ho, Cindy, thank you for coming in," Katie said, still trying to sound like Santa.

"Katie?" Cindy said. "My lord. Look at you."

"Are you sick?" Mrs. Parker asked Cindy.

"Yes, but Katie said I needed to come in and help."

Mrs. Parker looked at Katie then back at Cindy.

"My throat hurts, and I'm congested, but I figured free candy canes would help," Cindy said with her nasally voice.

"That is good of you, Cindy. But, go home and rest. No need getting all of us sick, too. I canceled my day and am filling in here. Cathy, Barbara and I can do it, with Katie as Santa." Mrs. Parker said, glancing at Katie, "You are about the shortest Santa we have ever had, but I think the girls have pinned you in nicely. Can you walk in those oversized boots?"

"Not very well," Katie said as she shuffled about.

"No good having Santa fall flat on his face. Maybe we will cancel the walk about, just stay in your chair and let the kiddies come to you."

"We can walk about, Mrs. Parker," Cathy said, "We will just tell them Santa is ready and waiting."

The crinkling sound of Cindy opening a candy cane drew everyone's attention.

"I feel a little better, now that I'm here," Cindy said, sheepishly sticking the candy cane in her mouth. "I can stay and help."

"Hmmm," Mrs. Parker sighed, considering. "Let me get some tissues from the supply clerk. Try not to touch anything."

"Yes, ma'am," Cindy said, and for the first time all season, she didn't sound sarcastic. Was it her cold, or did she feel some Santa camaraderie?

"Good job, Katie, you can do it," Mrs. Parker said, as Katie nervously walked out to the big, red padded chair, a throne for the king of the elves. Hours and hours every day for more than two weeks she had photographed and managed that chair with Santa Tony or Santa Bob, but now she was playing a bigger role than she had all Christmas season.

·‹‹●●›·

And *why* hadn't she studied the Santa handbook more thoroughly? Playing Santa was a grand and lofty responsibility. There were rules and tips.

"Welcome," she said, arms out as the first children came forth. A little girl pulled her younger brother dutifully up to Katie Santa's waiting lap. She was all business, and knew her role in this charade. Her little brother was reticent, his arms pulled in tight to his chest, lest Santa actually touch him.

"I want an easy-bake oven, a big stuffed dog and a real kitten," she said with a big smile, knowing that saying was getting. She wanted to believe.

"And you," Katie Santa said to her brother. He just stared, his lips quivering.

"He wants Hot Wheels and the Snoopy Astronaut," the big sister said for her brother.

"You do?" Katie Santa asked him.

He managed to nod his head.

Katie Santa reached into the basket of candy canes for each of them.

"Let's look at the camera and get a nice photo for you and your parents," she said, realizing as the children started to open the candy canes, she had broken one of the cardinal rules of good Santaship. Candy canes *after* the photo. Oh dear.

After that, the morning went smoothly. So many children, so many wishes.

Santa Katie saw the little girl in line with her sister. What excellent parents she had. The little girl was dressed in clean blue jeans, a shirt and vest and cowboy hat, the kiddie kind with the plastic trim laced around the brim. She was adorable, dressed as Katie had wished to be when she was that age. Her sister was equally cute. Thank goodness she had a line, courtesy of Santa Tony, for this little cowgirl.

In the meantime, she listened to more wishes for Hot Wheels, Barbies, crayons, plush animal toys, dollhouses, the new tape recorders, train sets, and transistor radios.

Then the little cowgirl and her sister were in her lap. *Who first?* Santa Katie wondered. Usually, siblings had the order worked out: oldest first, or most assertive. The kids knew, and Katie went along with it.

The cowgirl went first.

"Dear Santa," she said, as if she had written a letter and rehearsed it. "I want a real pony. I promise to take care of it and ride every day. I know they need to eat and they poop. I will take care of a real pony," she said, studying Katie's face, her eyes wide, imploring and questioning? Did she recognize Katie was not a man?

"Well, what is your name?" Santa Katie asked in her most masculine voice.

"Marsha," the girl answered.

"Marsha, when I was a child. A very, very long time ago. I wanted a pony too."

Both Marsha and her sister's eyes grew wide. They didn't expect Santa to have a childhood.

"I wanted a pony I could ride, but all I got were reindeer. A pony couldn't survive in the North Pole. No matter how much I wished. My reindeer are magical and fly me all over the world in one night. But I still can't ride them. Ponies need to live on a ranch, in the country. Maybe someday you will have that pony."

Marsha was both intrigued and crestfallen.

"And what is your name," Santa Katie asked her sister wearing a red plaid dress.

"Suzanne, and I want to meet the Beatles and be a famous singer," she said.

What focused little girls, my goodness.

"Well, how about some records?" Santa Katie asked.

"Of my own? Oh yes!" Suzanne said.

"Let's look at the camera and get a nice photo," Santa Katie said, pointing to Mrs. Parker with the camera. Photo done, she gave the sisters their candy canes.

"There is something different about you, Santa," Marsha said.

"Different from the other Santas," Suzanne agreed.

"Have a very Merry Christmas, Marsha and Suzanne," Santa Katie said, as they got off her lap and headed to the exit.

"Mom, Santa is a woman!" Marsha yelled out as she walked down the ramp.

Oh no! Santa Katie thought, glancing at Mrs. Parker. *What now?*

"Ho, ho, ho, Merry Christmas!" Santa Katie said in a booming voice, as if nothing were wrong, and the comment forgotten. And, so it was. It seemed mothers and children alike just wanted their Santa moment. How many of them really, truly believed in Santa anyway? Make the magic for just this time together.

More children, more Hot Wheels, Barbies, baby dolls, race cars, toy horses, Snoopy Astronauts.

What a lucky day for her so far; not a single accident in her lap.

"Merry Christmas, what is your name?" Santa Katie asked the little boy, maybe five by her estimation, as she lifted him into her lap.

"My name is Douglas."

Douglas was a pensive little boy and didn't jump right into his wish list, as most did. Santa Katie waited for him. He looked down at his hands in his lap.

"I'm glad you're here, Douglas. I'll bet you have been a very good boy."

Oh, no, was he going to cry? It was hard to tell with his long, dark hair hanging over his eyes. Had he been naughty? Pulled someone's hair at school?

"Santa, can you make Daddy love Mommy again?"

How was she to deal with this? She fought her own tears. Her brain searched for an answer that no one had. This precious little boy. Mouth dry, she gave him a hug, and reached for a tissue for him and her.

"Douglas, I wish I had such magic for grown-ups. I will pray with all my heart for you. You are such a good boy. Don't forget that."

Breaking the rule, she offered him the candy cane first, hoping to get a smile for the camera with such petty bribery.

"Shall we smile at the camera anyway, Douglas?" she asked, pointing.

"Can I have Hot Wheels?" he asked, looking at the camera.

"Hot Wheels will be fun," she said with a sigh, as a thin smile formed.

She needed a break. The line was very short, only three kids left. She signaled to Mrs. Parker to put up the sign behind those last three. "Santa will be taking a short break to feed his reindeer."

Only three children left. She could do this. *Pull yourself together, Kate. You're Santa Claus.*

Next, a mother and toddler came up together.

Santa Katie knew to speak softly and not reach too quickly for the little girl who clung to her mother, large, brown eyes brimming with tears.

"Patty, darling, would you like to sit in Santa's lap and tell him what you want?" Her mother coaxed.

Patty shook her head and buried her face in her mother's leg.

"How about if I kneel down next to you?" she asked, kneeling down next to Katie.

"Patty, would you like to stand here with your mother? You don't have to sit in my lap if you don't want to," Santa Katie said in a low, soft voice. "Your mother is right next to you."

These were the moments when this whole ritual seemed to fly in the face of not talking to strangers or taking candy from them. Isn't that the mantra she grew up with? Katie didn't know all the answers, and life could be so challenging for children.

"Patty, I would like to wish you a very Merry Christmas and give you a candy cane, just for coming up here to see me." She didn't smile, but as she took the candy, Katie saw the flash of the camera.

"What do you say, Patty?" her mother asked. "Will you thank Santa?"

"You're welcome," Patty said, confusing the order of the expressions.

"Santa, may we try for one more photo?" the mother asked. "Just one more. My husband is in Vietnam, and I would like to have a photo to send him as well."

Such pain, such bravery. Again, Santa Katie had no words for this family. She and the mother had tears in their eyes. Katie held up her finger and mouthed *one more, please,* to Mrs. Parker. Usually she took several photos, and the parents had a choice or could buy them all.

"Jingle bells, jingle bells, jingle all the way," Santa Katie sang, hoping that would be less threatening. Again, the camera flashed.

"Thank you, Santa," the mother said, lifting Patty into her arms for the walk down the exit ramp.

"Thank you; thank your husband," Santa Katie said, feeling numb in her inability to absorb the enormity of their plight. The news was full of war images. The protestors screaming to stop the baby killing. Here was this mother and this child. Katie's heart ached for the pain and isolation so many felt. Here and in Vietnam.

"Ma'am, excuse me. Ma'am," Santa Katie said. She wanted to get up and escort the family down the ramp, but the last child was already approaching, her hopeful face beaming at her turn to speak with Santa.

The mother and Patty looked back at her, and she motioned with a finger that they return.

"Please, it isn't much, but tell Mrs. Parker there is no charge for your photos. They are my treat."

"I can't," she said, more tears in her eyes.

"You can, you may. Please. Merry Christmas and bless you," Santa Katie said. *Bless you? What had come over her? You are a Mall Santa, not God.*

Santa Katie was trembling when the next smiling little girl climbed into her lap.

"Merry Christmas, and what would you like?"

"I like you. The last Santa I saw smelled like cigarettes," she said, her blue eyes sparkling with satisfaction.

"Smoking is a terrible thing," Santa Katie said. "No one should smoke, ever. Can you imagine how dangerous it would be if elves smoked in a toy shop?"

The girl laughed and nodded her head in agreement. "You don't look like a boy," she said, not getting to her wish list at all.

Kids these days, Katie thought. She was heartbroken from the stories of two of the families today, and now this bright, observant, non-believer who was still willing to play along with some Christmas magic.

"Well, I'm an elf. A very old and wise elf, and we are kind and loving."

"Does Mrs. Claus look like a man?"

What is this, Miracle on 34th Street *in 1969, with a modern, cynical Suzy?* This must be added to the Santa handbook. No wonder there are Santa schools. Sears should hire those guys next year.

"She is a beautiful soul, a grandmother or, rather, grandelf to all. But how about you? What would you like for Christmas?" She almost said Suzy. This break could not come soon enough, and as much as she needed a cup—two cups—of coffee, that was nearly impossible, because she couldn't get another bathroom break for ages, and this costume was hard to get in and out of.

"A spirograph, a big box of crayons, a princess gown, and ballerina costume," she said.

"Well, I will see what we can do. Let's smile at the camera."

She skipped down the exit ramp, candy cane held high for her waiting mother to see.

Cathy Elf was explaining to people that Santa would be taking a twenty-minute break but would return. They were disappointed, but the children waved, not wishing to be perceived as naughty this close to Christmas. Only two days left for the children. The two hardest days of the year ... maybe the day AFTER Christmas was the hardest day, it was all over until next year.

‹‹ ● ● ● ››

Christmas Eve

The windshield wipers beat a fast rhythm, the rain blurring the Christmas lights in an amazing kaleidoscope of festivity on the residential streets as Katie made her way home at nine. Still, she felt obligated to peer into the sky, as millions of children did, searching for Santa's sleigh. The magic of Santa. Hoax or Hope? All beneath a midwinter moon.

Physically, she was exhausted from the two hard weeks of work and tonight's initial clean-up in anticipation of packing up all the splendor post-Christmas. The office was left in a mess that was upsetting to her sense of order and completion. She was not required to return and do the hard teardown and packing of the photo shop on Christmas Day. Relief.

More fatiguing was the emotional strain she felt: her concern for her workmates. Where would their lives take them? Would Cindy stay and finish high school? What about Santa Bob's new job? The news was still riveting and polarizing, cancer wards and stranded travelers on top of the war and protests. Could there ever be peace on Earth? The children. Katie could not stop thinking about Douglas and Patty. How many other children were spending miserable Christmases in broken or damaged families? Even Mrs. Parker was a divorced woman with two boys, her own mother doing the lion's share of raising them, while Mrs. Parker tried to be the bread-winner and find time to be a mom.

This was not how Christmas Eve was supposed to be, she thought, remembering her idyllic childhood surrounded by a loving family. This is how Christmas Eve was for so many. *And you have a decision to make*, she reminded herself. Important decisions, yet so minor in the face of so much hurt and need. Christmas Eve, and her soul was not at peace. It was not a silent night; it was a holey night full of wounds and want.

As Katie walked into the house, her mother stood cleaning at the kitchen sink. A whole day was spent preparing for tomorrow's family gathering. Aunts, uncles and cousins, and Uncle John was bringing Granny. Her father was at the stove, wearing his traditional Christmas apron.

"Our own Santa Katie is home," he said in welcome. "And don't you look beat,"

"Thanks, Dad. I am. It smells wonderful in here. Thanks, Mom, you must be beat, too," she said, as she set down her purse and hung up her coat.

"You are home, Santa Claus is making his rounds, and I insist we take a quiet moment before tomorrow's storm of activity," her father said, pouring scalded milk into the little Tom and Jerry mugs. Another beloved family tradition—these hot eggnog-type drinks. She watched him add overflowing jiggers of rum and brandy to each.

"Honey, I'll never finish cleaning after that," her mother said, taking her mug with a grateful smile all the same.

They took their mugs into the living room and sat on the couch, the only illumination coming from the tree.

"Another hard day?" her mother asked, sipping her drink.

"Yes and no," Katie said. "I was busy. The mall was frantic. When did Christmas shopping become a contact sport?" she asked with a laugh. "I had such a day," she continued, taking a sip of the warm drink in her hands. "At least I didn't have to play Santa again." Through tears and laughter, she retold the events of her day as Sear's Santa, again sharing her grief for Douglas, Patty, and the many suffering families.

After much consoling by her parents, they finished their drinks in silence. Her mother got up to clean the mugs for tomorrow, and Katie got up to help her.

After her parents went to bed, Katie washed off her rosy cheeks, laid out her graduate school letters and the unpaid writing opportunity, with her byline, Kate Thorn. Each had merit, each had promise, each required an answer. It did not feel very festive, but she couldn't rest. She must decide.

Business degree, MA in social work, or writing.

Career, income, Ireland.

Then she picked up each one, individually, pressing the letter to her heart and her head as if some cosmic telepathic energy would speak to her and reveal the correct choice.

Laying out her writing paper, she picked up her pen.

Dear Santa, I want ...

·‹‹ ● ●›› ·

Anne M. Beggs is writing a family saga set in Medieval Ireland. Archer's Grace is Book One. "Dear Santa" is based on a true story that she couldn't let go of. Katie Bennett evolved as a college student grappling with her future. Modern Katie and 13th century Eloise are both filled with questions, compassion and long to make a difference in the world. For more about Anne, see her website, www.AnneMBeggs.com and follow her on Facebook, Instagram, Goodreads, or Bookbub.

·‹‹ ● ●›› ·

The Greatest Love

CHRISTMAS
BY MICHAEL L. ROSS

Belgium
May 1994

J ohn Pasi gingerly climbed from the cab, favoring his wounded leg. The taxi roared away. He leaned on his cane, staring at the Bierstube. He breathed in the pungent pine and delicate floral scents of the forest, contrasting them with the smell of burnt trees and flesh, gunpowder, and diesel of that Christmas fifty years ago. The flagstone path still led to the beer hall and inn. The scene felt unreal, leaving him between two worlds—the here and now with its peace, and the one from long ago, when artillery shells and machine gun fire exploded around him. His leg ached with the memory. There were differences, such as new buildings, the bomb craters filled in, new roads, and the railroad bridge transformed to permit cars—indications that life had resumed. It was much warmer than in December 1944.

He looked up the path to the inn and wondered for the hundredth time what he was doing here. He was too old for flights of fancy. He should be home, tending his vegetable garden and following the Red Sox. It would be different if Lisa, his wife, were still alive. They should be bouncing grandchildren, attending baseball games, and planning vacations. But a heart attack is a cruel thief, stealing happiness and life. Now, loneliness was a constant companion, etched into the lines of his face.

It was madness to think Marie could be alive. But... What if he didn't take the chance? The tiny flame of hope burst into a flame of longing. If she were here... He took crumpled stationery from his overcoat pocket, put on his reading glasses, and read the letter again. After all these years, he remembered how well she spoke English, but didn't know if this was her writing. Could someone be playing a game?

> John,
>
> Perhaps you won't remember me, but I have little time left to live, and I would like to tell you goodbye. We never got the opportunity all those years ago, and now time is running out. Doubtless, you are now married and have your own life. But I cannot leave this earth without letting you know how much you mean to me. Those few weeks during the war, when Giselle and I spent time with you, have lingered in my memory and my heart.
>
> I am still in Bastogne. Since I never heard from you after the war, perhaps you have forgotten me. Yet, I cherish the hope that those days also meant something to you. I hope this letter finds you. I spent many hours tracing your whereabouts through your Army. At first, as I feared, they told me you were dead. Then, a

friend of yours toured the battlefield here and told me about the Army mixing up your identity with another soldier, who died in a German prison camp. He gave me this address.

If you ever think of me, perhaps you can spare time for a letter. I have cancer and have only weeks left. It would mean a lot to me to know that you remember.

With great fondness,
Marie Bernard

It had to be a cruel joke. He'd watched the infirmary explode, engulfed in flames. He'd watched her fly through the air from the force of the blast and hit a brick wall, falling lifeless. The Germans loaded him onto a truck, wounded, and he was taken to a P. O.W. labor camp. Yet, here was this letter. If there was a chance... That's why he'd come, wasn't it? Sending a simple reply by post would never do. On the heels of Lisa's death, this letter arrived. He had to know. Ignoring the pain in his leg, he slowly hobbled up the path toward the Bierstube.

‹‹ ● ●› ›

Bastogne, Belgium
December, 1944

Marie drummed her dark fingers on the polished wooden table, looking out at the curtain of snow. After the long voyage from the Belgian Congo, her father insisted that she rest. She was used to caring for patients, listening to the woes of the Bantu village wives,

199

and playing with their children. Exhausted, she was happy to be home for Christmas with her family. Yet, where she had hoped for respite, the inactivity was more stressful to her than helpful. It left too much time to think, to remember Henri. After being in Africa for three years in the heat among her mother's people, this blizzard and the numbing cold were difficult to take. The storm meant their inn had few guests. She'd thought it safe to come home, now that the Allies controlled France. Everyone viewed the German collapse as only a matter of time.

"Marie, why do you look so morose? Aren't you happy to be home?"

"Yes, *Père*."

"Then why do you look like your best friend died? You should get Giselle and Andre, dance and live a little!"

Probably because my best friend did die! thought Marie. "No, thanks, Père. Seeing them as a couple makes me ache for Henri. I'll see Giselle at the clinic. It's a long walk in this cold. We haven't the petrol to drive." She was happy for her half-sister Giselle, but missing Henri stabbed at her heart.

"I'm sorry," *Père* said gently. "I just want to help you. You've only been home a few days, and now this storm."

He walked over and put his hands on Marie's shoulders, giving her a comforting touch.

"Giselle can't help being happy, with Andre back from the front. I know it's hard, but many women have to face the fact that their fiancés or husbands aren't coming home. None of the Jews the Boche took have returned. You can't hold on forever, waiting for Henri."

"I don't want to talk about it. This stupid war, the Boche, it's a blight that ruins everything." Tears ran freely down her face, and she turned to embrace her father. "I am glad to see you. It's just... I've spent three years being constantly busy, to forget about Henri. I know he's never coming back. But being here, I expect to see him coming up the flagstone walk, riding his bicycle to market, or calling *'Come, ma cherie! The day will not wait for us.'* I know you mean well, but I would rather stitch a wound than sit by the fire."

"I doubt the clinic has many patients right now. It's been quiet the last two months."

"What's that noise? It sounds like machines rolling in."

Her father went to the window and peered out through the snow. "It's American tanks. I'm surprised they are moving in this weather."

"Soldiers come and go. As long as they aren't German, we're fine," said Marie. "One advantage is that the tanks will pack down the snow, and make it easier to get to town on your clunky bicycle. The storm prevented me from going to the market."

·‹‹●●›·

The heavy truck following the line of tank destroyers skidded about on the ice-covered road, engine complaining in much the same fashion as the men it carried. John pulled the blanket tighter around him, sitting across from his buddy Dominic Romano. He took a Lucky Strike from the pack and lit it, letting the hot smoke give him an illusion of warmth.

"Hey Dom, where do you think they'll put us this time?"

"Dunno. At least we're heading in the right direction, away from the Krauts. Two weeks in Germany is enough for me. I hope it's a nice sleepy little village, with a fire, grub, beer, and dames—not necessarily in that order."

John smirked, handing Dom the cigarette. "You left out beds. Nice soft ones."

Dom chuckled, "You're dreaming, as usual. But it's a nice dream. Might as well add a gorgeous blonde, too."

"Nah. We won't be here that long. Rumor is, enough to rest

and then get back to the front. Maybe we'll all be home by summer, if Fritz knows what's good for him."

"Maybe. Guess we'll see. Home sounds pretty good right now. They'd be putting up Christmas decorations in south Philly."

The truck ground to a stop. John and Dom heard the Major's voice.

"All right, outta there, you ice cubes. Nap time's over. Pasi, Romano—you guys check that inn, make sure it's clear. See if it could be used as an aid station."

John and Dom ambled up the steps, across the flagstones, alert all around them for signs of trouble. There probably wasn't a Kraut within ten miles of here, but you couldn't be too careful. If it was safe, the Major might join them for a beer. John held his M1 carbine off the shoulder, scanning the trees to the left. Dom did the same on the right, but they saw nothing. Looking at the inn, John thought he saw a woman peering out of the window. When they got to the front door, a sign said "*Ferme*", meaning closed.

Dom lifted his eyebrows. "Whattya think?"

John banged the heavy door knocker by way of answer. "The man said to check it out. Can't do that from out here."

After a few minutes, a Black, medium-height woman with wavy, dark hair answered the door.

"*Oui*?" she said. In his best high school French, John responded, stammering a little.

"*Madame? Parles-tu anglaise?*"

"Yes, soldier, I speak English, at least after a fashion. What do you want?"

"I'm sorry to bother you, considering you're closed."

He noticed her eyes brightened and crinkled at the corners, amused at his embarrassment. His eyes swept down her slim figure and then met her gaze.

"Well? It's cold, soldier, and we have limited fuel. State your business."

"The Major wants us to take a look around, for the safety of the troops. If you don't mind…" John shifted his weight back and forth, and the motion swung the gun muzzle toward the woman. She reached out and pushed it away.

"In this war, things happen whether I mind or not—like people pointing guns at me."

"Oh, sorry, ma'am. I didn't mean…"

"Come in," she said, standing aside. "Might as well get it over with. Though, I assure you, no Boche are hiding in the closets or under the beds. Thank God, the Nazis are gone. We're pretty empty right now."

"Yes, ma'am. I'm Captain John Pasi, and my friend here is Lieutenant Dominic Romano."

"I'm Mademoiselle Marie Bernard. This is my father's *salle à bière*."

"We'll be as brief as possible."

John and Dom went in, silently reveling in the warmth. They dutifully searched every room, looking behind doors, under beds, and even back outside in the chicken coop, but found nothing unusual.

"Satisfied?" asked Marie.

"Yes, Mademoiselle. Thank you."

"Well, since you are our liberators, I should invite you to stay for dinner, but I fear what you have in your—what do you call it? K-rations?—is better than what we have. Food is scarce enough."

John looked her in the eye to see if she was sincere. Not everyone in Belgium welcomed them.

"If you're serious, do you know a farmer who might be willing to part with a cow or a pig? I grew up on a farm, and we could supply you with some meat. We'd pay the farmer, of course, American dollars."

"Many farmers have little left—it would cost you dearly. My father is a veterinarian, in addition to running the inn. He often knows of available animals. I think Monsieur Deveraux might still have a cow. The Germans will take it, anyway, if they come back. Two kilometers up the road, on the left, yellow house."

"Much obliged, Mademoiselle. We'll do our best to make sure they don't come back. I'll speak to the Major—if he agrees, you might have fifteen for dinner." John started to walk away, then turned back. "You do still have beer?"

Marie grinned. "Yes, we do, and wine that we hid from the Boche."

John touched his helmet, saluted her, and motioned for Dom to follow.

‹‹ ‹ ● › ››

She'd wanted something to do, Marie mused. Fifteen Americans to wait on provided that, along with some much-needed francs and dollars. The Americans were a scruffy lot. It reminded her of taking in a large number of mud-spattered little brothers. The tall one at her door with the black hair, the one who talked—John was it? He was handsome. She'd seen the red cross symbol on his helmet. A doctor, perhaps? All the Americans were tired, hungry, and hadn't been around a woman for months. She'd grown up waiting on tables and dodging men's advances, making light banter. This situation felt normal, except that she had to think in English to deal with them. The kitchen hummed with long absent activity, as Monsieur Deveraux's cow roasted on a spit, and she hopped with Giselle to keep the men's beer tankards full while tending the cooking. One or two tried their luck with hands that went beyond banter, but the Major and the one called John shut them down with a growl. She smiled and joked with them, touched by John's protectiveness. Maybe, one day, this war would pass, and the inn would be back to hosting guests. Maybe, someday, the ache in her chest where her love for Henri still throbbed would pass away, and her heart would open to new possibilities.

The men's snow-covered boots made a mess of the inn's polished floors, but that was the price of having business. They'd be gone soon enough, she supposed. Some of the men had chopped wood and started the blazing fire that warmed the dining hall, to everyone's visible relief, as outdoor temperatures hovered at near -20°C.

Giselle, her beautiful, blonde half-sister, laughed and flirted with the men, slapping away a few hands as well. Marie had called Giselle to help with the meal. Marie knew Giselle was completely taken with Andre. The flirting meant nothing; a habit they'd learned as girls to keep customers coming back.

When the meal was over and cleared away, she saw John go to the corner and pick up the guitar leaning against the wall. She sucked in a breath—no one had played it since Henri was taken, three years ago. It sat in the corner, a silent reminder of its missing owner. Marie wanted to rush over and take it from him, but when he strummed the opening of the carol, *"He is born, the Divine Christ Child,"* she surprised herself with a feeling of longing, rather than anger. Their eyes met in a glance of warmth. Before long, the hall rang with bass and tenor voices, singing carols. Marie and her family joined the familiar tunes, mixing French and English in a celebration of peace.

A loud drone of engines stilled the singing, followed by an explosion. The men were on their feet and back outside to their trucks and tanks in seconds. The guitar lay forgotten on the table, with the sounds of carols replaced by machine gun fire. It had to be an air raid. Marie and her family crouched under tables. When there was a break in the firing, they sprinted to the basement for protection.

‹‹ ❬ ● ❭ ››

John and Dom ran for their troop truck, as others manned machine guns pointing up at the sky. Their best option was to get moving, to find cover. The Luftwaffe might return for another pass on the column. The trucks accelerated, heading for the main part of town, then again screeching to a halt as everyone jumped out, passing sandbags, setting up machine gun nests, and getting the trucks under cover. The cold bit into John's hands like a hungry wolf, but he had no time to pay attention. The planes did swing back around. The troops all jumped for cover—but this time they had defenses. Dom pointed a machine gun skyward and managed to shoot one down, watching as it exploded in flames.

After the skirmish was over, John and Dom helped carry the wounded on stretchers to the local clinic. The little hospital bustled with twenty patients, both civilian and military. The sun and the temperature dipped. John was surprised to see their waitress, Marie Bernard, busily moving among the beds, treating wounds and offering encouragement. He caught her eye, and she smiled before turning back to the shrapnel gash she was stitching. Then, he lost her in the hubbub as he returned to the outdoors, digging foxholes after thawing the frozen ground with flamethrowers. One man had the idea of exploding buried grenades to make foxholes more quickly.

Marie's face popped into his mind again. Obviously, she was more than a waitress. He told himself again that they'd only be here a short while, just like Paris. He'd resisted the overtures of women there. She was awfully pretty, though. She seemed smart and confident. After the letter from home, telling him his girl was leaving him... Nah, what was he thinking? He probably wouldn't even have time to get to know her, if he even saw her again. But, if he did, maybe he could offer her a ride back to the inn.

Dawn simply changed the shade of gray in the clouds, without real light getting through. The foxholes now had a few inches of snow in the bottom. Some soldiers pulled camouflaged plywood over the top for warmth, leaving only a slot open. John didn't see how anyone could sleep in this icebox. John poked Dom to wake him. The night had been quiet. He looked around and saw no threats. He pulled himself up out of the hole, M1 slung over his shoulder, just in time to see Marie coming down the steps of the clinic, yawning.

"You're a welcome vision for a guy to see in the morning." John smiled at her.

"If you slept in that foxhole all night, it's a wonder you aren't frozen," Marie said.

"Do you have a ride home, or are you staying in town?" asked John.

She hesitated, then said, "I planned to bike back to my parents'."

John saw an opportunity. "How about a Jeep, instead? We can throw your bicycle in the back."

"All right."

John spoke to another soldier, and within a minute, they were rolling back toward the Bierstube. Ordinarily, he wouldn't be so forward, but he decided that time was not on his side.

"Marie, I saw you taking care of the men in the clinic."

"I'm a nurse—it's what I do."

"I want to thank you—you're smart and beautiful." John felt

awkward. "Are you... married, or engaged? I'd like to get to know you better."

"I'm flattered. No, I am neither married nor engaged. I... I had a young man, Henri, but he was Jewish, and the Germans took him some time ago. I don't know if he will ever come back. But I don't do *une affaire de cœur*. It isn't easy for me. I'm not that kind of girl. You'll be gone soon. I would rather we remained friends."

"Oh. I understand. I meant no offense."

She smiled. "None taken. It's just that when you played the guitar the other day, it was Henri's guitar. No one has touched it since the SS took him. It stirred memories."

"I apologize. I thought Christmas music might cheer everyone, before a night in the cold."

"It was nice—it felt like Christmas might come this year. When the Boche were here, I thought it would never be Christmas again. It reminded me of going to Mass."

"It's hard to think of peace on Earth in the middle of the war. Someday..."

"Someday, there will be a midwinter moon, with no bombers flying under it."

·‹‹ ● ● ›·

December 16, 1944

Marie bicycled the next day, retrieving eggs from Giselle, checking on patients at the clinic, and posting letters to her friends in the Congo. Fog rolled in, obscuring the familiar roads, and with it, more snow. The cold reached out to strangle anyone bold enough to venture out in it. Marie came to a crossroads with three paths forking out of it. Truck and tank tracks were everywhere, making it difficult in the dense fog to tell where the right road was. The snow grew deeper, and she became disoriented. The bicycle wasn't helping. She dismounted and leaned it against a tree, preferring to walk. After perhaps an hour, knowing she should have been at Giselle's by now, she saw a form advancing toward her in the fog. As it grew closer, the figure appeared to carry a rifle —a soldier. She debated hiding, but she was thoroughly lost, and freezing to death didn't seem a good option. She walked closer. *I'll ask for directions,* she thought. The form resolved into an American soldier, who startled and pointed his rifle at her.

"Halt! *Arret!*"

"Please, I'm lost. I'm Marie Bernard. I live in Bastogne. I want to find my sister. I got lost in the storm. Can you point me back to Bastogne? Here are my papers."

The soldier glanced at them. "Ma'am, I don't know about your sister, but Bastogne is that way," he said, pointing. "About a mile straight down that path, you'll come to a stone church. You should be able to find your way from there. Get moving though— there's a lot of Krauts coming."

Marie was about to thank him when a shot rang out, and the soldier crumpled, bloodstains spreading across his chest. She froze, then looked around wildly to see where the shot came from, but the fog was a shroud. She knelt in the snow to see if she could help the soldier. She'd gotten his uniform open when a bullet pierced his helmet. Blood and brain matter splashed the front of her dress, and behind her, the sound of tanks and tracked vehicles rumbled through the fog. The Boche were here.

·‹‹ ● ● ● ● › ›·

John and Dom peered through the fog—there were reports of fighting, and they'd been ordered north of Bastogne to Noville. Dom used his gift of bartering and talked to units and civilians they met on the way, scoring a case of cognac for a case of Lucky

Strikes. John shook his head—it seemed Dom could conjure supplies from nothing, if he had something to trade.

"This isn't such a bad war," Dom said. "Did you see that brunette nurse in the aid station? Oo la la!"

"You mean the squeamish one that disappeared whenever there was blood? Renee something?"

"Yeah, her! She could sew me up any time. And the people seem so glad to see us; they're willing to trade anything. I even scored a pair of nylons for her."

John shook his head and grinned. "I think you should concentrate on not needing to get sewn up. I need you to get more sulfa and morphine. Save the nylons for after."

Dom looked ahead. "Can't see anything in this damn fog. You wonder if the fighting is just Fritz being lost, or if there's something to it?"

"General McAuliffe wouldn't call us to Noville for a Christmas party. And you'd better keep that cognac hidden. I hear he's kind of a hard ass—chewed out a soldier for how his tie was done in the middle of a mortar attack."

"I ain't puttin' anything in his stocking! We'll change the box to say hydrogen peroxide."

"Hey, what's that over there? About ten feet ahead..."

"It looks like a dame! Sprawled out on the ground. Hey, Private!" Dom called the driver of their half-track. "Stop a minute."

"Sir, with all due respect, that might be a decoy to get us to stop. And the general said to deliver you docs stat."

John didn't hesitate. "My authority, soldier. Stop and man the machine gun. Dom, get your rifle and be ready."

John looked around and, seeing nothing, dismounted the half-track and went to the figure in the snow. He took off his gloves and turned the woman over on her back. She was breathing. Her pulse felt thready. No telling how long she'd been there. Blood drenched the snow where her right shoulder had lain. She was probably in shock, with hypothermia setting in. With a jolt, John recognized her as Giselle, Marie's half-sister. What was she doing out here? As he dug around to lift her, his hand struck metal—a Luger. He grabbed it and hoisted her, carrying her to the half-track.

"Dom, help me get her in. Can't leave her out here, though it looks like someone did. We can't stay here."

Once Giselle was inside the M3, John crouched on the floor and checked her—the bleeding had stopped from the cold. It appeared to be mainly a flesh wound. The bullet had passed all the way through.

"Dom, gimme sulfa and some of that cognac."

John treated the wound, dressing it with a bandage, then covered her with several blankets to warm her. The half-track started again, and Giselle moaned as the bumps jostled her wound.

"How much farther?" yelled John.

"Should be about two clicks," replied the driver.

John cursed the rattling terrain and the slow speed of travel and prayed. Could she survive that long? What would he tell Marie if she didn't? He heard the crash and explosion of artillery shells, and what sounded like German .88s and machine gun fire. They were heading into hell, rather than running away from it.

·《 ● ● 》·

Marie reached the safety of the church as artillery shells landed all around her. Those in the church let her in, closing the doors in haste. She found the parish priest huddled with a few others in the basement. It was at least some protection from flying shrapnel. The earth quaked and rumbled under the onslaught of German tanks, all around the church, and they heard harsh German voices yelling commands. Marie trembled. The Boche hated Blacks. How long before she was found? Would they ship her to a camp like Henri this time? Was the Bierstube still standing? And what about Giselle? She had some involvement with the resistance; was she staying at home in the cellar, like a sensible person? Marie had never been in combat before. Her hands trembled, remembering the American soldier whose blood still coated her dress. He'd died before she had a chance to help. Was that all she could do in this storm, hide and hope not to be found?

Marie spent the night in the basement, alternating between fear and frustration. The Germans had bypassed the church without looking inside. In the morning, Marie and the priest peered out a basement window into the snow and fog, but couldn't tell whether the Germans were completely gone. Marie opened the door to the upstairs and tiptoed to an outside window. Seeing nothing threatening, she opened the door.

"Father Delvaux, can you point me in the direction of Bastogne, Ecole Street? I will return to my house and wait for word from my sister, rather than trying to go on."

The priest looked outside and considered, then gave her directions. "Promise me you'll hide if you see more Boche. They will kill you."

"I promise, Father."

He pressed rosary beads into her hand. "Go with God, child."

Marie debated how to travel, but then, seeing an abandoned bicycle, she mounted and pedaled through the snow toward town. The German vehicles had packed the snow.

"God, protect me and give my feet speed," she prayed. She clutched the rosary in her left hand and prayed the Our Father, continuing as she rode. When she reached home, her father came to greet her.

"Marie! I'm glad you're back. We were worried! The Boche are everywhere. Giselle is hurt and in the infirmary—that nice doctor sent word—and he said that if you're willing, you can go help the wounded. There aren't enough nurses. Maybe, if you help the Americans, they will protect you from the Boche."

"Giselle! What happened? How badly is she hurt?"

"Her resistance cell tried to stop the Germans. I didn't know she was going. They shot her in the shoulder. The doctor, John, and his friend, Dom, found her in the snow and brought her back to town. I'm sure he saved her life."

"Then I must go. If the Boche are back, you must hide everything you can."

"The phones aren't working, and power is flickering. Please send word about Giselle when you can."

Marie's heart thudded in her chest, heavy with worry for Giselle. Just as she closed the door of the Bierstube, a Jeep pulled up.

"Lieutenant—Dom—what are you doing here?"

"John sent me to ask if you're willing to come and help nurse soldiers. We brought in several wounded in addition to your sister. And bring any medical supplies you might have—bandages, sulfa, morphine, anything."

"I haven't much, but what I have is here," she said, pointing to her bag. "I'll come."

"Then don't worry about the bike—hop in and let's go."

Arriving back at the aid station, Marie ran to the ward.

"Giselle, how bad is it? Let me see." Marie peered at the bandaged shoulder and tried lifting her sister's hand. Giselle winced, and Marie gently let her hand back down.

"It's all right. The doctor said if I rest and don't try to use it, it should heal fast."

"I should go see him."

Marie searched the lines of pallets, wrinkling her nose at the smells of gangrene, urine, and body odor, eyes scanning for John.

She found him kneeling over a patient, feeling the back of his head. One of the soldier's eyes was dilated and unequal to the other.

"Anybody got a corkscrew?" called John.

An orderly nearby produced one. John poured alcohol over it, and screwed it into the patient's skull, causing a geyser of blood.

"Hold him here, will you?" said John to Marie.

She did, as blood coated her dress. After a few seconds, the blood flow stopped. Marie cleaned the wound and sutured it. John looked at her briefly and grinned. "We make a good team." They moved to the next patient and the next, without stopping, for hours. Outside, they could hear explosions as artillery proclaimed no peace on earth. A stream of corpsmen came in carrying more wounded. Marie and John worked together as if in a dance, where he led the treatment and she held, poked, and stitched as he cut and sawed. Without power, they worked by candlelight. They didn't speak more than necessary, but each grew in appreciation of the other's skill. Marie watched as John removed frostbitten toes and feet, extracted shrapnel and bullets, and cut out damaged organs. As he learned more about her skills, he left more of the sewing, sterilizing, and cleaning to her. Once or twice, she almost gagged and threw up, but she controlled it. Her fingers and back ached from the cold and constant crouching and sewing. Her arms felt numb after holding down so many soldiers without ether. When there was a short pause, Marie touched John's arm and got his attention.

"Thank you for saving my sister. Giselle is foolhardy at times, but she hates the Boche."

John shrugged. "As you say, it's what we do. You saved many lives this morning working with me. You're a good nurse."

She looked into his eyes as they stood together and, without thinking, wrapped him in her arms and gave a tentative kiss on his cheek.

·‹ ‹ ● ● ● › ›·

John had little time to think about her kiss. Two corpsmen came in carrying a stretcher—and they went back to work. As he opened the chest wound, one of the corpsmen said, "Doc, there's a group of about five paratroopers up the road that are in a bad way. I don't know how much longer they'll last—they're under heavy fire, and three were wounded when I left them."

"Do you have transport?" asked John.

"Yeah, got a half-track waiting."

"I'll be done here in about fifteen minutes. I'll need a nurse." He saw Renee at a nearby pallet. "How 'bout you, Renee? Willing to go out?"

Renee turned her back to him. "I have plenty of patients here."

Marie said, "I'll go. It's the least I can do."

"Are you sure?" asked John.

"I care for patients wherever there is a need. You wanted a nurse."

They finished taking the shrapnel out of the soldier, and Marie sewed him up. John gave instructions to an orderly, and then, they both followed the corpsman and a paratrooper toward the truck.

John stopped and yelled to Dom, "Hey, Dom! Why don't you come along? Sounds like multiple victims, and maybe not much time."

Dom joined them piling into the half-track.

About five kilometers outside Bastogne, they saw a copse of trees at the top of a hill, and muzzle flashes from guns in the surrounding forest. They got out onto the snow, crawling to the trees.

Five men lay on the ground, so they spread out, checking for signs of life. The first two, John decided, were too far gone. He closed their eyes and said a prayer. The next was a head wound.

John gave morphine, and Marie bandaged it as well as she could.

"Marie, can you get the litter from the half-track?"

Dom and the paratrooper had maintained a lookout. Mortar shell explosions grew closer as the Germans zeroed in on them. As Marie returned, the snow kicked up around her feet on each side from machine gun fire. She flattened herself on the snow behind a tree and waited. When there was another break, she finished dragging the litter over to John, assisting him to lift the wounded man onto it.

John busied himself stabilizing the last of the five soldiers. When he looked up, he saw that Marie had moved to the back side of the hill and was examining two more soldiers. They hadn't noticed them before because of their white uniforms against the snow, but now, he saw the spreading bloodstains.

·‹‹ ● ● ›·

Marie crawled with her medical kit down to the two in white. She assumed they were American, but when she was a few feet away, she saw the Wehrmacht markings. One groaned and lifted a hand. Marie paused, thinking, *Germans! But they are helpless. In this cold, they won't last an hour.* She lay still for a moment, both to avoid detection and to pray, making up her mind. She could leave them—no one would know. Except that she would know, and God would know. She couldn't see any weapons, but that didn't mean they weren't there.

"John! There's two more wounded," she called. "But they're Boche. What should we do?"

"Check them out. Someone will cover you." He motioned to

the paratrooper, who turned his M1 carbine to offer covering fire to Marie if needed.

Marie crawled closer to the downed German soldiers. One didn't move and looked dead. She held the wrist of the other, checking his pulse. His eyes flew open, and he stared at Marie, shouting, "*Geh weg von mir! Fass mich nicht an!*" and pulled his arm away, then in English "Dirty Black!"

The firing above stopped. Marie saw John walking toward her, having loaded the other surviving soldiers. He carried both his medical kit and his .45 service pistol.

"Marie, we have to go before they start firing again."

The German soldier looked at the red cross on John's helmet, and addressed him, "Please, I'm wounded."

"I can see that. I don't have time to treat you here, because of your buddies on the other side of the hill. Marie can patch you up enough for transport."

"No! I won't have a Black touching me. No *Schwarze* can care for soldiers of the Reich!"

John grimaced and said, "Then, you'll die here in the snow. I'm a doctor, but I can't risk my other patients for you. C'mon, Marie, we need to leave now!"

"John, you know they'll die. We can't just leave them."

John looked heavenward and sighed.

"All right. Dom!" John yelled. "Search these two for weapons. Let's get them loaded and get the hell out of here. Marie, get back to the half-track—and watch it. Those bastards in the forest may still fire on us."

John saw her sprint for the half-track. No one fired. Turning back to the Germans, he pointed the pistol at them and watched Dom and the paratrooper load the German who had talked to them. After the way they had spoken to Marie, John noted with some satisfaction that Dom was none too gentle. Within five minutes, they were on their way back to Bastogne.

Mortar shells began exploding around them as the Germans noticed the vehicle moving toward American lines. The paratrooper pushed the gas pedal to the floor, fishtailing some, even with the tank treads, but the M3 wasn't built for speed. Ahead of them, out of the forest, a German Panther IV tank pulled into the roadway, the main gun pointed squarely at them.

"Sir, I can't go too fast, but I can outrun that," said the paratrooper. "Let me reverse and go around them. They can't swivel that gun as fast as I can move."

"No, just stop. I'll talk to them. We're medical personnel transporting wounded. The Geneva Convention protects us."

Dom slammed a hand on the side of the vehicle. "John, don't you learn? That hole in your helmet through the cross—the sniper didn't give a rat's ass about the Geneva Convention."

They were out of time. The paratrooper followed orders, stopping. A German Kubel, like a jeep, roared up behind the half-track.

"*Raus!* Everyone come out slowly. No weapons. You are our prisoners," yelled a German officer. John went first, hands up, leaving his pistol in the half-track, followed by Dom, the paratrooper, and last, Marie. They clambered down beside the vehicle into the biting cold and snow.

John spoke for them, "We are a medical team. We are bringing the wounded to the hospital. The Geneva Convention says we're to go free and undisturbed."

The officer with the lightning bolts on his lapel seemed unimpressed. "You say you're a doctor?"

"I am a doctor, and we have several wounded in the track, including two of yours. We're trying to get them to treatment."

The officer motioned to a soldier, who climbed up and examined the interior of the M3.

"*Er spricht richtig,*" said the soldier, nodding at the officer.

John moved closer, offering his identification. From the corner of his eye, he saw Dom edge out of line, toward the half-track's far side.

"Your men are in critical condition. If you just let us proceed, they'll be well treated."

The officer motioned to two of his men, who went to the rear of the track and pulled out the two German soldiers, moving them to the Kubel.

Dom used the diversion, everyone watching the transfer of the soldiers, to climb up to the machine gun turret of the track, staying low.

The officer looked them over, considering, "But, perhaps I should keep you—we need doctors." Then he pointed at Marie. "What is she doing with you? She can't be medical personnel."

"She is a qualified nurse and my personal assistant. I assure you she is medical personnel."

The officer laughed and said, "I don't believe you. That means you are no doctor, except perhaps a witch doctor. No *Schwarze* could be a nurse."

He lifted the flap on his holster as if to draw his pistol.

Dom stood and said, "I wouldn't do that if I were you. You may get me—your tank friend may get all of us, but I promise, you'll go first." Dom aimed the machine gun straight at the officer, thumbs on the butterfly trigger.

John felt his stomach clench—but Dom was right.

"We can all die here," said John. "Or you can be a man of honor, observe the convention, and let us go."

The German officer's face tensed and then, he said, "I was trained and served with Field Marshall Rommel in North Africa. He taught us that we should always treat prisoners the way we would want to be treated. Take your wounded and go." He turned to the driver of the Kubel and said, *"Funken Sie den Panzer an. Sag ihnen, sie sollen zurücktreten, meine Autorität."*

John wasn't sure what that meant but noticed that, after a minute, the tank backed into the forest, and the Germans got into their Kubel. Marie, John, and the paratrooper got back into the M3 and sped toward Bastogne.

· ‹‹ ● ● ● › ›·

When they arrived at the aid station and unloaded the wounded, John felt Marie tug at his sleeve. He turned to face her. She took both his arms in her hands.

For a second, they looked at each other, eyes locked.

John tried to lighten the moment. He looked down and saw holes in Marie's gabardine nurse uniform. They were machine gun bullet holes.

"Looks like they almost got you. I'm glad they didn't."

"John, I want to thank you. You and Dom saved my life back there. You could have given me up to them."

"I would never do that. Looks like you need a new dress, though."

Marie laughed. "I guess I do."

"That was close."

"Oh, the Boche are just bad shots. If they wanted to hit me, this black face against white snow makes a pretty good target."

John reached out and enveloped her in a bear hug. He pushed back the urge to let tears escape for this woman who selflessly served others. For a few moments, time stood still as they embraced each other. Then he let go and turned back to the room full of patients, people who needed their skills.

‧‹ ‹ ● ● ● › ›‧

Food, medical supplies, and water grew scarcer. When John emerged from the closet where he'd caught a few hours of sleep, he noticed Marie in an Army uniform, complete with boots, pants with front pockets on the legs, and a medical armband. She smiled at him and went on working. He noticed Renee was already at work, too.

He grabbed coffee and K-rations and stepped outside. The air still stank of gunpowder, blood, and peroxide wafting from the aid station as he lit up a Lucky Strike, but the sun was a welcome surprise. The fog had lifted—and he heard the buzz of aircraft. Looking up, he could see American C47s and cargo planes. The sky filled with different colored parachutes. There were red, green, yellow, blue, pink, and white, the colors signifying the type of items dropped—medicine, food, ammunition, fuel—supplies of all types. As John watched, a white parachute floated down about fifty feet away. On impulse, he walked over to it and cut the fabric loose from the strings, using a bolo knife. He'd heard Renee voicing disappointment that she was always too late to get to a white parachute—the aid packages attracted a crowd. Dom told him she wanted it as fabric for a wedding dress. Once it was loose, he rolled it up and took it back with him to the aid station—he would surprise her and Dom with it for Christmas. White was the color for medical supplies, so he went back and hefted the footlocker into the aid station. People were emerging from shelters everywhere to collect the dropped supplies.

The air soon filled with the sounds of German anti-aircraft fire, short pauses followed by a loud pop, with puffs of smoke. He sent medical orderlies out to collect other supplies that had fallen from the sky. When he opened the box, Marie came over. Their hands touched briefly as they sorted the morphine, bandages, and other items. John caught the affection in her gaze but didn't acknowledge it verbally. Patients were waiting.

‹‹ ❬ ● ❭ ››

December 22, 1944

Word spread through the city, house to house—the Germans were demanding surrender. The town was surrounded. The Germans threatened total annihilation, with tanks, artillery, and bombing. The artillery shells stopped coming, and the flow of wounded into the aid station paused.

"If you have been on shift for more than twelve hours, get some food and sleep," John ordered. "There's no telling what may happen."

John took advantage of the lull to drive to another aid station and see how they fared, then stopped at Heintz Barracks, General McAuliffe's headquarters. The guards asked about his business but seemed jubilant.

"What're the smiles about? I could use something merry for Christmas," asked John.

"Word is, the General sent his answer to the Krauts—one word—NUTS!" grinned the guard.

"Nuts, huh?" John smiled back. "Wonder what they'll make of that. I better get back to my unit, in case they figure it out."

John arrived back at the aid station and found it all quiet. Two corpsmen made the rounds of patients and reported that Marie had gone home to get some sleep. John used the time to inventory and organize their supplies, in anticipation of more casualties.

Within a few hours, the ground began to shake. Artillery shells hit surrounding buildings. He prayed Marie's house would be safe.

‹‹●●››

December 24, 1944

Snow fell in fluffy clouds, and a scratchy wind-up gramophone in the corner of the aid station belted out Bing Crosby's *White Christmas*. The snow covered the scars of mortar and artillery craters. A few straggling Christmas decorations flapped in the arctic air. It wasn't much warmer inside than out, as supplies again ran low.

The wounded poured in as fast as the snowflakes fell. Renee and Dom were almost full-time on triage, prioritizing treatment, and comforting those who would obviously die. There was no time to write to the families of the dead—that would have to come later. Another doctor flew in by glider, and John was delighted with the extra pair of hands. He tended the cases of frostbite, trench foot, and minor gunshot or shrapnel wounds, because they would help more soldiers and get them back into combat by treating those than by spending two hours on a chest wound.

Renee was everywhere, a constant source of smiles and cheer. She gave the soldiers chocolate, teased them about their girlfriends, and listened to their stories of home. John suspected Dom was responsible for finding most of the chocolate, but it kept morale high. He reminded himself that both Renee and Marie were volunteers. They didn't have to be here.

In a supply closet, he had a brown paper package for Renee with her white parachute. He'd found a women's Army greatcoat for Marie as a Christmas present. Renee had scrounged an artificial Christmas tree from her father's hardware store, decorated with tin foil and surgical scissors, with other odds and ends. The cognac was gone, used as an antiseptic.

Toward the end of the day, Dom called from the doorway to the outside.

"Hey, John! Come out for a minute. I found you a present."

"I hope it's more morphine." He motioned to a corpsman to finish cleaning the chest wound he'd just closed. At the back of the aid station, near the few windows, he could see Marie sewing up a shrapnel wound. Renee went into the makeshift kitchen. Going over to Dom, he saw that he had a small wooden barrel and two wine glasses, no doubt "requisitioned" from an empty house.

He stepped outside and accepted the glass of champagne Dom handed him.

As he brought it to his lips, he heard the sound of many airplane engines, dim at first, and then growing louder. John assumed it must be another C47 drop. But then, there was the sound of machine gun fire, followed by incendiary bombs and explosions, turning the dark into day. Dom raced to bring a truck around as the aid station caught fire.

"Let's get the worst wounded into the truck. At least they won't burn to death in there," he said. "We can move them somewhere safe."

John dropped the champagne and moved to help. Renee and Dom started loading men onto the flatbed truck, after pulling it around back, closer to a door. Marie joined in, this time ignoring the protests of the men who didn't want to be touched by a Black woman. Breathless, raising puffs of air in the cold, they carried men out, one after another, urging those who could walk to move. The smoke from the fires grew thicker, along with their coughing.

Then, there was a new sound, a guttural roar John recognized as German heavy bombers.

Marie and Renee had just reentered the building. Dom sped

away with the wounded. Then, an explosion knocked John over, and he felt an intense pain in his leg as a shard of metal pierced it. He looked down to see metal sticking out of his calf and blood flowing. The aid station flew apart in fragments—brick, stone, glass. He saw Marie fly through the air and hit a brick wall as it disintegrated. Then, all went dark.

·‹ ‹ ● ◉ ● › ›·

When John awoke, he was in the back of a German troop truck, lying on the bed as it bumped down the road. There were other wounded POWs in the truck, and he felt in his pockets for morphine and bandages. He felt as though he would pass out again, but fought for consciousness. He pulled on the side of the truck to a sitting position. He found he still had bandages in his pockets and worked the piece of shrapnel out of his leg. He was sweating despite the cold. With his leg bandaged, he sat puffing clouds of steam for a few minutes, gathering strength. Then he remembered... Marie! She must be dead.

·‹ ‹ ● ◉ ● › ›·

Bastogne, Belgium
May 1994

John came to himself, urging his aged body up the flagstone path. He let the heavy knocker fall, as he had fifty years ago. *Can't find out from out here,* he remembered. He waited, perhaps five minutes, and then knocked again.

"*Minute papillon!*" an irritated voice came from the interior.

225

When the door opened, an old woman, once blonde but now mostly gray, answered, "*Oui?*"

"Do you speak English? Are you Giselle?"

"John? John Pasi? Is it you, after all these years?"

"Yes." He held out Marie's letter. "I got this... is Marie still alive?"

"Yes, yes, she is. But she's not here. The hospital sent her to hospice care. She will be wild with excitement to see you. I must warn you—she's very weak. You mustn't stay too long, but I will take you. Let me get my bonnet. An old woman like me can't stand too much sun."

John followed her to her car. His heart pounded, and his mouth went dry. She was alive! After half a century, what would he say to her?

John turned to Giselle as she drove. "I'm surprised you even remember me."

She snorted. "Not remember the man who picked me out of the snow and saved my life? Of course, I remember. We both look a little different, that's all."

"And you think Marie will remember, too?"

"Think? She's been in love with you ever since the war. She's never forgotten, not even for a minute. When the army said you were dead, she went into mourning. Eventually, she married and had a son."

They pulled into a parking lot, and John followed Giselle to the door.

"What... What do I say? I've thought she was dead all these years... She looked for me, but I didn't look for her. I was married too—I have a son—my wife died recently."

"She may not want to talk much about the war. After you were captured, they pulled her out from the rubble—only a hand was sticking up. When they looked for survivors, her fingers moved, hadn't frozen yet. Sometimes, she still has nightmares. Just be there. It's all she's wanted for years."

A nurse checked and told them Marie was awake. Giselle opened the door.

"I'll leave you two alone. Marie, he's come. John."

"John? Is it really you?"

He looked down at the gray hair with tinges of the old color, straightened from former days, spread out on the pillow. The creases on her neck and face showed her age, but her dimples were still there—and the eyes! The eyes showed her excitement, her humor, her love—just like the Marie he knew. She lifted bony hands and clasped his between them. Her face broke into a wide smile.

"Yes, Marie. I've come. I got your letter. I couldn't just write to you. I'm sorry... so sorry. All these years—I had no idea. After that night, that Christmas Eve, I thought..."

"I know. I thought you were dead, too. One of the corpsmen who was there that night told me about you. He got captured, too. He came back to see where it all happened. All that matters is you're here."

"Giselle told me—you lost your husband. My wife died."

"Shh... It doesn't matter, John. I've always loved you."

She coughed, spasming, and wiped away the blood.

"Those days... meant a lot to me, too. Is it really too late?" asked John.

"I've hung on, in case you wrote to me. I never expected you would come. Hold my hand?"

John gently grasped her hand and stroked it. He sat with her, watching her labored breathing, looking into her eyes when they were open.

"I don't want to trouble you, but I can't help remembering that last night. You and Renee, running back into that building on fire. Pulling out men who weighed more than you. I wanted to grab you, to tell you not to go back."

She shrugged. "I would have anyway. Renee didn't make it. So many died. But God spared me, to see you again."

"There is no greater love than to lay down your life for your friends," John whispered.

He gently kissed her cheek, as she had done to him decades earlier.

As he watched, her eyes closed, and she seemed to sleep. Giselle returned.

"We should go now. You can stay at the inn. We can come back tomorrow."

·‹‹●●●››·

When they returned the next morning, the nurse met them at the door.

"I'm sorry, but your sister passed away last night. When we checked her at midnight, she was gone."

John turned to Giselle and they embraced each other, John's face wet with tears.

·‹‹●●●››·

Author's Notes

Most of this story is true and happened to real people. I am indebted to Martin King and his two non-fiction books, *Voices of Bastogne* and *Searching for Augusta,* that compiled the interviews, diaries, and stories of so many soldiers that lived through the Battle of the Bulge.

John Pasi is based on the real-life Captain John "Jack" Prior, who wrote down his experiences. His son gave Martin King his father's diaries and notes. While much has been written about "The Angel of Bastogne," Renee Lemaire, and there is no intent to minimize her contributions, there was another Angel, who has gone largely unrecognized, Augusta Chiwy. The character of Marie Bernard is based on Augusta, the "Black Angel of Bastogne." Augusta did everything this story portrays, willingly going into harm's way as a volunteer when Renee refused, yet, Augusta was despised because of the color of her skin. Both U.S. and German troops alike sometimes refused to let her treat them. John Prior did defend her in these cases.

Some changes were made for the sake of the story. Augusta went to Belgium much earlier than depicted, after her mother died in the Congo. Her father was a veterinarian and a man of influence. He secured her education and admission to nursing school, despite her mixed race. She jokingly said she chose nursing because it was the one place where she could give orders to a white man and not get in trouble.

Giselle is fictional—Augusta had a white brother, Charles, who was involved in the French Resistance.

Dom Romano is based on Irving Lee Naftulin, who served with Jack and was a Jewish dentist. There wasn't a lot of tooth-pulling in the Battle of the Bulge, so he used his medical training to help Jack.

Medical personnel in WW2 were not usually armed. However, in the heat of battle, many things happened that weren't in the rule books. Jack did get a hole in his helmet, though marked with a red cross, from a German sniper. He had lifted it from his head for a short time after being advised the Germans were sighting in on it.

Jack wasn't captured. After Hitler himself ordered the air raid on Christmas Eve, Jack was the one who pulled both Augusta and Renee from the rubble of the aid station. Augusta's hand was sticking out of the bricks that covered her, and Jack again saved her life. Renee was literally cut in half by the blast, and Jack delivered her body to her parents, wrapped in the parachute he'd meant as a Christmas gift for her. Renee had wanted the parachute to make a wedding dress. Renee had a relationship, not with the Jewish dentist, but with another medical corpsman—to what extent is unknown. Certainly, it wasn't the one depicted in the Stephen Spielberg mini-series, *Band of Brothers*. Also in *Band of Brothers*, a Black nurse appears briefly in a few shots but isn't named, while Renee Lemaire (named Anna in the film) is prominently featured.

Martin King tracked down Augusta and her exploits, which were many more than depicted here. Martin received death threats and was told to stop looking for her, so strong was the prejudice. Martin's book *Searching for Augusta* went on to become a Netflix movie that earned an Emmy, but was banned in Belgium due to prejudice. Martin's publicity gained many honors for Augusta, including recognition from the King of Belgium, yet, she is still unknown to many people. Martin tracked Augusta to a nursing home and met with her for over a month. It took time to gain her trust and get her to talk about those days, but she eventually did, and he was able to hear her story from her own lips, backed by Jack's diaries and the witnesses of other soldiers. She died shortly after, in 2015.

Jack and Augusta had a bitter pill to swallow as the Battle of the Bulge wound down. Jack's fiancé back home had broken up with him. Augusta wanted to go home with him, but Jack didn't know that. She kept her love quiet, under the racial norms of the time, and Jack did the same. When Augusta wrote to him, through an Army foul-up, her letters were returned marked 'deceased.' She thought he was dead. Jack did track her down, and once he did, a flow of correspondence went on for decades. Both she and Jack had married and had children. Jack saw her again, along with Renee's sister, at the fiftieth anniversary commemoration of the Battle of the Bulge in Bastogne. Jack wrote up a commendation for Renee Lemaire and placed a plaque at the location of the former aid station—there's nothing left of the original building. Today, there's a Chinese restaurant there.

·‹‹ ● ● ›·

Michael L. Ross writes biographical fiction, taking real people, fictional characters, and making history come to life. His Across the Great Divide series (The Clouds of War, The Search, The Founding) follows Will Crump and his family through the Civil War, Red Cloud's War, and the founding of Lubbock, Texas. The series also shows Luther Clay's family escaping to freedom on the Underground Railroad, and their struggle for peace and land of their own, culminating in The Founding of Nicodemus, Kansas, a real life all-Black town that exists today. For more about Michael, find his books on his website at www.historicalnovelsrus.com, at www.chirpbooks.com, or at other online retailers.

·‹‹ ● ● ›·

Philippe's Epiphany

EPIPHANY
BY C.V. LEE

London, England
January 6, 1471

The sweet strains of the harp rose to a crescendo, and silence descended on the great hall as the minstrel struck the final chord. Hinges creaked as two servants, resplendent in green tunics embroidered with a gold crown on the left sleeve, threw open the tall double doors. Three men, dressed like kings in fur-lined purple cloaks, fastened at the neck with jeweled brooches, stood on the threshold. Each carried a small wooden chest. The eyes of every guest followed them as they entered and made their slow pilgrimage across the room.

Philippe had seen this play every year at the Feast of the Epiphany. In years past, he had watched in rapt silence. But this year, he struggled to keep his mind on the scene, his thoughts distracted by his wife, Margaret. He kept his countenance schooled, concealing the battle that raged between his sensibilities and his better judgment. Theirs was an arranged marriage, its beginning fraught with missteps and misunderstandings. It vexed him greatly that his affection for her was growing, despite his determination to protect his heart.

Margaret was proving a tough opponent, beguiling him with her charms, but he was at a loss to comprehend her true motives. Perchance she hoped to stave off her father's anger? After three months, their marriage yet unconsummated; Philippe still retained the right to demand an annulment. Such knowledge would displease her father, as a goodly portion of her dowry had been spent here in London.

Or did she seek to deceive him into believing she had forsaken her regard for her former beau, Clement? As long as his doubts remained, Philippe had no intention of making their marriage real.

To his annoyance, Margaret slid closer. Her lips brushed his ear, her sweet scent of roses permeating his space. Amongst guests, she knew he must keep up appearances and play the doting husband. And with all the Christmas festivities, she had taken advantage of every opportunity.

She slipped her hand through his arm. "Uncle Hareby makes a fine Magi. Do you not agree?"

Despite the hundreds of candles that lit the room, the faces of the Magi remained in shadow. He squinted to get a better look. "Indeed, he looks very wise."

"I reckon you are not even watching. What has my husband so preoccupied?"

Having no intention of sharing his thoughts, he disengaged from her hold and placed a finger to his lips. He edged away, careful not to jostle the dignified elderly lady seated on the bench to his right, wearing the tallest hennin he had ever seen. Determined not to look at Margaret, Philippe fixed his gaze on the players.

A few weeks before their wedding, he had asked to break the marriage contract on account of her indiscreet behavior. Her father had insisted Philippe was wrong to question her innocence, and thus, he had been persuaded to post the banns. However, his determination to start anew had crumbled when he caught her in a compromising situation with Clement during their wedding feast.

The next morning, Philippe and Margaret had traveled to London. In the months that followed, a regard had grown between them, and Philippe had nearly dismissed his lingering doubts. Then, three weeks ago, a letter arrived containing unexpected news about Clement. Her distressed reaction brought all the mistrust flooding back. A reminder that words are just that. Words. The mouth can profess whatever it pleases, but that does not make the utterance true, especially when the actions conflict with the confession.

The Magi placed the chests on the ground and knelt before the babe in the manger. Opening them, they presented their gifts. A murmur of appreciation rose from the guests as the candlelight reflected off the gold, and the earthy scent of frankincense and myrrh seeped across the room. As they began their journey back across the great hall, a loud voice spoke from the minstrel balcony above. "Depart another way. King Herod lies. He seeks not to worship the Christ child, but to kill him." Slowly, the three Magi turned and departed through another door.

Philippe's thoughts returned to the problem of Margaret. Nigh a fortnight ago, on Christmas Eve, she had pleaded with him to give their marriage a chance. He had promised an answer by the day after the Epiphany feast, and his time was rapidly slipping away. With all the celebrations, he had lacked the solitude needed to examine his thoughts. She was eager for his answer, too often close at hand, trying to convince him of her loyalty. But, like words, a person can calculate their actions to deceive.

The biggest difficulty lay in his growing affection for his wife, while his pride railed against giving in. Hence, his predicament.

Should he give up the woman he was growing to love? Or accept a wife who loved another?

The guests clapped, startling Philippe out of his brooding. A cry of delight arose from the guests when a baker entered, bearing a platter laden with a kings' cake topped with a crown.

Philippe's eyes widened as he stared at it. "I did not know the kings' cake was part of the English tradition."

"It is not, but I understand 'tis a tradition your mother brought to Jersey from Normandy," Margaret said.

Crossing to the lord's table, the baker placed the cake in front of the host, Lord Stanley, and bowed low, making a grand flourish with his hands. Removing the crown, Stanley presented it to his wife. The baker pulled a knife from his apron and cut the cake.

Philippe scanned the room, his gaze alighting on Alice, Margaret's grandmother. She winked at him. "I suspect this is Alice's doing. But how did she have it made and delivered without my knowledge?"

"She asked Uncle Hareby's baker to oblige her." Margaret leaned forward, a hint of a smile on her face as she watched the servants darting about the room, delivering pieces of cake to each guest. "This promises to be fun."

The lady to his right leaned in, gesturing toward the cake. "You seem knowledgeable of this unusual happening. Pray enlighten me."

"'Tis a kings' cake in honor of the Magi," Philippe replied. "Hidden within are three items: a bean, a clove, and a twig. Whoever finds the bean is king for the day, the clove the villain, and the poor soul finding the twig is the unfortunate fool."

"And what is the benefit of being king?" the lady asked.

"That person gets to wear the crown and makes decrees the guests must follow."

"Strange, I have never encountered this tradition afore." Turning away, the veil of her hennin fluttered across Philippe's face. Unmindful of the situation, she explained the king's cake tradition to the gentleman beside her.

Margaret nudged Philippe's arm, her eyes sparkling. "You must hope I am not the king, for then I shall be able to decree many things of my husband."

"Do you mean to frighten me?" A smile tugged at Philippe's mouth as he pushed the veil out of his eyes.

"Have no fear," Margaret laughed. "I have no wish to start a war."

The servants presented Philippe and Margaret with trenchers, each bearing a slice of cake. Eager to savor the delectable confection made with butter and eggs and sweetened with honey, Philippe breathed in the delicious aroma of almonds.

When all the guests had been served, their host took the first bite. Philippe broke off a morsel and popped it in his mouth, detecting the subtle flavors of pear and ginger. "*C'est délicieux.* I must compliment your Uncle Hareby on the skill of his baker."

Margaret picked up her slice and nibbled it, chewing thoughtfully. "Most agreeable." When she finished her cake, she licked her fingers slowly, keeping her eyes on Philippe. "An excellent addition to the celebration. Alas, I am neither king nor villain on this day."

Philippe chewed his last bit and his breath caught. Something small and rough poked his tongue. He lifted a napkin to cover his mouth as he removed the offending object. *The twig. I am the unfortunate fool.* His face heated. *Is this the Fates giving me a sign?*

He held up the twig, faking a smile. The guests clapped and hooted, and he wished he could disappear beneath the table. Margaret touched his arm. "I do not think you a fool. 'Tis but a stupid twig. It means nothing."

Philippe studied the offending bit of wood. "Time will prove whether the warning portends my future."

Margaret's eyes widened. "You are a smart man. You cannot possibly believe such nonsense."

Philippe fidgeted with his napkin. "Of course not." But, he was not ready to discount the legend, recalling another Epiphany feast when Clement delighted at finding the clove. Since then, he could scarcely remember a time when that man had not attempted to make his life miserable, but the reason had always escaped him.

The minstrels raised their instruments and the notes of a familiar psalm filled the air, signaling dinner was over. Guests rose from the benches and wandered about the room. Philippe's eyes veered to the door. Finally, he could escape to a quiet place to contemplate his next move. He stammered his excuses and strode out of the manor. The faint glow of the sun behind the clouds indicated a few more hours of daylight remained.

He headed for the stable. There, no one would bother him as he wrestled with his apprehensions about Margaret. He shivered; in his haste, he had forgotten his cloak. He quickened his step as he picked his way along the treacherous path, avoiding the puddles and slick mud.

Opening the stable door, he stepped inside, relieved to be out of the icy wind that penetrated to the bone. The smell of horses and hay greeted him like an old friend. On his right, a shelf held saddles with bridles hung beneath, along with an array of grooming brushes. To his left, a grain barrel stood beside a low bench. He grabbed a handful of oats and ambled down the line of stalls until he reached Hareby's gray mare. Lifting the latch, he opened the gate and stepped inside. The mare nuzzled his hand, nibbling daintily until every morsel was gone.

Philippe rubbed her nose. "I wish human relations were this easy."

The mare nickered back softly and nudged him playfully.

"I want a ride too, but 'twould be rude to desert the celebration entirely."

Rushes crunched, warning Philippe he was no longer alone.

The footsteps stopped outside the stall. Philippe glanced over, surprised and dismayed to see Margaret.

"There you are." Margaret sounded relieved. "I have been looking all over for you." She stepped into the stall and stroked the mare's nose.

Their gaze locked, her look of concern evident. "I needed to be alone," Philippe replied. "I find I think best around horses."

"They are marvelous creatures. Sadly, I have never had a horse of my own."

"Surprising, indeed, given your riding ability."

"King Edward kept a large stable." Margaret glanced toward the bench. "Can we speak?"

Philippe gave a curt nod and, latching the stall, moved to the bench and sat. "There was no need for you to venture out into the cold when we could talk later at home."

Margaret dropped onto the bench, pulling something out from under her mantle. "I saw you depart. When you did not come back, I thought you might wish for your cloak."

Philippe mumbled his thanks as she draped it across his lap. Her hand brushed his thigh, and his body tensed. The silence stretched between them as he grappled with what to say.

"Why did you leave?" Margaret asked. "Is something the matter?"

"I am uncomfortable around so many strangers," he said, setting the cloak beside him on the bench.

"How odd." Margaret put her hand in his. "Many of these people are my friends, but I—Well I—I would rather be with you."

Her cheeks flushed as she stared at their entwined hands. His heart quickened. A warm glow filled his body, and the chilly dampness seemed to disappear. Fearing the closeness in this moment would vanish, Philippe did not respond.

"So, have you nothing to say?" Margaret asked.

Philippe swallowed hard. Being an only child and then holed up behind castle walls for so long, he had never learned the ways of conversing with a maiden. "It was very thoughtful of Alice and Hareby to surprise me with the kings' cake."

"'Twas my doing. I wanted you to feel more at home."

"Thank you, I guess. I don't know that it worked. It was embarrassing when everyone laughed at me."

"Is that really how you see it?" Margaret's shoulders slumped and somehow, she seemed to shrink beside him. "Why is it everything I do for you goes awry?"

Philippe shuffled his feet. How did one answer such a question? To claim it was not so would be deceitful. But to agree would harm her sensibilities unnecessarily.

"No need to answer," Margaret said, her tone defeated. "Let us speak of other things."

The amiable mood shattered, leaving Philippe confounded as to a response. "What do you wish to talk about?"

"Well, your fortnight is up tomorrow. I was hoping you had made a decision."

Philippe shook his head. "With all the Christmas festivities, I have not had a chance to turn my mind to it. Can you grant me another week?"

Margaret withdrew her hand and stood, hands on her hips. "Do I mean that little to you? Can you not comprehend the anguish I have suffered these months, not knowing your intentions?" Her voice rose with each question. "Or the humiliation I shall suffer if you turn me away?"

"What of my distress?" Philippe retorted. "I hold a position of import on Jersey. Am I to endure a lifetime of humiliation, being made a cuckold by a man who despises me? Maybe you should have fought harder to have our marriage contract revoked."

"How many times must I assure you Clement means nothing to me?" Standing, she looked resigned. "Because I wanted our

240

marriage to succeed, I have endured your hurtful suspicions. Honestly, what else can I say or do to get through to you?" Head held high, she glided to the door. She turned back, her eyes filled with pain. "Do as you please, for I no longer care. My apologies for trespassing on your privacy."

Philippe waited several minutes, until he believed her gone, before jumping to his feet and clenching his fists, groaning his vexation. He needed to be doing something. He grabbed a brush from the shelf and, returning to the stall, began grooming Hareby's mare. Women were mysterious creatures, and the coldness between his parents provided no clues about how to navigate this scary territory. It seemed he always said something stupid. *I must learn to harness my tongue.*

The rushes crackled again. Obviously, the stable was a far busier place than he had expected. Momentarily, Hareby appeared at the door of the stall and leaned against the gatepost.

"Philippe! What are you doing here?" Hareby asked. "You should be at the house enjoying the festivities."

"Says the man who has also made his escape," Philippe replied. "I hope you do not mind me grooming your steed."

"I am headed home," Hareby replied. "As to the grooming, I never complain about free labor." He held up a brush. "I shall join you." Together, they groomed the steed; only the snorts of the mare and the swish of her tail broke the silence. Finally, Hareby spoke. "You never gave me an answer. Why are you here instead of inside with the other guests?"

Philippe shrugged. "I felt awkward. These folks are Margaret's friends. When they laughed at me, I felt as though I did not belong. Horses accept me for who I am."

"Quite a deep thought for such a young man."

"I have experienced more than most."

Hareby's voice softened. "I am sorry about your father's death. So much responsibility to shoulder for a man of eighteen.

You are most fortunate Margaret will be at your side to share the load."

"Unlikely." The bitterness in his spirit revealed itself in the tone of his voice. Philippe drew in a quick breath, horrified by what had just slipped past his lips.

Hareby circled the mare and stood before him, his forehead furrowed. "That was an odd thing to say."

"It came out wrong."

"I do not believe that for a moment. In unguarded moments, the heart speaks." Hareby placed his hands on his hips. "What is your meaning?"

Philippe returned to brushing the horse. He would not trust Hareby with his innermost insecurities. The man was a mere acquaintance and Margaret's uncle. His loyalty would always be to her. "Please give your baker my compliments on the delicious kings' cake."

"Happy to oblige, but how is it relevant to our conversation?"

"My problems are none of your concern." Philippe presented his back and brushed down the mare's leg. "You played the Magi remarkably well. Are you given that part every year?"

"'Twas not my first time, but you are changing the subject."

Feeling his ire rise, Philippe responded, "Did Margaret put you up to this?"

"Most certainly not." Hareby huffed and crossed his arms. "I demand you explain yourself."

"I am not a man to speak my heart. Especially not to someone who will run back to my wife and tattle."

Philippe picked up the steed's leg and examined the hoof. Leaving the stall, he searched the stable until he found a pick and a stool. Returning, he busied himself removing dirt and pebbles from the hoof.

"It will do you no good to ignore me." Hareby said. "I shall wait all day and night and into the next if I must."

"You may wait forever. But I doubt you intend to follow me around London."

Hareby squatted beside him and spoke in a hushed tone. "I can see you are troubled. There is no need to bear every burden alone. We are family now. I promise to keep your confidence, and perchance, I may provide some wise counsel."

Philippe dropped the horse's leg and slumped against the wall. The weight of his worries felt heavier than before. "Forsooth, our marriage was a mistake. I said it. Are you satisfied?"

"A mistake! How so?" Grasping Philippe's elbow, Hareby steered him out of the stall to the low bench beside the wall.

Philippe took a deep breath. "Margaret loves another man." He stared at his boots. "I could accept her indifference, or even just a friendship, because our marriage may never be anything more. But knowing she pines for another, 'tis too much."

Hareby cocked his head. "I surmise you speak of Clement Le Hardy. Do you know this for a certainty?"

"I overheard them talking after our wedding."

"And what did they say?"

"I will never forget his expression." Philippe's throat swelled as he choked out the words. "He proclaimed his heart would wither and die for want to lie with Margaret and know her sweet love again."

"And how did she respond?"

Meeting Hareby's gaze, Philippe replied, "She said, 'I am not having this discussion with you. You are stewed.' 'Tis hardly a denial."

A hint of a smile ticked at Hareby's mouth. "I think you have fallen in love with her."

Philippe glanced away, slowly letting out a breath, conscious of Hareby studying him. "Is it that obvious?"

Hareby nodded. "I believe so. Why do you not just tell her?"

"I—Well—She—" Philippe stopped, not sure how to answer.

Hareby's voice was soft and filled with concern. "Just say what you are thinking."

Philippe's neck warmed. "If she knew my true feelings—that the man she loves hates the very sight of me. He seeks to hurt me at every turn. I have heard of people that do despicable things for love. What if he uses her to plot revenge against me? If she knew of my affection, she would have power over me."

"Do you hear yourself?" Hareby asked. "You sound like you are devising a stratagem for war. This is your wife we are talking about. Can I give you a modicum of advice?"

Philippe nodded.

"As you heard only a portion of their conversation, you may have missed pertinent information," Hareby said. "What if you had a way to know how she really feels about your supposed rival?"

"Her attempts to convince me are suspect."

Hareby opened his pouch and withdrew a parchment with a broken seal and handed it to Philippe. "The Fates have smiled on you today. I have in my possession a letter from my niece, written before you met."

Philippe eyed him suspiciously, but unfolded the wrinkled parchment and began reading the contents.

My dearest Uncle Hareby,

I hope you do not tire of my writing so often. Although I find Jersey quaint, there is little to occupy my time. I am counting the days until I am permitted to return to London. Sadly, my father has not seen fit to apprise me of how long my sojourn will last.

I spend many days in the company of a man named Clement, ten years my senior. Like me, you enjoy a delightful diversion. If only you were here to see him, we could laugh together. A freeman, he struts about in his too-tight doublet and thinning hose, as if he believes himself a gentleman. Although handsome and possessing charming manners, his attentions and flattery are both artful and insincere, and have become quite tedious. But, what is a girl to do when few on the island speak English and even fewer have time to spare to amuse me?

I do not know how much more I can bear. I beg you write my father and impress upon him that I am needed in London.

Yours, Margaret

Philippe folded the parchment, eyeing Hareby suspiciously. "How came you to have this letter in your possession today?"

"I was curious if Margaret's sentiments about her new island home were the same now she is married."

"And—" When Hareby did not reply, Philippe continued. "Does she still wish to live in London?"

"She remains uncertain, for Jersey has yet to feel like home. I plead your thoughts on the contents of the letter."

"It proves nothing. Sensibilities can change."

Hareby sighed. "My boy, I fear you are sadly ignorant of the ways of love. You see what you want to see. I have seen many a maiden in love, and Margaret's actions are not those of a woman enamored of another man. No, 'tis you who has captured my niece's heart."

"Perchance 'tis all a pretense, for she has not declared her regard."

"Maybe she is unsure of your affections and intentions.

Margaret is not deceitful. Accept the battle is over, and you have won."

"But I know what I saw," Philippe said weakly, not ready to concede fault in his convictions.

Hareby stood and strode to the opposite end of the stable. Returning with a saddle, he shoved it into Philippe's hands. "Help me saddle my steed." While Hareby slipped the bit into the mare's mouth and pulled the bridle over her nose, Philippe hefted the saddle onto her back and tightened the girth.

"One last thought that may help with your decision. Margaret is headstrong and determined to get her way. If she preferred this other swain, she would have voiced her objections until her father relented."

"How do I know I can trust what you say?" Philippe patted the horse's flank and stepped away.

Hareby hoisted himself into the saddle and clicked his tongue. The mare moved forward. "You have eyes. Prove what I said for yourself."

Once again alone in the stable, Philippe settled back onto the bench, head in his hands, mulling over their conversation. Looking back, he recalled the many times Margaret had been thoughtful of his feelings. Even today, rather than remain near the warmth of the fire, she had braved the cold to be with him. Those little smiles during dinner, as if she had some secret thought she wanted to share. Indeed, she had often sought his company, claiming she needed to speak with him when she had nothing of import to tell. The gentle touches that sent a thrill through his body, and the look on her face was proof she felt it, too.

God's bones. Hareby is right. How have I not seen it before? His stomach knotted. *Fie on my doubts and insecurities. Must I cling desperately to a falsehood rather than admit my folly?*

He leaned back against the wall and closed his eyes. *The Fates have chosen right again. I am a fool.* He kicked at the rushes to vent his frustration, worried his stupidity had ruined everything. *She is my wife. Why can I not just apologize?* But he already knew the answer. What if she thought less of him? Or his clumsy attempts made it worse? The thought of seeing disdain in her eyes, not to mention the profound embarrassment he would suffer, would be unbearable.

He caught sight of his cloak, folded neatly on the bench. Picking it up, he drew it around his shoulders and wrapped it tightly around him, breathing in his wife's lingering aroma of roses. A horse nickered. Of course. He would buy Margaret her own horse. Such a gift would declare his intentions without saying a word. He smiled, grateful for the epiphany of his wife's true feelings, and for the unsuspecting steed revealing the perfect way to make amends.

·‹‹ ● ●› ›·

C.V. Lee pens tales about forgotten heroes and heroines of the past. Her latest novel, Betrayal of Trust, tells the unforgettable true love story of Philippe and Margaret. For more information about C.V. Lee, check out her website atwww.cvlee.com. You can follow her on Facebook and Instagram.

Read the amazing love story of Philippe and Margaret in C.V. Lee's novel, *Betrayal of Trust,* based on real people and true events.

Stitchwork

◦⟡◦

SAINT NICHOLAS DAY
BY KATHRYN PRITCHETT

Lenzburg, Switzerland
December 6, 1869

Snow blew off the mountains in great white gusts, like starched linens thrown across the Frost King's icy bed. Prisca pulled down her worn hat and wrapped her thin shawl tighter around her slight shoulders as she hurried towards the rooms she shared with her aging mother.

"*Wie geht es dir?*" She kissed Frau Weber, who sat in front of a dying fire, before placing the day's rolls in the kitchen. She set the wedge of cheese and crock of milk on the windowsill, noting the snow crystals piling into small drifts outside the panes. Since she'd spent their last francs on this meal, there wouldn't be more until she'd finished the task at hand. She shivered as she took off her shawl and carefully draped it over her mother, then added one of the few remaining logs to the embers. After lighting the lone candle in the table lantern, she picked up her stitchwork, making sure not to let it fall into the ashes.

At least Prisca's legs would be warm, draped with the heavy, red velvet of Herr Kohler's *Samichlaus* costume. When he'd worn it last—or maybe during the year it had hung in his closet—the hood had torn away from the body of the cloak, and the thread that held the neck ribbons had unraveled. Strange, it almost appeared as though they'd been ripped loose.

She reattached the hood and pinned the ribbons to the crimson fabric—such beautiful trim from Herr Kohler's own factory—before drawing the threaded needle through the multiple layers. Running her finger over the golden threads, she allowed herself a moment of reverie. To wear such ribbon, to *own* such ribbon! She shook her head and got back to work. Herr Kohler would not accept anything less than perfection.

She grew uneasy thinking about the mayor's yearly admonitions to the children (but really all the townspeople) about their duties. How they must be honorable and never disobey those in authority. He would wear this robe when he delivered his annual sermon, to ensure the children would polish their shoes and set them by the door on St. Nicholas Day. At least, the ones who remained.

Many families had abandoned their farms for better-paying jobs in Zurich or Basel, but her father had stayed and worked for Herr Kohler. That is, until an accident at the factory cost him his left hand and, when that turned gangrenous, his life. At the funeral, Herr Kohler promised he'd provide work for her older brother, Bruno. When the mayor arranged for a military position —one with little risk of fighting—the future looked brighter. Until the night Bruno was assigned to patrol a small encampment of French soldiers on the border and one sauntered over asking for water, then dispatched him with a hidden knife.

That left two women to fend for themselves—one too old to be of any use, the other too young to have any power. Prisca should be grateful her stitching allowed them the bit of food they needed to sustain life. Yet, she didn't feel grateful; she felt angry. So angry, she wanted to scream. But girls didn't scream. They stayed quiet to show they'd be good, respectful wives.

Pfui! She'd lost focus and created a clumsy knot that needed to be snipped. After all, stitchwork was about taking things apart as well as putting them back together again. Prisca reached for her mother's sharp sewing scissors, the handles decorated with a little boy and girl gathering flowers, like she and Bruno had done when they were children. In her haste, she pricked her finger on the tips. She sighed with relief when the ruby drop of blood landed on the underside of the velvet, where it wouldn't be seen.

‹‹●●●››

The next morning, Prisca navigated the uncleared snow drifts to deliver the cloak to the mayor's home. Herr Kohler's daughter, Greta, took it and carefully examined the repair, a frown creasing her brow. Prisca's heart beat fast, like a hummingbird lured indoors by a vase of Alpen rose. She forced herself to take a deep breath, warding off worries about the drop of blood, even as she wondered why Greta hadn't repaired the cloak herself. Must be nice to hire out work any able-bodied woman could do.

Greta took the robe inside and returned with a jingling envelope, sealed with the mayor's own seal. It was all Prisca could do not to grab it before Greta handed it to her.

"Danke Sehr," she whispered.

Greta avoided Prisca's eyes and dabbed at her nose with a finely embroidered handkerchief. "You'll be at the children's parade this afternoon?"

"I hope to be," said Prisca. "If Mother doesn't need me."

"How is Frau Weber doing?"

"As good as can be expected." Prisca was eager to get back to her now.

Greta tucked the handkerchief in her pocket and turned to go inside. "The festivities will surely lift her spirits."

Prisca bowed her head and backed away. She didn't share that her mother's knees would ache even more from the cold if she attended the parade. And her cough would be all the worse for breathing the frigid air. No, it was best if she remained inside. Prisca would stay with her until she fell asleep. If there was time, she'd stop by the parade on her way to buy more food.

The snow had melted and iced over again as the wind picked up, causing her to stumble as she made her way home. It crunched beneath her boots, threatening to tear a hole in the worn soles. She remembered the fur-lined boots she'd outgrown, the ones she'd once worn in the children's parade. Her feet had been warm then, and her arms snug in a colorful sweater as they lifted to carry a cheerful *Iffelen*, an oversized paper hat patterned after a bishop's miter. Despite the dark of winter, life had been so full of light.

When she opened the door, she found her mother weeping. "St. Nicholas Day, and I haven't a thing for my daughter," she said.

"Hush, hush," said Prisca. "Look, I have the payment from Herr Kohler. Tonight, we will celebrate with a little treat." She shook the envelope, and the coins made a jolly sound. "Here is his very seal." She showed her mother the dark red wax and ran her finger over the raised "K." But when she opened the envelope, she discovered there were fewer coins than expected.

She turned away to hide her despair. Not only would they have a meager St. Nicholas Day, but they would also starve—or freeze—before year's end. She had failed her mother completely.

"What a wonderful daughter you are," said Frau Weber. "Let us eat!"

Prisca sliced half the cheese and put it on a small plate with the next-to-last roll. She forced a cheerful reply. "*Ja, Mutter,* we shall be merry that we've survived another year." She kissed her mother on the cheek and fetched a glass of water for her, hoping she wouldn't notice that she did not share in their little feast. After-wards, she tucked her into bed, placed the last log on the fire and quietly slipped out in search of Greta Kohler.

‹‹ ● ● ● ››

Children in white robes and red sashes filled the streets. They carried large *Iffelen* decorated with brightly colored stars or a cheerful depiction of *Samichlaus*. Some bore an illustration of a dark *Schmutzli* holding the reins of a donkey. The two key figures of the celebration—the giver of gifts and the enforcer of punish-ments—were linked forever.

Beneath the *Iffelen*, Prisca spied intricately patterned caps knitted by adoring mothers. Thick sweaters peeked out from the robes, and warm boots covered their shins. Ah, to still be one of these cared-for children. But now, even if she had new boots, or constructed a beautiful lantern, there was no place in the parade for a grown woman like Prisca. She wasn't a child anymore. Nor a young rabble-rouser like the boys who cracked the small whips at the front of the parade.

Samichlaus was the last one to appear. Herr Kohler looked grand in his gold miter and the repaired red robe. He waved at the parents assembled on the side, while a lone *Schmutzli* half-heart-edly threatened the crowd, scaring the children into good behavior so *Samichlaus* didn't have to.

The full force of the *Schmutzlis* would be unveiled that evening at the night parade. Dressed in black robes, these robed demons would bang their drums, wave their birch brooms, and terrorize bystanders with their shouts and jeers. Every child knew to be good or a *Schmutzli* might steal them away. When she was little, Prisca had feared the black-robed boys and men. Even Bruno, who had once had the honor of serving as a *Schmutzli*, frightened her when he donned the dusky robe and bushy beard.

But, this afternoon, it was the twin demons of hunger and cold that taunted her and propelled her to hunt down the mayor's daughter. She spotted Greta wrapped in a navy wool cloak, standing in front of the bakery. She pushed her way through to her side. The smell of freshly baked gingerbread caused her mouth to water, and she stumbled over her greeting.

"Fräulein Kohler, you... you look lovely in that blue cloak."

"*Danke Sehr*," said Greta. "And you look..." She paused, as though not certain how to compliment someone like Prisca, whose worn clothes and pinched face were better ignored. Eventually, she settled on a curt, "Happy St. Nicholas Day."

"Your father—he was pleased with the robe?" asked Prisca hungrily.

Greta didn't answer at first, just nodded at the charming rows of children circling the plaza. "Aren't they lovely?"

"Indeed. But Herr Kohler, what did he think of my work?"

Greta pursed her lips, then turned to look at Prisca. "Herr Kohler and I found the work acceptable, but not exceptional. I gave you what we felt your work was worth."

Prisca inhaled sharply. "But we agreed on a payment. More than what appeared in the envelope."

Greta said nothing, just smiled at the children as they passed.

Eventually, she reached into her pocket and dropped a few more coins into Prisca's hand. This time, Prisca checked immediately to see what she'd been paid. Her stomach dropped. All totaled, this was half of what she'd hoped to receive.

"But this is... not enough."

"This is all Herr Kohler will pay," said Greta. "Good day."

And with that, she joined her father and beamed as the red-robed mayor presented the children with a gingerbread square and an orange.

‹‹ (● ●) ››

The fire had gone out by the time Prisca returned home. *"Mutter?"* cried Prisca. She'd hoped to surprise her with a bit of gingerbread. But, given how little Greta Kohler had paid her, she'd had no money for such luxuries. She'd hardly had enough for one more roll and an even smaller hunk of cheese than she'd bought the day before.

Frau Weber remained in bed but didn't acknowledge her daughter's return. Prisca yanked off her mittens and pressed her hand to her mother's face. Her cheeks were cold, her breath barely visible. Prisca folded her half of the comforter onto her mother, knowing it still wouldn't be enough to keep her warm. She threw open the lid to the old trunk and rifled around until she found Hugo's military jacket. She removed it to add another layer, then spied the old *Schmutzli* robe at the bottom. One might have mistaken it for a harmless pile of rags and the accompanying beard for a rat's nest.

She shook out the hooded robe made of rough black home-spun and recalled carefully stitching it together—even for a monster, there'd be fine stitchwork. She remembered Bruno dancing around as she fit it to him, raising his arms and grimacing, bringing her to tears.

Her mother had hooted and cautioned Bruno not to take on airs. She told them that when she'd grown up in Austria, it was women who roamed the streets terrorizing villagers during the winter festivals. "The *Pertchln* were fierce! With ash-smudged cheeks and dark robes, they'd even let a breast hang out."

"*Nein!*" cried Bruno and Prisca, horrified.

Their mother had chuckled. "Indeed. No one could be identified, so there was no need to be ashamed."

She went on to tell them the story of Perchta—Old Mother Frost, the leader of the Wild Hunt. Though the Frost King ruled the mountains, it was Perchta who sent the snow flying when she shook out her feather bed.

"During the summer, Perchta was a beautiful woman who walked the hills with her golden spindle, gathering flax from the shepherds. But in winter, she would turn into a violent hag dragging a swan foot, sure to punish those who had not finished spinning the flax." Her mother hobbled around the room.

Captivated, Prisca pressed for more details. "So, the women in the parade—these were Perchta's acolytes? "

"*Ja*, they made certain you finished your spinning and weaving by Christmas. If you'd finished, you'd get a shiny coin and be granted a vision of Perchta in her summer glory. But, if you were slothful, you'd see a terrible old woman who would slit you open and stuff you with rubbish!" She reached out with claw-like hands.

Prisca gasped and covered her belly.

"Surely you didn't believe such tales?" said Bruno.

Frau Weber wagged a finger at her cheeky son. "Only a fool would question Perchta."

The audacious tale had shocked Prisca. But later, she had wondered what it would be like to be a *Pertchln*, a woman as bold as a *Schmutzli*.

·‹‹ ●◉● ›·

As she laid Bruno's jacket over her shivering mother, something snapped inside her. She untied her apron and added it to the covers. Then, she unlaced her dirndl and let it drop to the floor, followed by her blouse. The cold air stung her exposed skin, and she quickly pulled the rough black robe over her head. The sleeves were long but could be easily rolled. The hem grazed the ground, but with the help of the rope belt, she could hike it up enough to walk, while still covering her woman's boots. For once, she was grateful she was tall for a girl. She knelt by the now-cold fire and scooped up some ash to complete her disguise. At last, she secured the scratchy black beard behind her ears.

Looking in the small mirror that hung on the back of the door, she saw her tear-stained eyes glowing red in the fading light. She bared her teeth and growled, as Bruno had done. Then, she pulled the hood over her head and grabbed their birch broom. At the last minute, she tucked the small sewing scissors into her pocket. She would go to the men's parade under the cover of darkness.

When she arrived, she saw the grown men with their longer sheep whips, followed by the younger men bearing enormous *Iffelen* with candle-lit cutouts, like the *Kirche's* stained glass windows. Behind them came the torchbearers that surrounded Herr Kohler and now, a whole band of *Schmutzlis*. Trumpeters followed, then men in white farmers' shirts swinging huge cow bells from heavy straps. More white-shirted men carrying cow horns brought up the rear.

A cannon fired, the whips cracked, and the instruments sounded to begin the parade. Prisca maneuvered through the crowd to join the *Schmutzlis*.

"Ready to make some noise?" hollered one of the boys.

"*Naturlich!*" cried the others as they waved their birch brooms and cheered. Soon enough, they started roaming the streets, poking children up past their bedtime or lewdly teasing pretty young girls that dared cross their paths.

Prisca followed one of the smaller robed figures, zigging and zagging among the crowd. At first, she was silent, merely mimicking his movements. But the parade's cacophony gave her the courage to cry out. Lowering her voice to avoid detection, she bellowed at what was wrong in the world. "*Gib act!* Beware!" When her voice gave out, a guttural growl erupted, and a rush of power flooded her slim frame.

The parade wound through the streets, past the shadowy hillside castle and into the fields where a bonfire had been lit.

The villagers drank and sang. Someone handed Prisca a mug of beer. Thirsty, she drank it down. Emboldened, she ran in circles beneath the crescent moon until she charged into a mountain of red velvet and her hood slipped back, exposing the long braids that uncoiled from the top of her head.

Herr Kohler grabbed her by the shoulders. "Who are you?" From the sour smell of his breath, he'd also been drinking. He shook her until she whimpered for him to stop. He dropped his hands and barked. "No *Schmutzli* is a girl. *Nach hause gehen!*"

Go home? Home, where her mother shivered in the cold? Home, where she had failed her so? She glared at the weaving mayor in his *Samichlaus* costume. Her fury at not being paid roared back. "*Nein.* Not until you give me what I'm owed."

Herr Kohler squinted at this impudent imposter. "Give you what you're owed? What a naughty child. If I had one of my real *Schmutzlis* here, he'd throw you in his sack and carry you off to the woods where you'd never be found."

Prisca doubled over and sobbed.

"*Mist!*" Herr Kohler rustled about in his pockets. "Now, now. You want an orange? A piece of gingerbread?"

Prisca's stomach growled at his drunken offerings. But, even in the fog of her hunger, she knew the sweets would provide only a temporary reprieve. She shoved her chapped hands in her pockets and felt the cold points of the little sewing scissors. She thrust them up to the silver moon and saw the blades twinkle alongside the stars.

One of the horn bearers blew a long, deafening note, which caused her to charge at Herr Kohler, the sharp scissor tips aimed at the golden neck ribbons.

Even in his condition, the mayor dodged her assault, easily stepping aside. He grabbed her by her arm and twisted it behind her, causing her to drop her unlikely weapon. "Again, who are you and what cause do you have to harm me?" he hissed.

The list was long, but she settled on the latest offense. "I repaired the robe you wear. And yet, you wouldn't pay me for my work."

He cursed her as he threw her aside and rubbed his head like a bear woken too early from its winter nap. "You talk of robes and sewing, but I know no *Schmutzli* that wields a needle and thread —or such treacherous scissors."

Prisca straightened up. "Ahh, but I am no *Schmutzli*—I am a *Pertchln*. And I demand payment for the stitches sewn on your behalf. Also, for the father, husband, brother, and son my mother and I have lost."

Herr Kohler staggered back and wiped his eyes. "Nothing can compensate for losing a son," he said.

Prisca froze.

A lost son. Herr Kohler's only son had abandoned his father —as well as a pregnant wife and two children. He'd run off to Australia the year before without even saying good-bye. Not long after, the wife and *kinder* had fled to America with some traveling missionaries. The mayor, too, had known loss. Still, he was warm and fed and alive. Unlike her and her mother, he had enough.

"You wear a false robe," she said, the breath cold in her lungs. "*Samichlaus* gives gifts, but you, you give nothing."

He shook his head, but his eyes confirmed his guilt.

"Here, take these." He reached into one pocket and threw

some coins at her feet. Then, from the other, he pulled out a small piece of gingerbread. "That's all I have for you, my strange *Schmutzli*." He stumbled back towards the fire.

Prisca gulped down the spiced cake. Then, she picked up the coins and the scissors bearing images of happier times. "It's not nearly enough," she cried as she fled to the top of the hill where the old castle stood.

Tears froze on her cheeks as she gasped for breath and looked over the village. She should return to her mother, lie beside her to share what little warmth she could give. Prepare for the consequences that surely awaited her in the morning. No woman could threaten a man as powerful as Herr Kohler and not pay for it. She must apologize. Beg for mercy.

A cry down below—perhaps from another *Schmutzli* or maybe one of his victims—startled her. She looked up at the menacing outline of a golden dragon atop a turret and brought the scissors to her throat.

"Never!"

With a yell as fierce as the trumpeting horns, she slashed a long diagonal down the front of the black robe and let the icy beam of the winter moon puncture her bared breast.

The world grew silent as her breath shone bright in the moonlight. Once again, she raised the little scissors. "Tomorrow, I will stitch our lives together," she told the glittering stars. "I will mend what has been rent asunder." And with that, she marched down the hill, warmed by the flurry of snowflakes that dropped like feathers from the ebony sky.

‹‹ ● ● ● ››

Kathryn Pritchett writes about women forged in the American West. She is seeking representation for her debut novel, *The Casket*

Maker's Other Wife, in which Herr Kohler strikes a terrible bargain with his daughter-in-law Anna before she emigrates from Switzerland to Utah Territory and becomes a second wife in a polygamous marriage. You can find out more about Kathryn at www.thingselemental.com and read her short story *The Happy Heart* in the Paper Lantern Writer's anthology <u>Unlocked</u>.

·‹‹ ● ● ● ›·

Also By Paper Lantern Writers

Unlocked

Beneath a Midwinter Moon

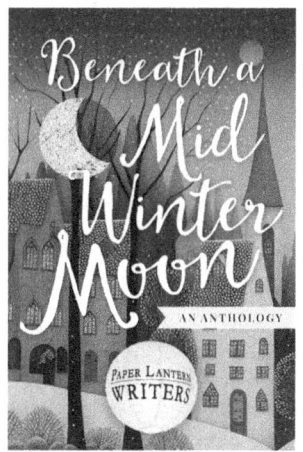

Destiny Comes Due

Crafting Stories from the Past: A How-To Guide for Writing Historical Fiction

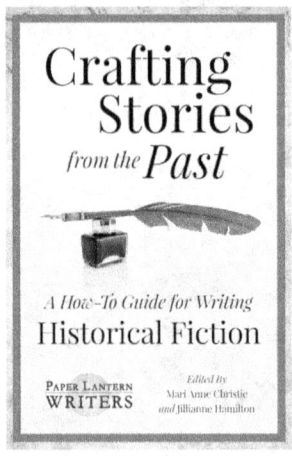

Find us at www.paperlanternwriters.com